Ian Richardson

City Crime

novum ◢ pro

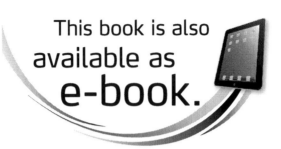

This book is also
available as
e-book.

www.novum-publishing.co.uk

© 2018 novum publishing

ISBN 978-3-99064-321-1
Editing: Julie Hoyle, B.Ed (Hons)
Cover photo:
negativespace.co | www.pexels.com
Cover design, layout & typesetting:
novum publishing

www.novum-publishing.co.uk

Chapter 1

Fred Tassell stood on the bank of the Grand Union Canal in Mile End and looked vacantly at the dirty water. For the first time for many weeks in this bleak summer of 1992 the sun was shining. He told himself that if it continued much longer he would take the step of removing his raincoat. He was used to rain seeping under the collar of his raincoat as he held his fishing rod out in the vain hope of catching something. As he looked up, it occurred to him that the greyness of the concrete in front of him was bathed in warm sun and looked almost welcoming. Then he looked sadly at the litter-strewn canal path and reassured himself that things were still going downhill. He often took it upon himself to pick up rubbish dropped by passers-by and enjoyed writing to the local paper about the amount of litter around the canal.

Tassell often wondered why he chose to come out to fish this canal, but then reminded himself that anything would be better than being cooped up in the vandalised tower block where he lived. He could not remember when the lifts had last been working and it was a strain at his age walking up and down all those flights of stairs. Still, there were times when he felt like a breath of what passed for fresh air in this run-down part of the East End and today he had to admit to himself life was just about tolerable.

Just then something unusual floating along the canal caught his eye. It looked like a loose piece of material in the distance and as it floated closer, Tassell squinted at it in idle curiosity. Suddenly he started in surprise. As it floated by, he could tell it was a dead body, bloated from being in the water for several weeks. A crow perched on its face, pecking at its eyes. Tassell threw a stone to scare the bird off, and stretching out his rod, managed to pull it slightly out of the water to stop it drifting away.

The stench from the body made Tassell turn away in disgust. He had been a soldier and had seen plenty of dead bodies in his long life, and he calmly decided what to do. He had heard of mobile phones that were becoming popular but had never seen one, so he walked as fast as he could to his nearby council flat to call the police. In the entrance hall he pressed the button for the lift, then cursed under his breath when there was no response. He walked as quickly as he could up five flights of stairs then dropped the key in his excitement as he tried to open the door of his flat. After more cursing to himself, he succeeded in letting himself in and rushed to the old-fashioned black phone.

Tassell waited impatiently for the emergency operator to answer. "Police, of course … I've found a body in the canal … Right near here … At the end of Mile End Road. My name's Tassell. I'm on the fifth floor of the flats nearby."

An hour later, Tassell ventured out again to see if the police had taken any notice of his call. When he reached the canal, the body he had discovered was stretched out on the towpath. Behind a cordon, a doctor was closing his bag obviously having performed the redundant but legally necessary task of declaring the man dead. A young uniformed constable and an older man in plain clothes were looking through the pockets of the corpse's suit. This had probably once been of the finest quality but was now little more than threads. A single brick was tied to one leg.

"That wouldn't be enough to weigh him down," the officer in plain clothes was saying. "I bet there were other bricks, but the ropes have worn away or been eaten by fish. Together with the air in the body that must have been enough to bring it to the surface." Just then he noticed Tassell standing nearby smoking a pipe. "Can you keep walking please, sir. It's not a pretty sight."

"I know," Tassell replied, proudly. "I found it."

"You were the man who called 999? Mr Tassell, isn't it?"

"That's right."

"I hope it wasn't too much of a shock. It must have been distressing for you."

Tassell snorted with scorn. "It would take more than that to distress me. I was here during the War. We saw worse sights than that every time there was an air raid." Tassell grew enthusiastic as he told of excitements of long ago. "The whole canal was in flames one night …"

"Well, perhaps you can help me," the detective interrupted quickly, probably anxious not to hear any war reminiscences. "I'm Detective Sergeant Clement. Can you tell me which direction the body was coming from?"

Tassell silently lit a match and, after shaking it out, threw it into the canal where it slowly floated southward. "The North, of course. Everything round here flows down into the Thames."

"How fast was it floating?"

"As fast as that matchstick," Tassell replied, enjoying displaying his knowledge of the canal.

"And I suppose it could have been dumped anywhere from here to Liverpool."

"No, it would have to be within about a mile upstream of here."

"How do you work that out?"

"There's a lock about a mile upstream. It couldn't have floated over that."

"Is there anything else you can tell me? Have you seen anything suspicious around here recently?"

"Not exactly," Tassell replied after a moment's thought. "The other night I did see a big black car drive slowly round, but that's all."

"How do you know it was black if it was night? Did you see the make?"

"I don't know. It just seemed black to me. All cars look the same to me nowadays, but it seemed expensive, the way it glided around. You don't see many cars like that around here, unless they've been nicked."

Clement made another note. "A big black car. Thank you, Mr Tassell. If there's nothing else you can tell me, we will take over now. Please come down to the station in the next three days and make a statement."

"We don't often see the police around here. Do you think you could do something about the litter? You wouldn't believe the amount of rubbish I have to pick up every day. I've got plastic bags full of it. I'm saving it up to show the council."

"Perhaps you could raise the litter issue with them, sir. I'm sure they'll be able to help. Now I do have a murder inquiry to deal with …" Tassell nodded and started to walk back to his flat. He was looking forward to telling his friends how he had performed his civic duty as well as making Clement look a fool in front of the constable.

Clement waited for Tassell to walk out of earshot. "Thank God the golden oldie's gone. Does he think I'm going to drop a murder case to look into litter? And I can't put a big black car through the computer. I'd be a laughing stock. I'd probably end up arresting the Queen," Clement picked up something caught in the remains of the corpse's suit. "Now that's interesting." He produced a credit-card sized piece of plastic with the words 'MacGregor and Company, City of London Auditors' on it. "That looks like one of those new electronic keys they give you in hotels or fancy offices. If he was murdered in the City and dumped in the canal, then this is the City boys' case. I'll give them a ring as soon as the body's been identified. It'll give them something real to do for once," Clement said, cheering up for the first time as he saw the chance to pass this workload onto another force.

"It might not be murder. Perhaps it's a suicide, sarge," suggested the constable. "He may have weighted himself down to make sure he couldn't swim to safety."

Detective Sergeant Clement looked down at the dirty water and shook his head. "I don't think so somehow. No one could ever get desperate enough to throw themselves into that."

Chapter 2

Detective Chief Inspector David Gould of the City of London police woke in his Barbican flat with a dry sensation in his mouth. It was matched by the ache in his back from the uncomfortable settee on which he was lying. He wondered what had woken him up. After a worried moment, he was relieved to discover that the ringing in his ears came from the telephone on the coffee table nearby. Gould reached out his hand and picked up the receiver.

"Gould, here." There was a long pause. "Isn't that the Met's area? ... Yes, I see. It might be worth checking out. I'll be right there." Gould put the phone down and stretched himself awkwardly. He told himself it was an absurd cliché for a married man to be sleeping on a sofa in the living room after a row with his wife. As he stood up and looked from his twelfth-floor window at the life going on down below, he reflected on how far his married life had degenerated. Audrey had accused him of being more interested in investigating the criminal life of the City of London than in her. He could not remember when he had last been so annoyed by a remark; in part his annoyance stemmed from the fact that his wife's remark was largely true.

Gould was one of the few City officers who lived in the Square Mile. He was born and brought up in the City and could not imagine living anywhere else. He enjoyed watching the commuters stream out of Moorgate tube station at nine o'clock in the morning and home again at five in the evening. Despite the veneer of civilisation in the financial world of the City, he knew better than anyone how much crime took place in the offices he could see below him. He had resisted all invitations to move to the Metropolitan Police. He loved the strange anachronism of the City with its distinctive police uniforms and the ritual surrounding the ancient office of the Lord Mayor. His own modern flat contrasted sharply with the many Wren churches he could see below.

Gould grabbed his clothes and started dressing in his tailor-made suit. In order to blend into his exclusive manor, he dressed with more style than most police officers, which set him apart from his colleagues in other forces. He had spent the previous day in South Wales interviewing some teenage hacker who claimed to have information about drug dealing at a travel agency in the City called Harvey and Ward. It had probably been a waste of time and his mood had not been improved by the implication of the local police that he was some overpaid interloper from London.

When Gould was ready to leave the flat, he knocked on the bedroom door. "I'm out on a call."

No reply came from the bedroom. He knew his wife was getting ready for her work as a primary school teacher. He knew from experience that the silence meant the row between them was continuing. Deciding it was best to let the row blow over, he shrugged his shoulders and left the flat to visit Mile End.

Gould's job provided him with the advantage of his own parking spot close to the Barbican. After a few minutes, he drove out of the City and was soon in some of the poorest neighbourhoods in London. He managed to find Mile End police station with its barred windows in one of the roughest parts of the East End. Gould was relieved to find there was space to park his car in the protected yard.

Gould decided to walk around the side of the police station to the front door. He looked up and down the road, his designer suit out of place among the tatty shops around him. His policeman's eye ensured he could recall every important thing he saw without effort. Once inside the station, Gould was directed into Detective Sergeant Clement's office. Clement immediately stood up respectfully when he saw the imposing blond, rather handsome, detective chief inspector enter.

"DS Clement? I'm DCI Gould," the visitor said as the two men shook hands. "Thanks for calling me into this case. What have you got?"

Clement showed Gould some photographs of the corpse. "We have a body that might interest you. This is how it looked when we arrived. Some old codger fishing in the canal found it. The methane inside the corpse must have pushed it to the surface. We think it was in the water for about three weeks – the skin was beginning to burst open. It looks as if bricks had weighed it down but only one of them was left – probably some fish had eaten the other ropes. According to the pathologist, death was by garrotting – the marks are still around his neck – look there. All together it looks like a professional killing. The corpse must have been dumped up to a mile upstream of where it was found, but it's a busy towpath, and we have not found any other witnesses." Clement was happy to use the benefit of Tassell's knowledge of the canal. "It's not an area where we get much help from the public."

"Have you got any identification yet?" Gould asked.

"His name was Hugh Marks," Clement replied, looking at his notes. "He had been reported missing three weeks ago. There was an electronic key in what was left of his pocket, which helped us. Marks was twenty-five years old and worked for MacGregor and Sons, which is a firm of auditors in the City. That's why we called you."

"Fine. What have you found out? What about his home life?" Gould asked.

"He was very conventional," Clement replied. "He lived with his girlfriend in Enfield, which would be about ten miles away from where he was found. They were planning to get married later in the year. Marks's parents are dead. I had to tell his girlfriend – I hate that part of our job. We can't find any connection with Mile End at all, and there's nothing suspicious in his background. He was part-qualified as an accountant and well thought of by his employers and everyone we've spoken to."

"Somebody didn't think well of him," Gould said, looking at the photographs of the bloated corpse. "This is a very professional killing. He seems to have crossed some dangerous people. Did he owe any debts? Did he gamble at all?"

"Not as far as we can see," Clement said. "His bank account was all in order."

"Was there any evidence of drugs?"

"There were no needle marks and no other evidence of drugs in the body. Mind you, the pathologist said any traces would have vanished by the time the body was found."

"Have you managed to interview Marks's girlfriend?" Gould asked.

"Yes, since I broke the news to her she's been in a state of shock. I feel sure she's not involved. I asked around the neighbours, but there wasn't anything out of the way," Clement replied. "They've known each other for years, and everyone says they seemed well matched and happy. Even if they did have a row and she wanted to kill him, I can't imagine a young girl garrotting a larger man then dumping his body in a canal. It must have taken at least a couple of men – professional criminals, I'd say."

"The most likely motive seems his work in that case," Gould said. "As his firm was in the City, I'll look into the victim's work side."

"That's very good of you, Chief Inspector," Clement exclaimed, relieved to have passed on this responsibility.

"I'd like to meet Marks's girlfriend first," Gould said. "It might be better if you come with me."

****

An hour and a half later, Gould and Clement knocked on the door of a terraced house in Enfield. After a while, a greying middle-aged woman came to the door. Gould guessed she was probably no more than forty-five, but her face was already lined by work and worry.

"Mrs Fitzsimons, I'm sorry to disturb you again," Clement began. "This is Detective Chief Inspector Gould of the City of London police. He'll be taking over this case. Is Natalie in, please?"

"Yes, of course she's in," Mrs Fitzsimons snapped in a strong Irish accent. "She never leaves her room nowadays – not since Hugh went missing. It's worse now you've found his body. I don't want her upset again. I daren't leave her – I've had to give up my cleaning job so I can stay at home all day. Please find whoever did it, Mr Clement," she added, grabbing his hand.

"We realise this is a difficult time for you, Mrs Fitzsimons," Gould interrupted. "We think the murder could be connected to Hugh's work and it may help us find the killers if I could speak to your daughter."

"Very well, come in," Mrs Fitzsimons said, as she ushered them into what was obviously the smarter of the two downstairs rooms. "If it helps find Hugh's killer, I'll fetch Natalie for you."

Gould and Clement sat on the armchairs and looked through the back window to a beautifully maintained garden. Some tulips were starting to bloom. A glance at the neighbouring gardens showed Gould how unusual this level of care was in the neighbourhood.

"Mr Clement." Gould's attention was drawn to a blond young woman dressed in a robe covering a nightdress. Her red eyes spoiled what must normally have been a very pretty face. "I'm sorry I'm not dressed and made up. There doesn't seem much point these days."

"I understand, Natalie," Clement replied, as he ushered her to an armchair. Gould was impressed with how well Clement's avuncular manner put Natalie at her ease. "This is Detective Chief Inspector Gould of the City of London police."

Gould stood up. "How do you do, Miss Fitzsimons. Thank you for seeing us, I realise how upsetting this has been. I'll have to ask some questions you may have been asked before. May I call you Natalie?" The young woman nodded, as they both sat down. "I'm involved in the investigation, Natalie, because I understand your fiancé worked in the City."

"Yes, that's right. He was studying for his accountancy exams. He worked for MacGregor and Sons – they're a firm of accountants in Eastcheap. He used to audit companies' accounts. He was always travelling to different firms." Natalie's enthusiastic description of her fiancé's work showed no trace of her mother's Irish accent.

"The last time you saw Hugh was 14 May, you said in your statement. Can you tell me which firms he was working for when he went missing?"

Natalie looked surprised at the question. "I don't know. We were saving for a home of our own. Hugh used to work very hard to get lots of overtime money for a deposit. He used to audit lots of firms, but he never spoke about his work much. I think he was glad to forget about it."

"Who was his direct manager at work, do you know, Natalie?" Gould asked.

"It was a Mr Miles. Hugh always said he was a bit stuffy, but he always got on well with him."

"Is there anything else you can think of to help us? Was there anything Hugh was worried about at work? Did he have any disagreements there? Could anyone have a grievance against him? That's the area we're concentrating on at the moment."

"No, they were all respectable companies, and seemed nice people." Natalie stopped, then continued after a pause. "He did mention a travel agency he was auditing. He once said it would be a good cover for drug smuggling. It was while we were walking back from seeing some thriller or other at the cinema. I used to tease him about liking thrillers with lots of blood and gore."

"What was the name of the travel agency, Natalie?" Gould asked sharply.

"Oh, Hugh did mention the name, but I'd never heard of it before, so it didn't stick in my mind. I think he was just fantasising though. Hugh always said exciting things didn't happen to accountants. I used to tease him about that Monty Python sketch – the one about accountants having safe and boring lives. I suppose I was wrong there, wasn't I? Something exciting happened to him." Natalie started to cry.

Gould and Clement were both experienced enough to realise Natalie's answers had run to their natural end and they drew the interview to a close. They both knew any further probing might push her nerves to breaking point. As they stood up ready to leave, Natalie took Gould's hand. Her quiet voice made him automatically lean down and take her arm. "You will catch whoever did this, won't you, Chief Inspector? If I could just know the person's behind bars that would help me to start living again."

"I'll do my best, Natalie. But whatever happens, start living again. You're too young to spend all your life in your room." Gould shook Natalie's hand and he followed Clement to the car.

"She seems a nice girl," said Clement as he turned on the ignition of the car. "I hate this job sometimes. All I've done so far is tell her that her boyfriend's dead, then ask her loads of questions."

"On the contrary, it's cases like this that make our job worthwhile," Gould said, surprised by the sensitivity of Clement's remark. "That girl's looking for us to find her fi-ancé's killer. I'm going to do that if it kills me," Gould added, looking through the car windows at the terraced streets they were passing.

****

The next day, Gould was sitting opposite Mr Miles, the managing director of MacGregor and Sons. His office was located in one of the few old-fashioned blocks left in the City. Mr Miles seemed the very embodiment of City respectability as he suavely expressed his regrets. He adjusted the sleeve of his suit jacket so his gold cufflinks were displayed to their best advantage.

"We were all very sorry to hear about Hugh Marks's death, Chief Inspector. It must have been some horrible accident or perhaps a random attack. There's such a lot of street crime these days."

"I'm afraid it was not random, Mr Miles," Gould replied. "There's no doubt he was murdered in a very professional way. I'm interested in any way he could have come into contact with criminals in his work."

"This is a very respectable company, Chief Inspector," Mr Miles said in an aggrieved tone. "All our staff must have excellent references before we employ them. He could not have encountered criminals here. It must be some personal secret that we weren't aware of."

"Please don't be offended, Mr Miles," Gould replied, in as emollient a tone as he could manage. "Gangs are invading all types of respectable companies and we have to investigate every possibility. Now please tell me a little bit more about Hugh's work," he continued more firmly.

"Well, he was training as an auditor," Mr Miles continued, apparently pacified. "He visited our clients' offices and inspected their books."

"Could I see a list of those companies, please, Mr Miles?"

"Yes, I have them here," Mr Miles replied, taking a file from a drawer and opening it on his desk. "This is his personnel file. His workload is shown just there. As you can see, they're all highly respectable companies."

"Could I keep this, please, Mr Miles?" Gould asked in a tone of command. Mr Miles meekly nodded. "Yes, they do all seem well-known firms," Gould continued running down the list. "Which company was Hugh auditing when he went missing?" Gould asked.

Mr Miles stood up and looked over Gould's shoulder. "That would be Harvey and Ward – they're a firm of travel agents in the City. They have a very impressive list of clients – most of the top companies use them."

Gould stopped reading Marks's personnel file. "Harvey and Ward did you say? I've heard of that company recently."

"They've just announced record profits," Mr Miles replied, in the excitement of a financial expert. "It was in all the financial pages. You must have seen it."

"I don't read the financial pages, Mr Miles. It was something in my line of work. It came up when I went to Wales. I'm sure it did," Gould said to himself.

"I hardly think so, Chief Inspector," Mr Miles replied with a polite smile. "Harvey and Ward's only office is in the City."

"Yes, but this new internet is a wonderful thing, isn't it, Mr Miles," Gould said, standing up, to conclude the interview.

"Yes, people can sit in the City and do business all over the world," Mr Miles agreed, showing Gould out.

"Yes, but it works the other way, doesn't it, Mr Miles," Gould replied, standing at the door of Mr Miles's office. "People from all over the world can do business in the City – and not all of them are honest."

★★★★

Later that day, Gould was seated opposite a tall elegant woman in the office of Harvey and Ward.

"I'm investigating the murder of Hugh Marks, Miss Lane," Gould began. "He worked for MacGregor and Sons and was auditing your company's accounts. Is there anything you can help me with at all?"

"Call me Margaret. No, I keep records of all our employees of course. But this man wasn't an employee. Auditors visit our offices for a few days at a time. I can't really see how I can help you. His name doesn't mean anything to me."

Just then, the phone rang on Miss Lane's desk, and she picked it up with an apologetic nod to Gould. "Yes, we want a secretary to start on Monday… Yes, I know they don't last long with us… We've been with your company for a long time. I'm sure you can find someone. Yes. Thank you," Miss Lane slammed the phone down. "Honestly, we've been clients of Eastcheap Recruitment Agency for years – you'd think they know the sort of people we want. I'm sorry – please continue."

"Is there anyone working here who may have information on Hugh Marks, Miss Lane?" Gould asked.

"No, I'm sure not. I assume he audited lots of companies' accounts. Why don't you try one of them?"

Gould stood up. "Yes, I'm sure you're right, Miss Lane. I will try somewhere else, but please phone me immediately if anything occurs to you."

Miss Lane stood up with obvious relief. "I'll show you out, Chief Inspector. It's always a pleasure to help the police." Gould allowed Miss Lane to show him out. Her anxiety to see him out was enough to raise suspicions in his mind.

****

The next day, Detective Sergeant Clement stood looking out of the windows of the City of London police station at the glossy skyscrapers around him. He looked uncomfortable at the immense wealth around him.

"I'm not sure I could do your job, Chief Inspector," he told his host. "I don't often have any need to come up to the City. It's such a different world from my manor." The worn old-fashioned blazer he was wearing emphasised how out-of-place he seemed.

"There's just as much crime in the Square Mile as anywhere else," Gould told him. "The criminals wear suits but, believe me, they can be just as unpleasant."

"I can believe it," Clement replied with the cynicism based on his long years of police experience. "But I think I prefer my criminals with dirty fingernails. What's the next stage on the Marks murder?" he asked, anxious to return to the point of the case conference.

"Well, I've agreed with the Commissioner that I'll take over the lead in the work side of this case. I'm sure Marks must have upset someone through his work in the City."

"That's very good of you, sir," Clement said with obvious relief. "But I'd still like to be kept in touch with the case. How are you going to take it forward?"

"Well, Marks was auditing several companies' accounts and we need to follow up on all of them. I've got my suspicions about one of them – it's an upmarket travel agency called Harvey and Ward. The South Wales police told me about some teenage hacker noticing a lot of mentions of Colombia in e-mail traffic from Harvey and Ward.

There's been some new source of cocaine in the City dealing rooms lately and the Drugs Squad are trying to track it down."

"And you think there's a connection between the two?" Clement suggested.

"It seems well worth investigating," Gould replied. "I went to see them and they claimed not to know anything about it. That made me suspicious. Someone with a lot of influence and money had Marks killed, and I wouldn't mind betting drugs are behind it. I'm going to send an officer undercover to check this company out."

"Why don't you just go through the front door and throw your weight about? That's what I'd do. You've got enough to go on."

"No, I know the criminals around here," Gould replied, shaking his head. "One sniff of the police and they'll have some expensive brief round complaining of harassment. What have we got to go on after all? Marks was auditing lots of companies when he was killed and any of them could have been involved. No, it's only a hunch that Harvey and Ward's is the one and it's best to send someone undercover."

"Well, good luck. I hope your man does well," Clement said, standing up as the case conference came to an end.

"I didn't say it was a man," Gould replied. "I think a woman might fit in better. I've got one in mind. She's just moved over from doing family work, so none of the drug dealers will recognise her. I think she should do very well."

★★★★

Later that day, a slim attractive dark-haired young woman came into Gould's office and put her head around the door. "It's DS Cottrell, sir. You asked to see me."

Gould stood up and politely directed her to a chair and sat opposite. "Hello, Philippa, congratulations on passing your sergeant's board." Gould shook her hand then, once she had sat down, picked up a manila folder. "Well, as you know, you've been assigned to the Serious Crime Squad, so we'll be working closely together from now on."

"I'm looking forward to the challenge of working here, sir," Philippa replied stiffly.

Gould picked up a paper file and placed it on the desk in front of him. "I have your personnel file here, but I'd like to hear about you in your own words. First, why did you join the police force? The police must have been quite a change from your previous work."

"Well, I started as a secretary here in the City. I liked the work, but I felt I needed something more rewarding. So I joined the City police force. All my friends were shocked. Perhaps I'm not the normal police officer, but I love it."

"Looking at your file, you've been involved in family matters and crime prevention. Mainly office work, I think, or dealing with mothers and children. It's very different to the cases we have here."

"I realise I have a lot to learn on the serious crime side, sir. I'll do my best," Philippa replied defensively, detecting a reservation in Gould's voice.

"No, don't apologise," Gould said, looking at her up and down. He told himself that anyone passing Philippa in the street would imagine she was one of the many thousands of female office workers in the City. Anyone looking less like a police officer would be hard to imagine. "You could be just the sort of person for some undercover work I have in mind. You don't look like the average police officer, and your experience of office work should be ideal. I've persuaded a company called Eastcheap Recruitment to co-operate – they didn't have much choice really. You're to work in a company called Harvey and Ward's. Your experience as a secretary should help. You're to report to a Margaret Lane. I've met her once, and she was very keen to see me off the premises. That, together with the intelligence we've received from a drugs raid in South Wales, makes me suspicious. There's been a recent murder in Mile End of a man auditing the company, and I've decided that an undercover investigation is needed…" Philippa listened intently as Gould continued to describe her first assignment in the City of London Serious Crimes Squad.

Chapter 3

On Monday, the newly promoted Detective Sergeant Cottrell stood on the pavement outside the City of London sky-scraper that towered high above her. The rush-hour crowds streamed past, but she was too preoccupied to notice the occasional male passer-by casting an appreciative glance in her direction as he scurried off to work. Despite the warm weather, Philippa Cottrell shivered inside the sensible skirt and cardigan that she had chosen to suit the secretarial role she was about to take. Philippa had always been nervous when starting a new assignment, but, now she was pro-moted, she especially wanted to make a good impression on Gould and convince him she was tough enough to cope with a career in the Serious Crimes Squad.

Philippa looked at the note, which she had been given by the employment agency, which the force had arranged for her. '10 am report to Mr Ward of Harvey and Ward', it said. She placed the note in her handbag and walked as con-fidently as she could into the foyer of the huge building. It took a while to see her would-be employer's name among all the other companies listed on the board inside the door. Eventually, she spotted an elderly man in commissionaire's uniform behind one of the desks dotted around the foyer. He was engrossed in the sports pages of that morning's paper and did not look up as Philippa approached. After a couple of minutes, he put the paper down wearily when she man-aged to attract his attention.

"Excuse me. My name's Philippa Maxwell," she said. She had agreed with Gould that she should use her real first name with a fictional surname for the assignment. "I'm due to start work here this morning."

The man grunted and ran his pencil down a long list of names until he eventually found Philippa's.

"Ah, yes," he said. "You're to be Mr Ward's secretary for today."

"Oh, no," she protested. "It's not just for today – it's permanent."

The man laughed unpleasantly as he pressed the intercom and announced Philippa's name. After a moment, he turned back to her.

"You're to go to the twentieth floor, love," he said. "Miss Margaret Lane will be waiting for you there."

She thanked him and turned to go to the lifts. As she waited for one to arrive, she heard the man behind her laughing to himself. She turned around sharply but he had returned to his sports page. After what seemed a long wait, an express lift came to take her to the twentieth floor. When she arrived there, a tall elegant woman, wearing heavy make-up, was waiting for her.

"You must be Philippa Maxwell," she said. "My name is Margaret Lane. Welcome to Harvey and Ward's. Would you come with me, please?" Philippa recognised the name from Gould's report. She found it hard to guess Margaret's age – at least ten years older than herself, so at least in her mid-thirties, she imagined – but the tightness around her eyes indicated she could be older. The well-dressed woman stretched out her hand.

Philippa thanked her and followed her along a plushly-carpeted corridor until they turned a corner and suddenly came to a locked glass door. Margaret Lane tapped some numbers into a console on the wall.

"I'm afraid we have to be very careful with security here, Philippa. We'll give you a code for entering in due course." Margaret continued to talk as they walked along the corridor. "As I expect you know, we're the top travel agency in the City – all the major companies know they can rely on us to be discreet and efficient. We're a partnership – Neil Harvey is senior, and Reg Ward is the junior. They go back a long time – they were at school together. I'll take you straight along to see Reg Ward. I'm sure you'll get on well with him. Don't let his manner put you off."

Philippa politely listened to the woman's introductory talk, though in fact Gould had filled her in with the company's background, and she knew a great deal more about the company's activities than Margaret realised. As they came close to one office, which was much larger and more expensively furnished than the others, they could hear raised voices, which were echoing down the corridor. As they passed the open door, Philippa saw a senior-looking well-dressed middle-aged man standing up and angrily addressing another man of about the same age, obviously his junior, who was sitting nervously in an uncomfortable chair.

"I'm fed up with this," the senior man was shouting, his face becoming steadily redder. "Do you know how many of your secretaries have left in the last three months? I've been counting them – you've had eight, and six of them have complained to a tribunal. You'd better keep the one who's coming today, or you'll be the one who's out."

Margaret Lane gave no indication of having heard the conversation, but she quietly closed the door as they went past, and Philippa could hear no more of what was being said. Margaret walked to a desk a few feet further along.

"Well, welcome to Harvey and Ward, Philippa," she said. "This will be your desk. Mr Ward will be here shortly."

As she spoke, a flustered man rushed along the corridor. Philippa recognised him as the man who was being shouted at in the office the two women had passed earlier. He kept his eyes down as he came up to Margaret.

"Ah, Reg," she said. "This is Philippa – Philippa Maxwell."

"How do you do, Philippa." Reg Ward shook her hand politely. He was around fifty years old and struck Philippa as looking rather dissolute, but still handsome, resembling a matinee idol who has gone to seed. Ward's hair was greased back in the fashion of several decades before. She was reminded vaguely of the later films of Clark Gable, when the actor was a sad reminder of the leading man he had once been. Philippa suppressed a shudder as she took Ward's hand.

"I'm pleased to meet you, Mr Ward," Philippa replied as politely she could. "I'm looking forward to working here."

Until then, Reg Ward had kept his eyes down. Then, something in Philippa's voice made him look at her face. He held her hand a little longer than necessary, as he looked her up and down. Philippa sensed with mixed feelings that she had met with Ward's approval.

****

Later that day, Philippa was seated at her new desk outside Ward's room, when the phone rang and she picked it up. She was busy in the normal type of secretarial duties and had so far exchanged only a few words with her new boss. She was concentrating on learning her new role for Harvey and Ward, and so far, had noticed nothing to interest the City police.

"Harvey here. Come and see me at once." An abrupt order came down the phone. Philippa recognised the voice of the man she had heard shouting at Ward that morning. Philippa picked up her notepad and pencil and knocked on Ward's door.

"I've been asked to see Mr Harvey," she said.

"Harvey wants to see you? That's odd. He's never asked to see any of my other secretaries," Ward said, looking puzzled, and Philippa thought, worried. Philippa easily found Harvey's office. She knocked on the door and went in.

"You asked to see me, Mr Harvey," she said as she entered. Harvey was a large, florid man, dressed in an expensive suit, obviously tailored to hide his considerable bulk.

"Yes, come in," Harvey stood up as she took a seat. "I like to meet all new staff when they arrive." Philippa knew from what Ward had said that this was not true, but she waited for Harvey to continue.

"I see you have good references from your previous employers. I was quite impressed. In fact, I know one of the people whose signature was on them," he continued, as Philippa shifted uneasily in her chair. "I phoned him up today and told him we had one of his former staff. And do you know what he said?"

"Not really, Mr Harvey," she replied.

"He said he'd never heard of you." Harvey leaned forward, adjusted his gold cufflinks, and came close to Philippa. "How do you explain that?"

"I suppose he must have forgotten me," she replied, conscious of how lame her reply would seem to Harvey.

"I don't think so," Harvey took a deep breath. "So, let's review the situation. There are hundreds of secretarial jobs available in the City. Here we have a young woman who goes to a great deal of trouble to forge references for a job in my company. What do you think I should make of that?"

"I don't know, Mr Harvey," she stammered. Tears unconsciously came to her eyes as she realised how close she was to being uncovered on her first assignment in the Serious Crimes Squad. "I'm desperate for a job, that's all."

"I expect loyalty from people who work for me. I won't tolerate spies from outside poking their noses into my affairs." Harvey's voice was becoming steadily louder. Then he suddenly paused. He seemed pleased with himself for bringing Philippa to tears. For some reason, he decided to relent, possibly deciding she was not a threat. "I'd like you to come back and see me tomorrow and explain why I shouldn't sack you immediately. Do you understand?"

"Yes, Mr Harvey. Thank you," Philippa said as she stood up, turned around and rushed out of the room. Out in the corridor she took a deep breath. It was very obvious her cover was in danger of being blown and she still needed to find more about what was going on inside this company. She returned to her desk and decided to consult Gould that evening as to what action she should take.

★★★★

After Philippa had left his office, Harvey gave a satisfied smile, picked up his phone and dialled a number. When he started to speak, his voice changed completely. "Hello,

Samantha. I have booked somewhere a bit special tonight. I think you'll like it. See you at eight then." Harvey put down the phone with a complacent smile. He stood up and combed his hair in the wall mirror above his desk. He felt several years younger as he looked forward to his evening date. He had decided to cultivate a younger image and rather thought the modern abstract painting on the wall that he had bought a few days ago added to the effect.

****

For the rest of the day, Philippa kept to her role of a loyal secretary learning the details of her new job. As soon as she arrived home in her Greenwich flat, she spoke to Gould on the phone. "Whoever set up those forged references for me screwed up, sir. Neil Harvey knows one of the people listed and they've told him they've never heard of me."

Philippa could hear a muffled oath from the other end of the line. "We cleared it with the companies' personnel departments," Gould said, "but something must have gone wrong. There's always a danger of this happening. Still, how do you want to play it now? We need to find more about what's going on in Harvey and Ward."

"As I see it, we have two options," Philippa replied. "The first is we pull the plug and call the whole operation off."

"I don't want to do that. We could be on the track of a murderer in that company."

"The other option is we ask someone inside to co-operate."
"Who?"
"My vote is to get Ward to help us."

"Ward? What do we know about him?" Gould asked. "What if he's involved in the Marks' murder or the drugs smuggling? Then we're back where we started."

"Not really. If we pull out now, the whole operation's wasted anyway. Ward's got no form and at least we'll have someone to question if he won't help. I'll make it clear he has a choice of co-operating with us or going down with the rest when we move in. I can't see him being involved in murder or drugs. From what I can see, there's no love lost between Ward and Harvey. I think we ought to risk it."

"And you think he'll co-operate?"

"From what I've seen, he'd co-operate with anyone female and reasonably attractive," Philippa replied, recalling the way he leaned over her earlier in the day.

"Very well," Gould said after a pause, "getting Ward's co-operation may be the best course. It's risky but every other option seems worse. I'm taking your advice, but it'll be on your head if this whole investigation collapses."

"OK. I'll report back tomorrow evening," Philippa replied, before putting the handset down. She gazed at her reflection in the mirror in her hall and reflected that her first undercover assignment was proving to be tougher than she could have imagined.

Chapter 4

While Philippa was reporting to Gould, Neil Harvey was in the dining room of a Pall Mall directors' club smiling complacently. He was seated opposite a young woman with artificially blond hair. Harvey was conscious of the jealous glances of the other men in the restaurant and relished the feeling. He realised from the hostile looks from the other women there that they assumed Samantha was some sort of high-class call girl. In fact, he felt like telling them that he had not paid Samantha a penny. They had had sex several times, which had been better than anything he had experienced before, and if she did not enjoy it, she certainly had not objected.

Having turned fifty, Harvey felt he was doing rather well attracting a girl like Samantha. He clicked his fingers for the bill that came remarkably quickly. As the waiters hovered, Harvey left a fifty pounds tip on the table and the couple were ushered out in an appropriately obsequious manner.

After a taxi ride, the two arrived in Battersea and climbed the stairs to Samantha's attic flat. Harvey was in a mellow mood as Samantha switched on all the lights in the sitting room. It was large and well-furnished and, not for the first time, Harvey wondered how Samantha could afford the rent. She told him she worked as a receptionist, which seemed unlikely to pay much. A thought crossed his mind that only one profession would pay for such a flat. Harvey shook his head to banish the thought – if a girl like Samantha was willing to offer sex free of charge, he saw no reason to refuse.

"Do you fancy a drink, love?" Samantha asked in her Liverpudlian accent as she unzipped the back of her dress. Harvey sat on the settee opposite, watching. He was too aroused even to reply but distractedly nodded his head.

"Are you enjoying yourself, love?" Samantha continued as she stepped out of her dress. She unclipped her bra; she obviously had enough experience to know just how long to suspend the bra in front of her before letting the skimpy garment fall to the ground.

Harvey was too fascinated by the performance to say any more. Samantha stepped out of her panties and walked toward Harvey. "Shall we do it the same way this time?" she said and without waiting for an answer, unzipped Harvey's trousers and with a provocative wiggle, sat on him in a way designed to give him the ultimate physical sensation.

Some ten minutes later while Harvey and Samantha were dressing themselves, the door of Samantha's flat banged open and a small wiry-looking man came in. Harvey gaped at the man in astonishment.

"What's going on? Who the hell are you?" Harvey demanded.

"Just call me Miller. I'm sorry to disturb you," said the man, who spoke with authority in a cockney accent. "But I think you should know that your performance tonight has been videoed." He indicated a large mirror on the back of the bed.

"Do you know this man?" Harvey turned to Samantha.

"Yes, love," replied Samantha. "I'm afraid he's right. I think you ought to listen to him."

"What is this? Blackmail?" Harvey demanded, staring at Samantha and Miller in turn. "If it is, you can both go to hell. I'm not paying anything."

"It's nothing so crude as money," Samantha said. "All you've got to do is meet an old friend of yours."

"What are you talking about?" Harvey shouted at Samantha, his fists clenched.

"We both work for someone you went to school with," Samantha replied. She looked to Miller for support. "He'd like to make you a business proposition. It's nothing to be worried about, love, I'm just a gift for old time's sake. You can still see me, but please take me somewhere a bit more exciting next time," Samantha continued with a half-smile, as Miller came between Harvey and Samantha. Miller had the look of an experienced street fighter and Harvey quickly abandoned any thought of violence against Samantha.

"I'm not taking any more of this," Harvey said, walking towards to the door of Samantha's flat. Before he could turn the handle, a well-dressed man of about Harvey's age walked in.

"Don't you remember me, Neil?" the man asked.

"No, I certainly don't," Harvey snapped, though something about the man's face seemed familiar from somewhere in his past.

"Let me give you a clue," the man said, putting his hand out to stop Harvey. Even though the unknown man was shorter than Harvey, the force of the intruder's personality kept Harvey from moving. "You were the only boy at school to stand up to me."

A distant memory from childhood came to Harvey's mind. "My God, you're Spendlove, aren't you? Jack Spendlove. Are you behind all this?" Harvey said. "I hope you're not expecting me to say that I'm pleased to see you. I didn't like you then and I don't like you now."

Miller moved forward with a threatening gesture, but Spendlove brushed him aside. "Don't worry, Nick," Spendlove said to Miller. "I can see this is a shock for Mr Harvey." Spendlove turned to Harvey and sat down. "The thing is, Neil, that we've both done rather well in our chosen careers. I've been admiring the success of your travel agency business from afar."

"What business are you in now?" Harvey sneered. "Blackmail, by the look of things," he said, nodding at Samantha, who was now dressed.

"Not primarily," Spendlove answered, with a sinister smile, "but I hope you enjoyed Samantha's services. Don't worry about payment – it's all on the house," he laughed.

"What do you want then?" Harvey asked, his eyes gazing at Spendlove suspiciously.

"A fusion of our businesses," Spendlove replied. "Your access to travel routes will complement my knowledge of the fastest growing leisure market in the West."

"What market's that?"

"Cocaine," answered Spendlove, with obvious pride. "It's the market of the future, Neil. Half the dealers in the City are clients of mine."

"Drugs?" Harvey echoed. "I might have known you'd get involved in something like that. And you expect me to help you? Are you out of your mind? I could get twenty years in jail getting involved in that."

"There's no need to worry, Neil. I will take care of all the hard work and take all the risks," said Spendlove. "You just have to turn a blind eye and count your profits. And you have continued access to Samantha – or one of my other girls if you'd like a change."

"Go to hell, Spendlove. I'm reporting all this to the police." Harvey picked up his jacket and walked toward the door.

"That's your choice, Neil," Spendlove replied. "Miller here will send these photos we've taken to your wife – Kathleen, isn't it? Your children might be interested as well – Cassandra and Jason are their names, I think. We've got both stills and a video with sound – quite artistic, they are. I have your home address from Companies House. The only snag is you left off your postcode. Can you give it to us now then the photos will get there that bit quicker?" Spendlove laughed without mirth. "The three of us will just sit here and watch the video. Samantha has some good tricks, doesn't she? Perhaps your wife might learn a few things from watching it. Do you think she'll appreciate it, Neil?"

Harvey stood at the door of Samantha's flat and looked dubiously at Miller and Spendlove. Harvey looked at the unmade bed and shuddered with embarrassment as he imagined what was on the video and how his wife would react when she saw the images of him with Samantha.

"What do you want me to do exactly?" he asked in a defeated tone.

"You won't have to do anything very much," Spendlove replied. "In fact, nothing at all. I have one of my employees working in your firm now. His name's Charles Anson. I think you know him."

"Yes, I know Anson," Harvey said trying to keep his voice calm. "What about him? What do you want me to do?"

"You don't have to do anything. Just leave him alone to do his work – that's all we ask. One of your colleagues started sniffing around too much just recently and he paid the price."

"What do you mean? Let's just say he won't be talking to anyone again and leave it like that," Spendlove paused to make sure that Harvey looked sufficiently terrified. "Now, we don't want any more unpleasantness, do we, Neil? Are you prepared to co-operate?"

Harvey looked at Spendlove, Miller and Samantha in turn. He shivered as he considered his position.

****

Later that evening, Neil Harvey drove his Jaguar up the long drive of his Haslemere home into his garage and turned off the engine. He realised he had many factors to consider in planning his next move. Picking up his briefcase, he unlocked the front door and walked as quietly as he could along the carpet in the hall. He had already warned his wife, Kathleen, not to expect him for dinner. They slept in separate bedrooms so he hoped he could climb into bed unnoticed, but he saw a light in the kitchen. He knew the family's au pair sometimes worked late there. He reminded himself that she was very pretty and he had hopes of making a bit of progress with her. He entered the kitchen with what he hoped was a charming smile.

"Ah, Mr Harvey. You made me jump," Tania, the au pair, edged away from Harvey. She was dressed in a robe, and instinctively drew it tighter around her.

"I'm sorry to startle you, my dear. I was hoping to find you here," Harvey walked towards Tania. He was telling himself how lucky he felt to find Tania on her own, when an unwelcome voice came from the hall.

"Neil, you're back late."

Harvey winced as he heard the familiar sounds of his wife's voice. He wondered if he had ever found it attractive, then decided probably not. He had married Kathleen for money, not for love. He enjoyed the trappings of luxury his job gave him, but, in fact, most of the assets of his home life were in his wife's name. He often told himself that a comfortable lifestyle made a loveless marriage tolerable, but there were times when he doubted it. He managed to compose his expression into a dutiful smile by the time his wife entered the kitchen.

"Ah, Kathleen, I thought you would be in bed," Harvey said, dutifully kissing his wife's forehead.

"I realised that, Neil. You can go to bed now, Tania." She paused until Tania left the kitchen. "I hope you're not too disappointed to find me up."

"No. of course not. I'm just glad to be home. You won't believe what a hard day I've had."

"That smells like alcohol on your breath."

"Yes, well I met a few mates at the club – just socialising for the business. You know how it is."

"Oh, I know all right. After all, it's my business." Kathleen knew how Harvey hated to be reminded that the bulk of the money to finance his business came from her father.

"Well, all the more reason why you should welcome me working late. I'll be off to bed. I've eaten already and don't want anything more." Harvey left the kitchen and went up to his bedroom and threw his case on the floor. As he undressed, he cast his thoughts over the various women in his life. They seemed to exist in different contexts. Kathleen – his wife, who was little more than a source of funds. Margaret Lane – his loyal PA and occasional mistress. Samantha – who it now appeared was a prostitute, paid by Spendlove. His daughter, Cassandra, was working well in his firm, and he did not want her contaminated by any dubious activities organised by Spendlove. He decided he needed to take some decisive action tomorrow to keep all these women from knowing about each other.

As he turned out the light, he looked wistfully out of his window to the other wing where the au pair, Tania, slept. He had appreciated the sight of her in her robe, and he had a mental image of her taking a shower after her day's work and the water cascading off her naked body. But he shook his head. He felt he had more than enough problems at present, without inviting any more complications into his life.

Chapter 5

When Philippa arrived for work the next day, a woman she did not recognise was talking to Reg Ward, around his open office door. She seemed in her mid-twenties – roughly Philippa's age- but it was obvious the two had nothing else in common. Everything about the unknown woman spelt money – from her bronzed skin to the highlights in her blond hair. Her gold earrings and necklaces clanged together as she moved. Philippa knew it would take several months of her own wages to buy the beautifully-tailored trouser suit the woman was wearing.

The woman was a fascinating sight and Philippa had to stop herself from staring at her. Reg Ward, however, felt no such constraint and was obviously entranced, nodding at everything she said. Philippa pulled some papers from the drawer of her desk and had started to type when the woman came out of the office, closely followed by Ward.

"Hello, you must be the new girl," the woman announced in a refined public-school accent. Philippa felt a duchess would have used the same tone to address a new kitchen maid.

"Yes, this is Philippa." Ward introduced them. "This is Cassandra, Philippa, Mr Harvey's daughter." Philippa fought off a ridiculous urge to curtsey and they shook hands politely. A mental image of two boxers shaking hands before a fight crossed Philippa's mind.

"Cassandra has an important marketing role here," said Ward.

"Yes, I can imagine," Philippa replied, with a fixed polite smile.

"Well, I have won quite a few contracts, if I say so myself. I hope you'll be successful, Philippa, while you are with us … I'll see you at that meeting at eleven, Reg," Cassandra said as she turned to go back to her own office, leaving a whiff of expensive perfume.

"Should I put that meeting in your diary, Mr Ward?" Philippa asked.

"Call me, Reg, Philippa," he replied. He leaned unnecessarily close as he indicated how to log the meeting on the computer system. Philippa instinctively leant back from his arm, which stretched close to her breasts. "By the way, would you like to come along to keep track of what's decided? I think I'm going to need all the support I can get."

****

While Philippa was being introduced to Cassandra, Neil Harvey sat in his office and thought about the events of the previous night and how they affected his daughter. He had no wish to have her involved in any way with the drugs trafficking that he had just learnt was going on in the company, but he was not sure of the best way to keep her away from it. He knew that she was seeing a lot of Anson, and to him they seemed close to moving in together. He knew his daughter well enough to know that any suggestion he made that she should drop her friendship with Charles Anson would have the opposite effect.

He felt sure that Cassandra was not involved in Anson's drug dealing, but he knew she would need proof before believing her father before her current boyfriend. There was only one thing for it, he decided, and that was to get Cassandra out of the company in some other way. He was unsure how he was going to respond to Spendlove's blackmail, but he was certain he wanted his daughter out of harm's way. He mentally planned what he would say at the regular weekly progress meeting.

****

When Philippa went into the conference room soon before eleven that morning with Reg Ward, Cassandra was already there, talking to a man Philippa had not met. If Ward had been fawning on Cassandra earlier, it was clear that this time the position was reversed. Cassandra gazed on this man with unfeigned admiration.

"We have to make your father see sense …" the man was saying before he noticed they were no longer alone.

"Charles," Ward said, attracting the man's attention. "This is Philippa."

When Anson stood up, it was evident what it was about the man that caught Cassandra's attention. Philippa told herself it seemed strange to call a man beautiful, but Philippa felt that was the best word to describe Charles Anson. He was tall, aged about thirty, with perfectly even features, resembling some walking advert for male cosmetics. Philippa found it hard not to stare at him, but she managed to look demurely down as they shook hands.

"Charles organises many of the most important trips for our clients," Ward explained, but before he could say more, Harvey came in, followed at a respectful distance by Margaret Lane. The force of his personality stopped any other conversation as the rest of those present meekly took their seats. Philippa carefully sat as far away from Harvey as she could, hoping he would forget about her forged references.

"Good morning," boomed Harvey as he looked around the room. The rest of the meeting instinctively looked down – only Cassandra seemed unimpressed. Harvey addressed his next remarks to her.

"I'm afraid I have some bad news," Harvey continued. "We have lost one of our biggest contracts – for the Stock Exchange itself." He glared around the room – in the light of their conversation the previous day, Philippa did her best to seem invisible. "This is not good enough. Cassandra, you were in charge of this contract. How did we manage to lose it?"

"Well, there was a lot of competition, Dad … er, Mr Harvey," Cassandra replied. Her usual air of confidence seemed to be disappearing under her father's interrogation.

"There was a lot of competition, was there?" Harvey echoed. "Let me tell you, young lady, I am not interested how much competition there is. I just want to win. Only losers come second. What do you have to say to that?"

"I'm sorry, Dad," Cassandra said, her eyes cast down. "We'll just have to do better next time."

"No doubt you are sorry." By now Harvey's face was puce with anger. "I think you know by now that anyone who works for me is allowed to make one mistake. You've just made yours. The rule applies to my family as much as anyone else. You're dismissed." There was a collective intake of breath by the others at the meeting as their eyes unconsciously turned to see how Harvey's daughter would react.

After a moment's pause while she absorbed what her father had said, Cassandra rose to her feet, and walked towards him. "You can't sack me, I've just resigned." With some dignity, she turned to walk towards the door.

"Where do you think you're going?" Harvey was shouting. "You'd be nothing without my money."

Cassandra opened her mouth as if to speak, but merely left the room, slamming the door behind her. Nobody in the room made a sound.

"Well, thank you for coming, ladies and gentlemen," Harvey said, standing up. "Let's have no more failures. Winning is the only option in any company I run. Good day." Harvey left the room.

There was a long pause before anyone spoke. To relieve the tension, Philippa eventually asked a question. "Is Mr Harvey always like that?" she asked.

"No, Philippa, this morning was bad, even for Harvey. Something must really have upset him – he was quite cheerful yesterday," replied Ward.

"How could anyone talk to their daughter like that in public?" Anson's question did not receive a reply. Instead Margaret Lane got to her feet.

"Well. I'm on Neil's side. I'm sick of you all talking behind his back like that," Margaret shouted. "He's a great and good man. You don't understand the pressure he's under." She ran out of the room. The others could hear her go into Harvey's room and the sound of the door being locked.

"There speaks the voice of true love," said Anson, with a cynical laugh.

"What do you mean?" Philippa asked.

"Mr Harvey and Margaret are what you might call a pair, Philippa," Reg Ward replied.

"Yes, nobody knows what goes on in his room when they're together over lunch," Anson replied. "All we know is that Margaret's clothing is a good deal more crumpled in the afternoon than in the morning …" Anson laughed. "Anyway, I ought to see how Cassandra is." Charles Anson rose to go, leaving just Reg and Philippa behind.

"Well, come on, Philippa, the show's over," said Reg. "You've seen how the organisation works. Now let's get some work done."

As they walked back along the corridor, Philippa asked Ward what he thought would happen to Cassandra.

"Oh, she'll be all right," he assured Philippa. "The storm will probably blow over soon."

"I'm not sure," Philippa replied. "I've only just met Cassandra, but she looked very upset when she left. How close is she to Charles Anson?"

"They go around together," Reg said. "That's all I really know. She's keen on him as you've noticed, but he's only in love with himself. There doesn't seem much future in it."

"What is his job exactly?" Philippa asked.

"Most of the dealing firms employ us to arrange airline tickets for their staff," Reg answered. "Anson's the man on the ground meeting the customers."

They walked on in silence. There were a few things Philippa knew about Charles Anson already. He was, as Ward implied, good-looking, vain, and he dressed a good deal more expensively than his position justified. Philippa's police training had made her notice that his nostrils were enlarged and reddened – the classic signs of the cocaine addict. Philippa was already mentally rehearsing the report she would file that night for Detective Chief Inspector Gould.

Chapter 6

At lunchtime, Philippa followed some of the other members of staff to a nearby wine bar. She bought herself an expensive orange juice and looked around. Philippa recalled a military saying that time spent on reconnaissance is seldom wasted and she was content to just look around the wine bar, quietly soaking up the atmosphere. She expected to be spending some time working undercover with these people, learning as much as she could about them. She smiled to herself when she realised she was sounding like an explorer in some distant country.

Just then she saw Cassandra sitting in the corner, sipping a glass of wine. Philippa went over to speak to her.

"May I join you?" Philippa asked, but received only a glare in response. "I'm really sorry that your father sacked you, Cassandra," Philippa continued. "Especially in front of everyone like that. You must feel awful."

Cassandra looked at Philippa with contempt. "What do you know about anything? You've only just joined. I don't want sympathy, least of all from someone like you," Cassandra replied.

"What are you going to do now?" Philippa asked in a conversational tone, forcing herself to ignore the woman's rudeness for the sake of the police investigation.

"Hell, I've no idea. I know those people," Cassandra indicated the Harvey and Ward employees clustered around the bar, "are talking about me. They think it's easy being the boss's daughter. Let me tell you, my father gives me a much harder time than he gives them." She paused while she sipped her wine. "I'm sorry if I was rude," she continued, calming down. "But I've had a lot to put up with. If my father thinks I'm going quietly, he can think again."

In the far corner of the bar, Philippa saw another group of young executives celebrating. One of them called over to Cassandra.

"Don't worry, Cassie. You can't win them all."

"Who's that?" Philippa asked.

"Can't you tell? That is my twin brother. He was christened Jason, but you can call him Judas. He's a traitor to Dad's firm. He resigned a few years ago to work for our main rivals. He takes delight in humiliating me every chance he gets."

"How does your father feel about that?"

"How would anyone feel? Betrayed, of course. Still, he seemed to have a grudging respect for him. I think Jason's hope is that Dad will invite him back once he's had a few years' experience. Then Jason will lord it over me." Cassandra shuddered. "It's an awful thought."

Just then, Charles Anson came in. "For God's sake, I've been looking for you everywhere. Where the hell have you been?" he demanded. He noticed Philippa who was getting up to leave. "What's she doing here?"

"Philippa's a friend," Cassandra responded. "She can stay as long as she likes."

"Yeah, well, I want to talk to you in private," Anson replied. "Here, buy us all a drink." He handed Philippa a twenty-pound note. "Cassandra will have the same again and I'll have a pint of lager. Keep the change."

"What do you think I am? Some sort of serving wench?" was the thought that came to Philippa's mind, as she took the note. In her civilian life, they would have been the words that came to her lips but she managed to restrain herself.

"Thank you, Charles," Philippa said, walking away to the bar and putting the note into her purse. She looked forward to sending that twenty-pound note for tests. If it proved to be heavily contaminated with cocaine it would be useful evidence. She told herself that while it might be an unprofessional feeling, putting Anson behind bars would give her a good deal of personal satisfaction.

****

Soon after lunch, Neil Harvey looked out of the window of his office at the skyscrapers around him. He pondered his position now that Cassandra was out of the way. He asked himself if he should simply sack Anson and tell the police what he knew. He would enjoy shopping Spendlove to the police, but then Harvey shuddered as he tried to imagine what would follow if Spendlove carried out his threat of sending Kathleen Harvey the photos of her husband in bed with Samantha.

His thoughts turned wistfully to the sex sessions with Samantha and how much he would miss them. He always knew she was attracted to him by his money and position, but the realisation that the sessions were paid for by his old adversary from school days was too much for him to bear. Perhaps he should simply divorce Kathleen? But that would mean giving away a large part of his money. Much of his income came from his wife and his lifestyle would go rapidly downhill once she had proof of his adultery with Samantha.

Harvey, anxious to make a decision, reached out and pressed the intercom. "Tell Anson to come in at once," he barked to Margaret. Whatever was going in, it was clear that Anson was involved, and Harvey was determined to find out what was happening within his company.

With a knock on the door, in a moment, Charles Anson came in. "You wanted to see me, Neil," Anson asked, as he sat down on the edge of his chair.

"Yes, I did. I've just had a meeting with someone I knew a long time ago – I won't call him a friend. His name's Jack Spendlove. I think you know him too."

Anson's face was a picture of polite bafflement. "Did you say Spendlove, Neil?" Anson paused in convincing head searching. "No, I've never heard of that name. Who is he?"

Harvey came out from behind his desk and stood close to Anson. "Spendlove told me what you've been up to. You work for me while you're here and no one else. Do you understand?"

Anson looked slightly scared as if Harvey had taken leave of his senses. "I assure you, Mr Harvey. I always do my best for the company. What am I supposed to have done wrong?"

"And do you really think I'm going to let my daughter go out with a drug dealing creep like you? I'm going to keep her as far away from you as I can."

"But I don't have anything to do with drugs, Mr Harvey."

"You shut up. If you ask my daughter out again, your life won't be worth living. Do you understand?" Harvey pointed to the door. "I know more of what's going on than you think. Now get out of my office before I throw you out."

Anson opened his mouth as if he wanted to say something, but changed his mind and opened the door to leave the office. Harvey gazed after the closed door once his visitor had left. Anson's apparent innocence seemed genuine, but Harvey was determined to find out more. He decided he would follow Anson when he next left the office.

★★★★

Back in his own office, Anson breathed heavily and locked the door behind him. That had been too close for comfort, he told himself. Harvey was definitely on to something, but he wondered who the hell was this Spendlove he was talking about. Anson received his regular payment from a small wiry man he knew only as Nick.

Anson unlocked the drawer of his desk. He moved some papers to one side then smiled with satisfaction as he saw a gun lying underneath. Somehow, he felt he might be needing it and he slipped it into an inside pocket. He checked on his electronic calendar – he was down to pick up a special client from Heathrow Airport. This was a euphemism for the more profitable of his two occupations. He picked up the keys of his executive car and walked out. As Anson pulled out into the traffic, he did not suspect that Harvey was in the taxi behind him.

★★★★

As Anson neared Heathrow airport, some carnations lay wrapped in polythened splendour on the floor of the cargo hold of a jet. It had arrived from Colombia an hour before and it was undergoing one of the routine checks given to all planes arriving from that country. The trained police spaniel sniffed along the floor but seemed baffled by the scent of the flowers. The animal eventually gave up and directed its handler away and on to the next plane.

The baggage-handler standing at the door of the hold breathed a sigh of relief as he saw the dog leave. He carefully picked up a vacuum-packed plastic bag of cocaine from inside the flowers and stashed it in his pocket. When he had finished unloading the rest of the cargo, he looked around to make sure he was not being followed and walked away. When he reached the gate, he flashed his valid identity card at the guard, walked through the terminal lounge and dropped it into a rubbish bin outside. From his vantage point, Neil Harvey saw Charles Anson get out of his car. With a smile of satisfaction Anson picked up the bag and took it into his car. Harvey waited until Anson was out of sight before he directed the taxi back to his office. He decided he had seen enough.

****

When Anson reached Hammersmith on the way from the airport, he parked and walked into a Macdonald's restaurant. After buying a coffee, he walked over to the furthest corner, passing a children's birthday party. When he sat down, he watched the children's high-pitched antics with obvious distaste. Anson's contact always chose a Macdonald's for their meetings – a different one every time for security. The contrast between the innocence of the children around him and the tawdry nature of his drug dealing always turned Anson's stomach. He was not sure if his contact noticed this or perhaps the incongruous surroundings amused him. Anson told himself it was not so many years since he had been the same age as the children at the party. He wondered what had happened to his life since that time, then shuddered at the thought. He told himself he was in the drugs business too deeply to turn back now. A firm hand on his shoulder interrupted Anson's musings.

"Charles, how are you?" Miller said, sitting down opposite Anson. Receiving no reply, Miller asked in a quieter voice. "Got the white stuff for me?"

"I've just had a rollicking from my boss," Anson replied, keeping his voice down. "He said I was working for some character called Spendlove. I didn't know what he was talking about. Are you Spendlove? You've never told me your name."

Miller laughed. "That was Neil Harvey talking, I suppose. I met him recently. I hope he's not going around talking to too many people. No, I'm not Spendlove. You can…"

"Call you Smith, I know," Anson continued. "Can we get this over with? I don't enjoy carrying a kilo of this stuff around London with me. Have you any idea how much work's involved in arranging for this stuff to be hidden inside loads of stupid flowers?"

"Just give me the consignment, Charles," Miller replied, ignoring Anson's words. "I'm not interested in your hard luck stories."

Anson obediently handed over an innocuous-looking carrier bag. Miller picked it up and placed it on the seat next to him. "Aren't you going to check it's the right amount?" Anson asked.

"I know you wouldn't dare play silly devils, Charles. You wouldn't have the guts."

"So, where's my payment?"

Miller nodded and silently passed over a small padded envelope. Anson eagerly opened it and held it up to his eyes. He saw the expected large bundle of money, and a clear plastic bag of white powder.

"That should keep your own customers happy," Miller said, before putting his hand over the envelope to stop Anson grabbing it. "We try to keep an eye on our staff, Charles."

Anson looked puzzled. "What's that supposed to mean?"

"Did you know that Neil Harvey followed you to the airport just now?" Miller continued, as Anson gaped at him. "I thought not. A few weeks ago, some character called Hugh Marks was following you as well. I'm not sure what he saw, but he won't be telling anyone anything now."

"Marks? Wasn't he the auditor who disappeared?"

"That's him," Miller nodded, then moved his face closer to Anson's. "I hope Harvey doesn't meet the same fate. Or if you get too careless, you might as well. Goodbye, Charles." Miller stood up and walked out of the restaurant.

Anson waited the agreed two minutes, then, in his rush to be away, brushed past the children on the next table. The birthday party continued in ignorance of the drug transaction between the two grown men.

****

When Harvey returned to the office, it was late in the afternoon. "Are you coming round tonight, Neil?" Margaret Lane asked as she prepared to go home.

Harvey, distracted by worries about Anson's drug dealing, looked at her with contempt. "No, I won't be coming round ever again, Margaret. I've decided to make some changes around here," he said. "It's over."

"What do you mean?"

"It means I want you out of your flat. The lease is in my name. You have a week to leave – otherwise you'll be trespassing."

Margaret looked around helplessly. "But why? What have I done?"

"Nothing, sweetie, but you're getting old. I need someone younger."

"You've found someone else, haven't you? I can tell you've been acting strangely. What's her name?"

Harvey sighed. "Her name's Samantha, if you must know. I've been honest in saying it's all over between you and me. Now, do you want to carry on working here or not?"

"Oh, yes, I'm still an employee of this company," Margaret said, with tears in her eyes. "Don't think I'm leaving quietly, Neil. I'll see you in hell before that. I know things that go on in this company that could put you behind bars for years."

"What are you talking about?"

Margaret picked up her handbag and started to leave the office. "That'll be for you to find out. Good night, Mr Harvey."

With the sarcastic use of his title, Margaret left the office, leaving Harvey to ponder his position. Margaret's threat was the least of his worries as he had no doubt Margaret could be eased out quietly with a generous severance payment.

However, he was still unsure what to do about Spendlove's blackmail. Now Harvey had evidence against Anson, the simplest option would be to sack him and call the police, but Harvey was scared of the consequences. From his past knowledge of Spendlove, Harvey had no doubt that he would carry out his threat to send the photos of the two lovers to Harvey's home address. For the hundredth time, Harvey shuddered as he visualised his wife's reaction if she ever saw the photos. He would not mind being divorced but Kathleen was still a major shareholder in the company, and Harvey had no wish to see control of the company in the hands of a vengeful wife. Somehow, he had to persuade Spendlove he was willing to co-operate, but the thought of a long prison sentence from being involved in drug trafficking filled Harvey with horror.

Harvey poured himself a Scotch and thought some more. Since his firm was already involved in drug dealing, without his knowledge, Harvey would be quite willing to make money out of it as long as his involvement was kept to the minimum. He drank the rest of his Scotch in one gulp and dialled the number he had for Spendlove Associates. "Spendlove," he said when he got through, "Harvey here. We need to talk about your offer. Come round to my office tonight."

****

Soon afterwards, as Philippa was putting on make-up in the ladies' room, Margaret Lane came in. She was flustered and on the edge of tears.

56

"What's wrong, Margaret?" Philippa asked.

Margaret dabbed her eyes with a tissue and looked at herself in the mirror. Her heavy make-up was starting to run, making her look much older and somehow pathetic.

"Oh, nothing, really," Margaret sniffed. "My whole life's coming to an end, that's all."

"What do you mean?" Philippa asked.

"Well, the great Mr Harvey wants to get rid of me," Margaret replied. "After all I've done for the company – and for him."

"Why's that?" Philippa inquired. "You seem to be doing a good job here."

"He says I'm too old," Margaret said, starting to cry. "Don't ever get old, will you, Philippa? Or he'll get rid of you as well."

"I don't think I'll have to wait that long. He wants to get rid of me now," Philippa replied. "There's been a problem over my references."

"Oh, I shouldn't worry about it," Margaret said. "He's probably forgotten about that already."

"Do you really think so?" Philippa asked, relieved. "I hope so, and don't you worry either," she continued. "I'm sure Mr Harvey can't get rid of you just like that."

Margaret had stopped crying now and was repairing her make-up. "Perhaps you're right, Philippa," Margaret said. "Anyway, I'll go down fighting if I have to go. I know most of what goes on in this firm. More than Neil thinks. Let's just say I can bring the whole company down if he gets nasty."

"What sort of things?" Philippa asked, trying to hide her police officer's interest in the company, but Margaret merely shook her head, grabbed her handbag and rushed out.

Philippa left the ladies' room to return to her desk. Despite Margaret's reassurance, Philippa was still worried about maintaining her cover story. As she sat down, she decided to take the step she had told Gould about and let Ward into her secret. The opportunity came when he was leaning over her to correct some of her typing, putting his arm around her shoulder.

"Reg," Philippa asked. "Can we have a word in private?"

"Yes, love. I was hoping you'd say that," Ward said, with a leer. He opened his mouth as if to make some facetious joke, but something in Philippa's expression stopped him. He just nodded and led her into his room and closed the door.

"Reg, there's something you should know. I'm a police officer. Here is my identification." Philippa showed her City of London Police warrant card to him. She had the satisfaction of watching Ward jump away as if a bee had stung him.

"But – but – why?" he stuttered in his surprise "What's it all about?"

"I'm not allowed to say what we are investigating," Philippa said. "But it is important. I hope you'll co-operate with us. It would be in your own interests. I've seen how Neil Harvey treats you. Whose side do you want to be on when everything comes to light? Ours or his?"

"I haven't done anything wrong," Ward replied. "And as far as I know, nor has Neil Harvey."

"Then neither of you have anything to fear, do you? Of course, if anyone here learns about this operation, my bosses will know who to blame, won't they?" Philippa replied, keeping her eyes fixed on Ward.

"I thought I was getting a secretary not a blackmailer," Ward complained. "Still, I'll help you any way I can. I've got nothing to hide."

"Now it's essential that you do not reveal my identity to anyone. Do you understand?" Philippa asked. Ward nodded, looking as if his world had collapsed. "It would help if you could arrange for me to go on one of the visits to the dealing rooms," Philippa continued.

"I expect I could arrange that," Ward replied, recovering his composure. "I'll have a word with Harvey – I'll make up a story. Perhaps we could both go to see him now."

Moments later, Philippa and Ward entered Mr Harvey's room. Philippa felt like a naughty schoolgirl. She hoped Ward had concocted a convincing lie to explain her imaginary career.

"Philippa has told me all about her references, Neil," Ward explained, as Philippa stared at him. "The problem was that she's changed her name. She's just been divorced and has gone back to her maiden name."

"Yes, that's right, Mr Harvey," Philippa lied, shaking her head vigorously. "If you phone up the companies now, they'll confirm my story." Gould had assured her he had put the fear of the law into the various companies she listed in her references and prayed they would support her bogus back history.

"Well, I'll take your word for it," said Harvey vaguely. "It's good to see people so keen to work with us. How are things going, Reg?"

"Oh, fine, Neil," said Reg. "I'm sure we won't have any trouble with Philippa. She's made a good start. One other thing – would it be all right for her to go with Charles Anson on one of his visits to customers? We both feel it would be good background for her."

"Yes, that seems a good idea," Harvey replied, picking up his gold-plated fountain pen. "Now, I have a lot to do…"

"Oh, yes, Neil," replied Ward, backing out of the office.

"Thank you very much, Mr Harvey," Philippa said, as she followed Ward into the corridor.

Reg Ward led Philippa to Charles Anson's office, knocking on the door and going straight in. Anson immediately slammed down his phone receiver, interrupting the phone call he was making.

"I'm sorry to interrupt you, Charles," said Ward. "Philippa wondered if she could come out on one of your trips this afternoon."

Anson's face fell. "Well, it's not very convenient, Reg."

"Why not?" asked Ward. "She won't be any trouble, will you, Philippa?"

"Oh, no, I'd love to learn more of how the company works," Philippa said as enthusiastically as she could.

"Oh, very well," replied Anson, making his reluctance plain. "You may as well come with me now."

"Thanks, Charles. I'll see you later, Philippa," said Ward, as he left.

"Come down to the garage with me," Anson said, when he and Philippa were alone. "We visit a lot of the dealing rooms on our trips. I don't know if you know much about the City. It's quite interesting."

Anson led her to the lifts and the two went down to the basement of the building. A van with the company logo on its side was waiting. Anson climbed into the driver's side and switched on the ignition as Philippa sat on the passenger seat.

"Obviously, I don't go on all the trips," Anson told her. "But I like to make sure the contracts are going well."

The first call was at a dealing room in Bishopsgate. Anson took in a large number of airline tickets. Several of the well-dressed young men stopped work and drifted over toward them. Everything seemed uneventful, but Philippa made sure she kept an eye on Anson. For a few minutes nothing happened, but then she saw what she had been expecting. Surreptitiously, Anson took money in exchange for a small envelope he had in his pocket. His customer opened it up to inspect it and Philippa could tell it contained a white powder.

Philippa decided she would arrange to have a colleague interview the people with whom Anson was trading, but she was confident she had succeeded in one of the purposes of her undercover investigation. She had uncovered at least one source of cocaine traffic in the City of London. But how far up the company structure did the illicit trading extend? And how did Marks's murder fit in – or was it coincidence? Before arresting Anson, she realised these were the main questions she had to answer.

Chapter 7

As Philippa and Anson travelled back through the City traffic, she was running through the various options that were open to her. Should she arrest Anson now or wait to see what other members of the conspiracy she could catch? Was there any connection with the murder of Hugh Marks in Mile End? She left Anson to park the van and walked to her office in Harvey and Ward, deep in thought.

When she opened the door to tell Reg Ward she was back, she saw him feeding documents through a shredder. He jumped guiltily when he saw her.

"Hello, Philippa," he said. "Did you have an interesting visit?"

"Yes, it was very useful, thank you," Philippa replied. "What are you doing?"

"Oh, just shredding a few old papers," he answered. "It's common practice here. By the way, what part of the police are you from?"

"I'm not allowed to say," she said. "Why do you ask?"

"No reason … It's not the fraud squad, is it?" he asked, with a worried expression.

"I'm a police officer, Reg. The police squads all work together," she said, gently. "It's your duty to tell me about any wrongdoing."

"You're nothing to do with the Inland Revenue, are you?"

"Not really, Reg," she answered. "Is that all you're worried about? Some tax fiddle or other?"

Ward looked relieved and turned off the shredder. "Yes, that's all." he said "Now are you a secretary or a policewoman this afternoon?"

"I'm happy to do some typing, Reg," she said, as she went back to her desk. Ward followed her out and gave her some letters to prepare.

★★★★

At her elegant home in Haslemere, Kathleen Harvey looked at the grandfather clock in the dining room and clucked disapprovingly. She was dressed elegantly, as she regarded dinner as a special occasion, even when she and her husband were dining alone, and she hated to be kept waiting. She was cross when Tania came in and echoed Kathleen's own thoughts.

"Do you think Mr Harvey will be home soon, Mrs Harvey?" Tania asked.

"I don't know, you stupid girl," Kathleen snapped. The au pair waited in a reproachful silence. "I'm sorry, it's not your fault. Oh, just serve me, will you, Tania? Neil will just have to go hungry when he comes in."

"Yes, Mrs Harvey," Tania replied, making a face when Kathleen's back was turned. As Tania served the dinner, they heard the sound of the front door being opened.

"I'll go," Kathleen said, standing up and walking into the hall. She had prepared a sharp reprimand for her husband but was startled to see her daughter standing there. It had been raining and Cassandra's normal immaculate hairstyle was a sodden mess. "Cassandra," Kathleen said, taking in her daughter's unusual lack of style. "Whatever's the matter?"

For the first time Kathleen could remember since childhood, Cassandra burst into tears. "Daddy's sacked me," she said, through her tears.

Kathleen rushed forward and took her daughter in her arms. "Come and sit down," Kathleen said, leading her into the sitting room. "There must be some misunderstanding. I'm sure he didn't mean it."

Cassandra said, still sobbing. "Yes, he meant it. He sacked me in front of the whole office, too."

"Your father will be home soon," Kathleen said, looking again at the clock. "We can talk about it then. I'll give him a ring. I can't understand why he's so late."

While Cassandra poured herself a drink, Kathleen phoned her husband's office, but she received no reply. She slammed the phone down and turned to Cassandra. "I'm sure we'll persuade Neil to change his mind. In fact, as major shareholder, I can guarantee it," Kathleen continued, with a smile. "Come along, you may as well have your father's meal as he's so late."

****

Harvey waited at his desk and looked at the clock. It was about seven o'clock and the rest of the office seemed empty. His hands shook as he poured himself a glass of whisky. He stood up as he heard the doorbell ring and went to the door. Just before he left the room, his phone rang.

"Dad, it's me," the unwelcome voice of Cassandra's twin brother, Jason, came on the phone.

"Jason, what do you want?" Harvey asked in a sharp tone. He realised that any phone call from his son resulted in some plea for money.

"I've heard about Cassandra losing her job," Jason answered. "I wondered if I could take over. I did a better job than her on that Stock Exchange contract. She looked pretty sore about losing to us, when I saw her in the bar."

"For God's sake, Jason, I'm busy," Harvey exploded. "I have lots of things to think about at the moment."

"It's a serious suggestion. I could come back and do a damn good job for your firm. Could I at least come around later and talk about it?"

"Jason, you made your choice when you joined our competitors. You can go to the devil, before you get any money from me. I won't offer you a job until hell freezes over." Harvey slammed the phone down He heard a noise outside and went to allow his visitor into his office.

****

Unknown to Harvey, the office was not quite empty. Anson sat in his room in darkness. He told himself he was going to get to the bottom of Harvey's threats against him. Anson could see the lights on in Harvey's office. He did not know exactly why Harvey was working late but he was going to make it his business to find out. It might have a bearing on whether he would continue his drug dealing or whether he would be sacked or even sent to the police. Anson heard the bell at the security door ring and Harvey go to answer it. Anson stood behind the door so he could watch the corridor without being spotted. Harvey returned with a stranger, a short man who conveyed an air of controlled menace. Anson asked himself if this was the Spendlove that Harvey talked about. Once Harvey had closed the door behind him, Anson walked over to hear what was being discussed.

****

Harvey looked at the man seated opposite him and remained silent.

"Thank you for agreeing to see me, Neil," Spendlove said in a business-like tone. "I've brought that video I mentioned with me. I'm sure there's no reason for your wife to see it. We'll burn it together, shall we?"

"Yes, but it's very easy to mass produce videos nowadays, isn't it? How many copies have you made to humiliate me any time you choose?"

Spendlove smiled. "You always were smarter than me, Neil, but as long as you co-operate, it would be in my own interest to keep it quiet. I'm sure Samantha will give you a good time later. On what I pay her, I can guarantee it."

"What did you mean when you talked about a colleague of mine becoming too curious?" Harvey asked.

"I think his name was Marks – he was auditing your accounts. He said he'd seen something suspicious. One of my contacts at another firm where he worked heard him. A bad mistake. Still he won't be making it again."

"What happened to him?"

"Let's say he's part of the food chain. Very ecological it was the way we disposed of him." Spendlove laughed.

"Still we aren't interested in him, are we? Like I said, we can make a regular payment into any account you name. How about it?"

"I got the better of you before, Spendlove. Clear out of my office. I've got more on you than you have on me. Do anything with that video and I'll go to the police and tell them what I know about you."

Spendlove stood up. "As you wish, but you've made a mistake crossing me, Harvey. Why are you asking those questions anyway?" He walked behind Harvey's desk and pulled open all the drawers. The last one had a small tape recorder operating. "I thought so. You were planning to take that tape to the law, weren't you? No one double crosses me …"

Harvey screamed as Spendlove opened his attaché case. Anson rushed back to hide in his office.

Chapter 8

The following day Philippa came into the office at around eight o'clock. She knew this was earlier than normal office hours and was hoping to use the quiet period to investigate whether Anson had any accomplices. She had all the keys to Ward's office cabinets and was hoping to make progress in investigating the drug smuggling.

As soon as Philippa entered the corridor to go into her office, Margaret Lane grabbed her arm, looking distraught. Margaret was unrecognisable from the immaculately poised woman who had welcomed Philippa to the company two days before.

"What's happened, Margaret?" Philippa asked. Margaret stared wide-eyed until Philippa repeated the question.

"Someone's killed Neil," Margaret screamed. "When I came in this morning he was dead. There's blood everywhere."

"Dead?" Philippa echoed. "Are you sure?"

"Of course, I'm sure. He's not breathing."

For a moment Philippa gaped at the other woman in amazement. How could Neil Harvey be dead? But soon Philippa's police training asserted itself, and she was able to take over. Should she keep to her undercover role or become a policewoman? In a moment, she decided that the investigation of a murder had to take priority.

"Take me to him at once. Make sure you don't touch anything," Philippa barked orders to Margaret Lane's obvious amazement. "Do what I say. I am a police officer." She flashed her warrant card as she led the way to Harvey's office. "Is he in his office?"

"Er – yes," Margaret stammered. "He was lying across his desk."

Philippa entered Harvey's office, holding Margaret back from entering. Philippa saw Harvey lying on his side as Margaret had described. The jacket he was wearing was covered in blood and from the amount of blood in the room and the position of the body, there was no doubt Harvey was dead. It seemed obvious that a gun on the floor in the middle of the room was the murder weapon.

"I don't have my mobile with me," Philippa told Margaret, handing her a business card." Call this number, straightaway Make sure you ask for Detective Chief Inspector David Gould to come."

"Gould? Isn't he the man who came to see me last week?"

"Yes, that's right. He's my boss. Phone straight away. I'll stay here and make sure no one comes in." Margaret ran off – her customary efficiency taking over from the initial shock of finding the body. When she left, Philippa had time to compose her thoughts.

'What am I going to tell David Gould?' was her immediate reaction. She had been sent on this undercover mission to find who was behind a new stream of high-quality cocaine now flooding the City dealing rooms. She had a cast iron case against one dealer – Charles Anson. But she was no nearer to finding out who was controlling him. Was he a freelance or part of a gang? Was he controlled by someone more senior within the company? Had Anson murdered Marks? Had he now murdered Harvey?

Philippa knew that Gould would expect her to have an insight into who had shot Harvey. Although several people in the company had a motive, she had no idea which, if any, had in fact committed the murder. She mentally ran through the most obvious suspects. Perhaps Charles Anson had shot him because of some disagreement over drug dealing. Perhaps someone even higher in the drug chain than Harvey had ordered his killing for a reason of their own. Perhaps Harvey had stumbled onto the drug ring even though he was not involved himself, and had been killed to keep him quiet.

And how about the women in his life? She had never met his wife, but could this be some domestic dispute, which had got out of hand? It seemed unlikely but must be borne in mind as a possibility. Neither his daughter nor Margaret Lane, his mistress, would mourn his death, judging from what they had said about him in the last couple of days. Could one of them have killed Harvey? And why was Reg Ward looking so guilty the previous afternoon? Despite his womanising reputation, Philippa liked the man and wanted to believe he was innocent of murder, but objectively she had no reason to trust him. Perhaps Ward had finally tired of years of being subordinate to Harvey and had decided to kill him.

One important question was whether Harvey's murder connected with the killing of Hugh Marks. It seemed hard to believe that two deaths connected with the same firm in such a short period of time could be coincidence, but Philippa told herself how important it was to keep an open mind. While she was engrossed in these thoughts, staff had started to arrive for work. One of the first was Reg Ward, who noticed Philippa standing outside Harvey's office.

"What are you doing there, Philippa?" Ward asked, in a casual friendly tone.

"Neil Harvey's dead, and it looks suspicious. I must stay here to keep the evidence uncontaminated."

Ward stared at her in apparent shock. "I could stay here, while you call the police," he offered, after a pause.

"I don't think so, Reg," Philippa said. "It's important to keep the crime scene untouched. I don't want you to be accused of any tampering with the evidence, even if you're innocent. Everyone in the company has to be a suspect, including you. Margaret's calling the police."

Just then, Margaret Lane returned. "The police are on their way," she said. "And I asked for your Detective Chief Inspector Gould to come."

"I've just had to tell Margaret about my identity," Philippa explained to Ward.

"Did *you* know Philippa was from the police?" Margaret asked Ward.

"She told me yesterday," Ward explained. "But I still don't really know what she came for. She says we're all suspects in whatever it is."

"I'll tell you more when I can," Philippa replied. "But my assignment seems to have changed. Now please try to keep people away from this crime scene."

Margaret and Ward walked off, and, whatever their own thoughts, efficiently kept a crowd from gathering. In a very few minutes, two uniformed constables arrived.

"What are you doing here, Philippa?" asked one, with whom she had worked before.

"I'll leave DCI Gould to explain when he arrives," she said, shortly. "Until then, take over guarding this room. It's Mr Harvey, the head here. He's definitely dead and it looks like murder."

The constables stood outside Harvey's office as Philippa walked to her own desk to gather her thoughts. From the reaction she received when she walked along the corridor, it was obvious that rumours of her police role had leaked. She wondered whether from Ward or Margaret, or someone over-hearing their conversation. She realised that Gould would need a dedicated room for the investigation, and she walked along the corridor to ask Margaret Lane to arrange it. When Philippa went into Margaret's office, she found her crying.

"I never wanted this to happen, you know, Philippa," Margaret said, through her tears. "I loved him, really. You probably thought I was just his paid mistress, didn't you?"

"No, I'm sure nobody thought that," Philippa demurred as convincingly as she could. "Please take a rest – you must be in shock. I'm sorry to intrude, but Chief Inspector Gould will need a room when he arrives."

"Oh, you can use Cassandra's," Margaret explained. "I don't think she'll be coming back, now she's been sacked." She thought for a moment. "Mind you, if she inherits her father's stake, she may return permanently." She started to cry again.

Philippa thanked Margaret and said the police would use Cassandra's office. Philippa was in there moving a few papers off the desk, when Cassandra came in and stopped dead.

"What the hell do you think you're doing?" Cassandra asked, in an aggressive tone.

"Cassandra, I'm a police officer," Philippa said, flashing her warrant card.

"Police? But why?" Cassandra asked, open-mouthed. "What do you want?"

"I've got some bad news for you, Cassandra," Philippa said, keeping her eyes fixed on Cassandra's face. "I'm afraid your father's dead. It looks suspicious. It could be murder."

"Dead? Daddy?" Cassandra cried. "But he was fine yesterday. How could he be dead? It must have been some sort of accident. Who could have wanted to murder him?" Her legs seemed to go weak and she sat down on the nearby chair. Philippa watched her carefully – was there something a little phoney about Cassandra's reaction, or was Philippa being influenced by her dislike for the woman? Could Cassandra really be surprised her father was dead? Surely she must have seen or heard all the commotion in the corridor? Why had she come to work anyway, when Philippa knew she had been sacked the day before?

Philippa was preoccupied in these thoughts when she noticed Detective Chief Inspector David Gould standing in the hall, watching her with keen interest.

Chapter 9

When Gould arrived, Philippa immediately stood up – her police discipline seeming odd in the office surroundings. "Good morning, sir," she said. "We have a murder on our hands. The victim is Neil Harvey – he's the head of the company. This is the dead man's daughter – Cassandra Harvey. Cassandra, this is Detective Chief Inspector Gould."

"I'm sorry to hear about your father's death, Miss Harvey," said Gould, shaking hands. "We will do our best to find his killer. The news must be a shock. Is there anything practical I can do to help?" Philippa could tell Gould was evaluating Cassandra's reaction to her father's death. It would breach police rules to interview Cassandra if she was in a state of shock, but all detectives know is that is the time when suspects are most likely to be willing to say what they know.

Cassandra dried her eyes and blew her nose with a delicate lace handkerchief. "It's a shock to find someone's murdered your father, but I will be all right, thank you, Chief Inspector. I'll help in any way of course, but I see you have a woman on the spot already," she said, nodding at Philippa in an unfriendly way.

"We'll need to have the next of kin formally identify the body even though DS Cottrell's sure it's your father."

"You'll need to contact my mother in Haslemere, she'll have to come up. I don't think I could face looking at the body," replied Cassandra. "I gather you want to use my office. I'll find somewhere else." She left, as always trailing expensive perfume behind her. Gould closed the door behind her.

"Well, Philippa," Gould said. "You seem to have stumbled on something big here. Why don't you tell me about it? When the forensic boys have finished, we'll look at the murder scene together."

Philippa told Gould in summary form everything she had learned in her three days undercover in the company. He waited patiently until she finished.

"So, we're not sure who the murderer is, but we have a good case against this Anson character for drug dealing," Gould said.

"Yes, that's right," she confirmed. "Should we interview him first?"

"That seems a good idea," Gould confirmed. "But we'll see how the Scenes of Crime boys are getting on."

Philippa led the way out of Cassandra's office to where the dead man lay. Gould stood in the doorway and looked carefully at the scene. A doctor was examining the corpse and stood up when he saw Gould.

"I can confirm he's dead, David, shot through the head," the doctor said. "As far as I'm concerned, you can move the body when you like."

"Thank you, doctor, but the Scenes of Crime boys will want to keep it here for some time yet," Gould said. "Now, you know what I'm going to ask, don't you?"

"When was he killed? Well, you know estimating time of death is an inexact science," replied the doctor. "I examined the victim at ten o'clock this morning. There was nearly full body rigidity, which normally occurs after twelve hours. But he was overweight so it could have taken longer. I measured the temperature of the corpse and, assuming the room was this temperature all night, that also implies twelve hours. I would say he was shot last night – say between seven p.m. and midnight."

"OK, thank you, doctor," Gould replied, as the doctor left. "How are you all getting on?" he asked the Scenes of Crime Officers in their white polythene overalls as they busied themselves photographing the scene and dusting for fingerprints. Getting only a vague reply, Gould turned to Philippa. "Tell me what you can see. You won't have come across many murders in the family squad," he said.

"I'll do my best," Philippa said. She felt defensive as she summarised her reactions. "Harvey's lying over the desk. I'd guess he was standing when he was shot. It looks as if the murderer dropped the gun in the middle of the floor and ran out. It's a small light gun – anyone could use it. Either a woman or a man who wanted to conceal a small weapon. There are some papers on the desk, but we'll have to wait until the body's moved before we can see if they're relevant to the murder or not," she paused hesitantly.

"Not bad, Philippa," Gould replied. "But you have missed the most important thing."

She looked around again. "He's dressed in a smart suit – he has a jacket on as if he were going out. There's a bottle on the desk."

Philippa was about to say more, when one of the Scenes of Crime Officers jumped up with a cry of delight. It was obvious something very important had been found.

Chapter 10

The Scenes of Crime Officer stood close to the body holding a small cellophane packet containing a white powder.

"I found this in his pocket, sir," the man said. "We'll have to analyse it of course, but I've got a good idea what it is."

"Probably cocaine," Gould said. "Now, that doesn't surprise me. Does it you, Philippa?"

"Harvey could have been involved in the distribution, do you think, sir? Anson could have been doing the drug dealing for him," Philippa suggested. "I was hoping to investigate further to see how many other people knew about Anson's drug dealing."

"Harvey could be part of the gang," Gould said. "Unless the drugs were planted to make it look as if he was involved. That's always possible. What else can you tell me?" he asked the Scenes of Crime Officer.

"Well, Harvey was killed by a single shot to the head. There's no sign of him moving afterwards so he must have died instantly," the sergeant said. "There's an open bottle of whisky but oddly enough no glasses, though there were two rings on the table as if two people were drinking. I should try and find those glasses if I were you. Only the deceased's fingerprints were on the bottle." The sergeant paused while he checked his notes.

"There's blood up on the wall behind Harvey, indicating that the bullet was shot from low down – probably someone sitting in the chair. There's not much doubt it's Harvey's blood. We'll check of course but it takes a while for the DNA tests to come back. There are no fingerprints on the gun. A tissue has been dropped on the floor but I don't think we'll find anything useful from it. You saw we found a bag of what looks like cocaine in Harvey's right jacket pocket – there were no fingerprints on that, either. He was wearing a formal suit as if he was preparing to go out for the evening." The sergeant looked again at his notes. "That's about it."

"Very well, thank you," replied Gould. The sergeant walked away, still dressed in his incongruous white boiler suit.

Gould led Philippa back to Cassandra's office. "Call Anson in, will you, Philippa? I have a few questions to ask him. He must be a suspect. Even if he's not a murderer, we know he deals in drugs. Let's lock him away before he can destroy evidence."

Philippa went to Anson's office. He stood up languidly as she entered, his natural charm asserting itself.

"Charles Anson," she began, showing him her warrant card. "You should know that I am a police officer." The expression on his handsome face, which had been friendliness itself, became at first stunned and then scared. "I must ask you to come to see Detective Chief Inspector Gould – he's in Miss Harvey's office."

He seemed about to speak but thought better of it. He stood up silently and Philippa led him to Gould's temporary office. She indicated to one of the uniformed constables to come inside as well. Anson took his seat and Philippa picked up her pad to take notes.

"Mr Anson," Gould began. "Detective Sergeant Cottrell here has been on an undercover mission to find the source of a new supply of cocaine, which has been found in several City dealing rooms. Do you know anything about this matter?"

Anson looked coolly at Gould. "Nothing at all," he said.

"I should warn you that Detective Sergeant Cottrell saw you passing drugs yesterday," Gould said. "One of your customers is willing to testify against you." Philippa was professional enough to hide her surprise at Gould's lie.

"If he's a drug user," Anson replied. "I doubt if any jury would believe his word against mine."

"Mr Anson, I must warn you that you will be charged later today with illegal dealing of a controlled drug." Gould read out the formal words. "Do you have anything to say?"

"It's obviously a set up job," Anson replied. "This young lady," – the trite phrase was spat out like a swear word – "is – what's the phrase – an agent provocateur. I'll see you in court."

"Very well, Mr Anson" replied Gould. "If you don't wish to help yourself by assisting us – that is your affair." He called to the constable. "Benson, take this man into custody." The heavily-built officer took Anson by the arms and brought handcuffs from beneath his tunic. He put these on Anson and was about to lead him out, when Anson insisted on speaking to Gould.

"It wasn't just me," said Anson. "Harvey was behind it too. He supplied me with the drugs in the first place. Arrest him, why don't you?" Anson stopped struggling while Gould considered his reply.

"I'm afraid that will not be possible, Mr Anson," said Gould. "Neil Harvey was murdered last night. Which brings me onto another question – where were you between seven p.m. and midnight yesterday?"

While Anson paused before replying, it struck the police officers that Anson did not seem surprised to be told of Harvey's murder. "I was at home, of course," Anson said.

"You're trying to pin this one on me, aren't you? Well, I'm not going to stand for it."

"As you wish," Gould said, nodding at the uniformed constable at the door. "Mr Anson, you are under arrest for trading in controlled drugs. You are not obliged to say anything, but it may harm your defence if you fail to mention any relevant facts."

"I have nothing to say," replied Anson. "I demand to see my solicitor."

"That will be arranged," said Gould. "Take him to the station." Anson was escorted out of the room by the constable.

Gould turned to Philippa. "I think you've done enough here for the time being, Philippa. There's one important person neither of us has seen yet."

"Who's that?" she asked.

"The victim's wife," Gould replied. "She lives in Haslemere, I think his daughter said."

"Shall I get the local cops to tell her the news?" Philippa asked.

"I don't think so," Gould looked around him. "The SOCOs will be busy for a while and we've got men taking statements from the office staff. There's not much you can do here. Get the address from that Lane woman and go and see Mrs Harvey. I've got a feeling you'll learn more from going down there than staying here."

****

An hour or so later, Philippa drove her unmarked police car up the long drive of Harvey's house in the Surrey countryside. It was a large mock-Tudor mansion with a long tarmac drive. She looked over the beautiful views of the Downs, then gasped as she looked up at the scale of Harvey's house. The contrast between this house and her own flat in Greenwich suddenly depressed her.

"I wonder how much of this was legal money and how much was from drug-dealing," she asked herself aloud. Her ring on the bell was soon answered by a tall blond young woman. She stared at Philippa without speaking.

"I'm Detective Sergeant Cottrell of the City of London police," Philippa said, showing her warrant card. "Who are you?"

"My name's Tania. I am the au pair," the woman replied, in a Slavic accent.

"I'd like to see Mrs Harvey please? It's extremely important."

The au pair did not seem surprised at the visit and directed Philippa through to a lavishly appointed sitting room. A woman aged about fifty rose as they entered. Mrs Harvey was dressed immaculately in a lavender dress. The shoes matched perfectly and Philippa had no doubt the pearls in her necklace and earrings were genuine.

"Mrs Harvey, I am Detective Sergeant Cottrell. I am afraid I have some very bad news for you," Philippa began.

"Yes, I know, Cassandra phoned to tell me. I can't believe it," Mrs Harvey said. Her voice was flat, but her eyes looked as if she had been crying.

"In that case, I'm sorry to disturb you at such a sad time for your family, but I have to ask you some questions."

"I understand, Sergeant," replied Mrs Harvey. Her accent seemed out of place, betraying origins in, Philippa guessed, the East End of London. "Won't you take a seat?"

Philippa sat opposite Kathleen Harvey and took out her notebook.

"As Cassandra has told you, your husband's body was discovered in his office early this morning," Philippa began. "At the moment, we believe he was murdered sometime last night. I wonder if you could tell me if you have any ideas as to who could have committed the murder."

"No, my husband didn't have any enemies, Chief Inspector," Mrs Harvey replied. "I'm sure it must have been an intruder of some sort."

"I don't think so, Mrs Harvey," Philippa replied. "The building was very secure."

"Well, I'm afraid I didn't know very much about my husband's work, Sergeant. I don't go up to his office very often. If it was something to do with his work, I don't think I can help you."

"Where were you last night, Mrs Harvey?"

"I was here at home with Cassandra until late."

"Your daughter was here last night? Doesn't she live in London?" Philippa asked, surprised.

"She does, but she came to see me, as she was upset," Mrs Harvey paused as if uncertain whether to continue. "I suppose I may as well tell you. She'd had some silly row with Neil in the office yesterday and was hoping to make it up. She hoped I could help her."

"Your husband had sacked her," Philippa interrupted. Mrs Harvey looked startled. "I was working undercover in your husband's company at the time of the murder, Mrs Harvey," Philippa explained.

"Oh, how strange!" Mrs Harvey giggled in a girlish manner, which struck Philippa as artificial in a woman of her age. "Anyway, Cassandra was hoping to sort it out with my husband, but in the event, he didn't show up."

"Did you phone to see where he was?"

"Yes, but there was no reply. Weren't you worried when he didn't come home?"

"I was annoyed more than worried. He sometimes stayed in his club overnight, but he should have told me."

"Can you tell me anything about the relationship between your daughter and a man called Charles Anson?" Philippa asked.

"They were seeing each other, but I don't think it was anything serious. Mind you, now Cassandra's living in London, she doesn't tell me everything."

"Did you know Anson was dealing in drugs?"

Kathleen looked stunned. "No, I didn't," she replied, with convincing surprise. "I'm sure Cassandra will be shocked if what you say is true."

"Did your husband ever mention any worries he might have about drugs being sold at his office?"

Kathleen shook her head. "No, never."

"Do you know anything about a woman called Margaret Lane? She works at your company's firm."

"That woman!" Kathleen spat the words out. "Yes, I know about her. She wouldn't leave my husband alone."

"How do you mean, Mrs Harvey?"

"She was always phoning him at home. She wouldn't let a weekend go by without interrupting him with some trivial thing."

"I think I'll stop there for the moment. This will have been a terrible shock for you. Is there anyone we can call to keep you company at the moment?" Philippa asked. "Would you like your daughter to come down?"

"No, don't interrupt her at work. She'll have her hands full up there."

"Is there anyone else I could call?" Philippa asked. She felt momentarily ashamed of her questions, which were more designed to help gain a picture of the Harveys' home life than to look for companionship for the newly bereaved widow.

"I have a son as well – Jason – he's Cassandra's twin," Kathleen said.

"If you give me his phone number, I'll ring him for you." Philippa took the phone book from Kathleen's trembling fingers. "This is his work number, I imagine?"

"Yes, he works for another travel agent in the City. He had a row with my husband a few years ago and they're competitors now." Kathleen hesitated, as if she may have revealed too much to Philippa. "But he'll be devastated by Neil's death," Kathleen continued hurriedly.

"Yes, I'm sure," Philippa made a mental note of Jason's strained relationship with his father, which she had already heard about from other sources. Once she was connected with Jason, she continued. "Mr Harvey, this is Detective Sergeant Philippa Cottrell of the City of London police. I am with your mother, and she asked me to phone you … I'm afraid I have some bad news for you. There has been a suspicious death in your father's office. At the moment, we believe your father is dead … Could you come round to see your mother, please … Very well … Thank you."

"Thank you, Sergeant. That was a help."

"He will be here shortly," Philippa said, making a mental note to find Jason's address. "For the moment, I'll ask your au pair to look after you when I leave. Isn't there anyone else? Any neighbours, perhaps?"

"No, I don't think so. We keep ourselves to ourselves in this sort of area."

"Well, I think that will be all, Mrs Harvey." Philippa stood up. Mrs Harvey jumped out of her chair, obviously glad the interview was at end. "One other thing, do you know if your husband ever wrote a will?"

"No, I don't think so, no," Mrs Harvey said, ushering her visitor into the hall.

"Thank you, Mrs Harvey," Philippa said, handing her a business card as they reached the front door. "We'd like you to come to the station in Snow Hill in the City to identify the body and make a statement tomorrow morning." Mrs Harvey shut the door quickly behind her.

After her interview, Philippa drove out of sight of Mrs Harvey's house and briefed Gould, using her mobile. Philippa asked Gould what he thought of what Kathleen Harvey had said.

"Well, it's very convenient for Mrs Harvey if she has an alibi for the time of the murder. Convenient for Cassandra, too," said Gould. "They both have strong motives – Mrs Harvey will be a very wealthy woman if she inherits all this."

"And I felt Jason's response was very laid back when I told him about his father's death. We must find out where Jason was last night."

Chapter 11

The next morning, Gould and Philippa were back at Snow Hill police station. All available evidence had been collected from the crime scene, and Gould had decided to interview the other witnesses and possible suspects on his home ground. He enjoyed unsettling the witnesses, with the experience of a bleak interview room. The stench of the meat from the nearby Smithfield market could generally be relied on to intimidate the smoothest of City financiers. The two officers were drinking cups of coffee – Gould was relaxing comfortably, while Philippa was sitting slightly awkwardly on the edge of her hard chair.

"I'm looking to you to help me on this case, Philippa," Gould said.

"Yes, David." Philippa was feeling confident enough to use Gould's first name.

"You know these people. Who's coming to see us first?"

"Margaret Lane," Philippa replied, looking through her notes while Gould waited for her to continue. "She found the body. She's in charge of personnel. She seemed to be in love with Harvey – everyone says she was his mistress, but she denied it when I spoke to her."

"Does she count as a suspect?"

"She fits the bill. She told me Harvey was about to ditch her – said she was too old for him now. She said she was about to dish the dirt on Harvey's company, but I don't know if she knew about the drug dealing. It may just have been bravado."

"There must be a good reason Harvey ditched his mistress like that," replied Gould. "I'd love to know what it is. Anyway, we'll have to ask Miss Lane about her movements. Who's coming after her?"

"Reg Ward," Philippa replied.

"Your former boss. He's the only one who knew you're a police officer. Could he have panicked for some reason? Does he have a motive?"

"When I arrived, Harvey was giving him a hard time about all the secretaries he was getting through. He seemed to be trying to seduce most of them."

"Did he try it on you?" Gould asked.

"Well a bit, but I think he was on his best behaviour with me. Especially when he saw my warrant card," Philippa added with a smile.

"We can't do Ward for that. Does he have a believable motive for murder?"

"I hope not, but I suppose it can't have been easy working for Harvey. Ward might have suddenly blown a fuse and killed him." Philippa felt herself blushing defensively. "I quite liked Reg really. Still, I'd like to know what was in those documents he was shredding yesterday. He looked extremely guilty when I came in. He said he was worried about the Inland Revenue, so it could be some silly tax fiddle. Still we all know there are people who have murdered for less."

Philippa was about to say more when the phone rang on Gould's desk. He picked it up, listened and then put it down.

"It's our first visitor," Gould said. "Tell me more about Ward later."

Margaret Lane came in. It was obvious she had been crying.

"Please come in, Miss Lane," Gould said. "Take a seat. You know Detective Sergeant Cottrell already."

"Hello, Philippa," Margaret said. She smiled slightly "Things seem to have changed since Monday, don't they? I suppose we need a new secretary for Reg again now."

"I can see you're distressed," Gould said. "But I need to ask you a few questions." Margaret nodded. "I'll begin by asking you where you were between the hours of 7 p.m. and midnight the day before yesterday – the night of the murder."

"I went home at 6 p.m., the usual time. Mr Harvey was alive and well when I left."

"Are there any witnesses for your whereabouts last night, Miss Lane?"

"I'm afraid not," Margaret replied. "I live on my own and, as I wasn't going out, I didn't see anyone."

"How was Mr Harvey when you left?"

"He was going out that evening. I'd set out another jacket ready for him."

"Is that part of your normal functions?" Gould asked with incredulity.

"Not really, Chief Inspector," Margaret paused, blushing. "I suppose I'll have to tell you as you'll find out soon enough. Neil and I had been having an affair for three years."

"What sort of affair? Was it a happy, stable relationship?"

"Yes. I respected him, of course, and I like to think I helped him," Margaret replied. "I realised he couldn't leave his wife, even though they'd stopped sleeping together. He came round to my flat a couple of nights a week."

"You were content with this situation?" Gould failed to keep the incredulity out of his voice.

"Yes, I was. It suited both of us."

"Until the day before yesterday …" Gould prompted.

"How did you know about that?" Margaret snapped and then continued, after glaring at Philippa. "Oh, of course, your spy told you. Yes, Neil and I did have a row on Tuesday."

"What it was about?"

"I'd rather not say."

"This is a murder enquiry, Miss Lane," Gould replied firmly. "Please answer my question."

"Very well, Chief Inspector," Margaret said. "Neil wanted to finish our relationship."

"Did he say why?"

"He just said I was getting too old." Tears were coming to Margaret's eyes. "After all we'd been through," Margaret dried her eyes with a handkerchief. "But it's a very small thing, not something to worry your investigation. Just another seedy little story …"

David Gould stood up and looked out of the window. He was uncomfortable with displays of emotion, and there was something unbearably pathetic about the normally efficient Miss Lane, breaking down into tears. Philippa asked if there was anything she could do to help but Margaret shook her head and after about a minute, she became more composed. "I'm sorry, Chief Inspector. Please continue with your questions," Margaret said.

"Very well. Did Mr Harvey give any clues as to whether he had a new girlfriend?"

"He mentioned someone called Samantha, but I don't know anything about her."

"As far as you know, did Mrs Harvey know about your affair with her husband?" Gould asked, indicating for Philippa to make a note of Samantha's name.

"I never asked…I think she must have guessed or perhaps she just wasn't interested," Margaret replied.

"Margaret," Philippa began, "when I was undercover, you said that you were going to tell the truth about the things that went on at Harvey and Ward's. What did you mean by that?"

"Oh, nothing, really. I just wanted to threaten Neil. I was upset …" Margaret's voice tailed away.

"Is there anything you could think of that could help us find the murderer?" Philippa asked.

"No, nothing I can think of," Margaret said after a moment's thought.

"I'd like to go back in time. How did your relationship with Neil Harvey start?" Gould asked.

"I started working for Harvey and Ward ten years ago. Neil interviewed me for a job as a secretary. Then things just blossomed from there."

"What things?"

"My career first … Then we were often working late, I became his mistress. I hate that word, but it's what you wanted me to say, wasn't it?"

"We're just trying to find the truth behind Neil Harvey's murder. It's not up to us to judge you, Margaret," Philippa told her gently.

"If there's nothing else you wish to tell us, Miss Lane, can you tell us who had access to your offices the night of the murder?" Gould asked.

"Well, as I once told Philippa," Margaret nodded at her. "We are security conscious at Harvey and Ward. The only people given access are the people who work there, the cleaner – but she's very reliable – and Mrs Harvey – but I don't think she ever visited the office."

"Do you know anyone who would have had a motive to kill Mr Harvey?"

"I suppose Mrs Harvey could have, if she found out about us – or about Neil's replacement girlfriend."

"Anyone else?"

"No, I don't think so."

"How about yourself? It must have hurt being dumped like that."

"Me? Murder Neil? Because I'm a scorned woman?" Margaret Lane looked surprised. "All I can say is that I didn't kill him, even if I wanted to."

"Do you know anything about drug dealing at your firm, Miss Lane?"

"Certainly not."

"We have arrested one of your employees – Charles Anson – for trading in cocaine."

Margaret seemed genuinely shocked. "Are you sure? Charles is one of our most successful sales staff. That's terrible. I didn't know anything about it."

"Could you tell us about the events of yesterday morning, Miss Lane?"

"I came to work in the morning as usual. I took off my coat and switched on my computer. Neil's door was closed so I didn't suspect anything at first. I was just going to see if he had left any work for me to do. I opened the door and he was there. His body was across the desk. Just like you saw him." Margaret started to cry again.

"Did you touch anything when you came in to the office?" Gould asked. "Be careful before you answer."

Margaret stopped crying and thought. "No, I just opened the door, stepped inside and saw the body. I could see he wasn't breathing. I didn't want to touch him. I stopped, turned round, ran down the corridor and saw Philippa. I told her what had happened. She told me she was in the police and we went back to my office. Philippa can confirm all that."

"Yes, that's right. The crime scene was untouched from the time Margaret and I returned to Harvey's office," Philippa said.

"You say Mr Harvey was working at the office when you left last night, Miss Lane," Gould said. "Did he say he was expecting anyone?"

"No, he didn't. I thought he was going out somewhere," Margaret replied. She seemed about to stop, then continued as the police officers waited. "I usually look in to say good night before I go home, but I left in a huff last night. After he told me he was going to get rid of me for some tart called Samantha, I didn't feel like playing the efficient secretary. I shouldn't say it now he's dead, but it's how I felt. Is that awful of me?"

"It's not for me to say, Miss Lane." Gould stood up. "Well, if there's nothing else, thank you for coming," he said. "Let me know if you think of anything more that would help us with our inquiries."

Margaret stood up and quietly left. When she had gone, David Gould turned to his colleague. "What do you think, Philippa?" he asked.

"It's difficult when you have got to know these people," she replied, blushing slightly. "Margaret Lane did seem upset yesterday, and she could have done anything. I think she was in love with Harvey – God knows why, he seemed nothing more than a bully – and I suppose love can turn to hate."

"You saw Harvey's wife – is she still an attractive woman? Can you imagine Harvey and her staying in the same house and not sleeping together?"

"Not really," she replied. "But Harvey might have been lying about that and Margaret could just be repeating what she was told."

"We must really find out more about Harvey's background," Gould said. "What sort of a man could ditch his girlfriend like that?"

"From what I saw of Harvey, he was pretty brutal. Shall we see Reg Ward now?"

"Yes, ask him to come in, will you? I suppose he had a motive as well. It can't have been much fun – being a junior partner to a man like Harvey. Perhaps Ward was tired of being patronised by him. Could the worm finally have turned, do you think?" Gould asked.

"I can't see it, sir. He did look very shifty when he was shredding documents yesterday, but I can't imagine him as a murderer."

At that moment, a uniformed constable came in. "It's Anson, sir. He's asking to see you, as soon as possible."

"What does he want? Come on, Philippa, this should be interesting," Gould said, standing up.

"But what about Reg Ward? He's waiting outside."

"He'll have to wait longer. I want to hear about Anson's drug dealing first."

Chapter 12

When Gould and Philippa entered the cells located in the basement of the police station, they saw a Charles Anson almost unrecognisable from the dapper executive they had seen before.

His good looks were haggard and his expensive pinstripe suit, which looked so elegant in his office, seemed merely ridiculous in his present surroundings. He jumped up when he saw the two police officers.

"You've got to get me out of here, Chief Inspector," Anson yelled.

"You're under arrest for a serious offence. Why should I let you out?" asked Gould.

"OK, OK, I admit I was selling cocaine," Anson said impatiently. "But I was only doing what I was told."

"That was Eichmann's defence. It didn't do him much good, and it won't help you either," Gould replied. "Carry on, Mr Anson, Detective Sergeant Cottrell is taking notes. You've already been cautioned – tell me more."

"Neil Harvey put me up to it," said Anson. "He set up this travel agency as a front for drug dealing. It's an ideal cover for moving drugs from one country to another. Surely you know that?"

"Never mind, what we do and don't know. We'll ask the questions – you answer them. You're saying Harvey was behind your drug dealing, but he's dead now. We only have your word he was involved. We're looking for proof. Who else in the company do you claim knew about it?"

"No one as far as I know. I always dealt directly with Harvey. We each took half of the money I received."

"Were there any witnesses to these alleged transactions, Mr Anson?"

"No, of course not. Harvey always told me not to involve anyone else."

"So, we only have your word for this, and obeying an illegal order is still a crime." Gould gave a theatrical sigh. "Saying Harvey was involved doesn't help your defence at all. You're looking at a few years' imprisonment at the moment. Telling the truth and helping us find Harvey's murderer will look good. Now let's start again. Was Harvey involved in your drug running?"

Anson hesitated. "I suppose I ought to tell you the truth. I stayed late last night. I knew Harvey was staying late and I wanted to know what he was up to."

"Why was that?"

"He was acting oddly yesterday. He accused me of knowing someone called Spendlove, but I'd never heard of him. Harvey talked about sacking me. I thought I'd stay late and see what was going on."

"Why did he want to sack you?" Gould was careful not to show his recognition of Spendlove's name from police records.

"He must have found out I was selling cocaine. I don't know how." Anson paused as he saw Gould fold his arms in a display of scepticism. "Harvey wasn't really involved in drugs as far as I know. I just made that up."

"So, now you want us to believe Harvey wasn't involved in the drugs. Why should we believe this version?" Gould continued when Anson fell silent. "Still, I'm more interested in Harvey's murder at the moment. What did you find out when you stayed late the night of the murder?"

"Harvey let someone in. It was a stocky man in an expensive suit. He looked like a successful businessman, but I don't know who he was."

"Could you identify this man again?"

"I expect so. He was short and overweight. He had an air of power. You wouldn't want to cross him."

"Very well. What happened next?"

"I left while they were still talking."

"And you didn't try to find out what they were talking about?" Anson shook his head. "Did Harvey receive any other visitors while you were there?"

"Not as far as I know. Do you think this man could have murdered Harvey? Was he this Spendlove?" Anson asked excitedly.

"I'd be interested in that point as well. Come with us and look through some photographs to see if you recognise this man. There's one Spendlove known to us, but a visual identification would help. This man's obviously a suspect, but so is the other person who was there last night."

"Which other person?"

"You, Mr Anson," Gould said, seriously. "You were there at the right time and you have just mentioned a possible motive. You could have had an argument about drugs and shot Harvey. Let's say Harvey was innocent. He found out about your activities and was going to tell the police, so you killed him. Alternatively, you could both have been drug dealing and you shot him in a row about money. It happens all the time in the drugs world. You're our main suspect at the moment. It would be in your interest to cooperate with us unless you want to face murder charges."

Anson gulped. "I understand."

"Come up to my room, then. It'll be in your interest to cooperate. I have some pictures to show you." Anson looked relieved. "I must make it clear you are still being charged."

"But you will speak up for me if I help, won't you, Chief Inspector?"

"I'm not making any promises, but I'll see what I can do."

★★★★

A few minutes later, Anson was sitting in Gould's room, flipping through the Drug Squad's book of mug shots of suspected dealers. After some hesitation, he decided that one photograph was of the man he had seen entering the office to talk to Harvey on the night of his death.

"That's him," said Anson. "I'm quite sure it is."

"That's Jack Spendlove," Gould said. "That would explain a lot. He's the man Harvey mentioned to you before he died. We've been after Spendlove for years. If you confirm you saw him arrive last night that would be of great interest to us. Are you prepared to testify to that?"

"Yes."

"It would help you if you could give any more details of other people who were involved in drugs with you. Before you deny anything, I don't believe you were working completely on your own. Your sort never do."

"I arranged the transport of cocaine from Colombia by hiding it in flowers." Anson's words came out in a rush, as if he was glad to be finally confessing to his crimes. "A baggage handler was involved, but I only knew him by sight. Then I passed the stuff to someone called Nick. We used to meet in various Macdonald's. He would phone and arrange which one."

"Can you tell us anything more about this Nick?"

"I don't know his full name. He was small and wiry, aged about forty. He's another one you wouldn't to cross."

"Could you identify this Nick?"

"Oh, yes, I'm sure of it. I met him lots of times. I would give him the cocaine and he would give me some small amount to sell on."

"Thank you, Mr Anson," Gould said, nodding to the uniformed constable. "Take him away." After Anson had left, Gould turned to Philippa. "We need to keep a close watch on Anson. Once the news gets out he's helping us, his life may be in danger. Warn the custody sergeant to keep him apart from other prisoners."

"Yes, David."

"Then I'd like you to arrange an interview with Spendlove. His address is in the files."

"How about Reg Ward? We're due to interview him next."

"Ask him to come in, will you? You can lead the interview. Take your time. I think we should begin right from when Harvey and Ward first met," Gould said. "I think I read somewhere they were at school together – let's start with then." Philippa stepped out and found Reg Ward, waiting nervously in the corridor.

"Come in, Reg. Try not to worry," she said, taking pity on his concerned expression. She led him into the interview room.

Chapter 13

Philippa sat down opposite Ward and switched on the tape recorder. Gould sat silent next to her. Philippa felt uncomfortable interviewing someone she was close to regarding as a friend. Logically, though, she realised that her job as a police officer was to investigate a murder and this outweighed any personal feeling she had. She read out the formal time and details for the benefit of the tape.

"Now, Reg," Philippa began. "As you know, we are investigating the murder of Neil Harvey. I was working undercover at your company at the time of the murder. We'd like to go back as far in time as we can. To start with, can you tell me how you first came to meet Mr Harvey?"

Ward looked startled. "I thought you only wanted to ask about the murder."

"We feel the further we go back the more we'll know, Mr Ward," Gould said firmly. "Please answer Detective Sergeant Cottrell's questions."

Ward addressed himself to Philippa. "Do you really want to know how Neil and I met?" he asked "It was a long time ago. Before you were born," he added with a smile.

"Yes, take your time," Philippa said. "We're in no hurry. Any detail at all might be useful."

"Well, Neil and I first met at school," Reg Ward began. His eyes misted over as he recalled long-forgotten times from his past. "It's a funny thing, Philippa, but I always relate events in my schooldays to whatever Beatles record was current at the time. 'Day Tripper' was at number one in the charts when I first came into close contact with Neil Harvey. I was about sixteen."

"How old was Harvey?" Philippa asked.

"There's a difference of about two years in our ages so he was eighteen," Ward continued. "We were not exactly friends at that stage, but I soon had good reason to be grateful to him. The reason we met was through an eighteen-year-old thug. He had a father who was running a protection racket. The father was often up in court about it and the son seemed to be following his example."

"What was his name?"

"Spendlove. Jack Spendlove. Why do you ask?"

"His name is known to us," Philippa said, exchanging glances with Gould at the mention of Spendlove's name. "But please carry on."

"The teachers didn't take any action. Well, as long as the father paid the fees I don't think they minded much. Although the headmaster advertised it as a public school, it took most of its pupils from some of the rougher parts of Inner London. The parents were either hard-working couples who wanted to join the middle classes or well-off kids who had been rejected by other schools. This meant that there was a lot of bullying at the school. Most of the petty criminal element at the school left at fifteen, but Spendlove was the exception. He was a delinquent with brains. When he walked through the streets outside the school, he had a gang of cronies who floated around with him. They always reminded me of pilot fish swimming around a shark." Ward paused. "I don't know why I'm going on about Spendlove, but you asked me to tell you everything."

"Please go on, Reg," Philippa said. There was something fascinating about this middle-aged man recalling his schooldays, and she had no wish to interrupt. She was also more interested in Spendlove than Ward realised.

"Well, one of Spendlove's sidekicks, a boy called Rothenberg, often demanded money from the younger boys," Ward continued. "I was bigger and stronger than Rothenberg, so I could have refused him, but I always knew that he was just a messenger from Spendlove, who was well known to carry a knife. You didn't argue with him. I never saw the knife myself, but he still managed to frighten anyone who resisted his threats.

"This particular day – it must have been in the summer of 1965 – I remember how shocked I was when Rothenberg, who had never spoken to me before, stopped me in the playground and demanded five pounds. This was an unheard-of sum of money in those days and I had no idea what to do. Fortunately, Neil Harvey – he was a sixth former and bigger than I was – overheard the conversation and he told Rothenberg to leave me alone."

"What happened then?" Philippa asked.

"Rothenberg told him to mind his own business. Then Harvey asked him what he was going to do about it. It wouldn't have been much of a fight. You see Neil had the advantage of being about five inches taller and two years older than Rothenberg.

"'You know who this money's for, don't you?' Rothenberg said.

"'Jack Spendlove,' Harvey answered. 'I'm not scared of him and I'm certainly not scared of you.'

"Then I remember Rothenberg opened his mouth as if he was going to say something but, thinking better of it, he scuttled away rather like a frightened crab. I've never been so relieved in my life and I thanked Harvey for helping.

"'Oh, that's all right,' he told me. 'I've been wanting a chance to stand up to Jack Spendlove for years. If you stand up to people like him, they usually back down.'

"For the rest of the time that he was at the school, I was in awe of Harvey, and I made sure I stayed as close to him as possible. Luckily, Spendlove and Harvey left school at the same time. After that, I didn't feel threatened any more, once Spendlove's acolytes began to disperse. Rothenberg remained my enemy but without Spendlove to back him, he just looked pathetic."

"So, you've been friends with Harvey ever since?" Philippa prompted.

"No, not really," Reg Ward replied. "I'll just carry on with my life story, shall I? I did fairly well in my last couple of years at the school. I got good A-levels in Maths, which was enough to allow me to study for my accountancy exams. I got a manager's job at a travel agent's and settled down.

"I occasionally heard about my old schoolmates. Rothenberg became a clerk in a firm of solicitors working for some of the most dangerous criminals in the East End. Spendlove ran a chain of betting shops for his father and was sometimes seen driving an expensive car. Everyone said his career as a criminal continued into his adult life. After school Neil and I drifted apart for a while. The next time I saw Harvey was when he was about to marry Kathleen." Ward paused. "Could I have a coffee please?" he asked.

"Yes," Gould replied. "Can you get Mr Ward a cup of coffee, please, Philippa. You probably know how he takes it. And take a cigarette break yourself."

"Yes, sir," Philippa replied, using Gould's formal title as they were in front of a civilian. It was not part of her police duties to fetch cups of coffee, and she did not smoke, but she correctly interpreted Gould's request as an opportunity to interrogate Ward on his own, with the tape recorder turned off. She knew this often happened in interviews, but the witness did not realise there was a back-up tape recorder still working.

"Did you and Harvey go out with girls in those days, Mr Ward?"

"Not really. We were apart at that sort of time. I suppose I experienced the normal growing pains of a boy in the 1960s. Heathfield School was all boys, and I only started going out with girls when I left. I was an only child with old-fashioned parents and they tried to keep me at home a lot. Perhaps I was making up for lost time. I adopted a stamp collector's approach to girls and tried to go out with as many as I could." Ward stopped, as he realised he might have said too much.

"Don't be embarrassed, Mr Ward. We've all been there." Gould hoped Philippa would stay out of the room and leave Ward free to talk about his sexual history.

"Anyway, eventually I became engaged to Annabel, a petite dark sort of girl. She wasn't the prettiest girl I had ever gone out with, and everyone was surprised when we married, but that often happens, I suppose. She was an active Catholic and went to mass every Sunday. I could never see the point of religion but didn't mind her going if she wanted. We were married at a Catholic church in 1972, I think it was, when we were both twenty-two years old."

"I assume something went wrong with the marriage," Gould prompted. "DS Cottrell said you were divorced."

"Well, despite trying, we didn't have any children, and eventually doctors told us Annabel couldn't conceive. I didn't mind, but I could tell Annabel was upset. At work, I was advancing quite fast in the travel agency business. I wasn't academically bright, but I worked hard and passed my accountancy exams without too much trouble. By the age of twenty-four I was a manager of a branch of a chain of travel agents and doing quite well. The travel agency was prospering, and sometimes I was offered overseas trips to drum up business. I went with girls from the office and well you can probably imagine the rest …"

At this point, Philippa returned with a cup of coffee for Ward. Gould nodded that she could start the interview again. "There you are, Reg, I made it the same way as at the office."

Ward muttered his thanks as Philippa switched the tape recorder back on. "I'll continue, should I? By this time, I'd largely forgotten about my school friend. Then in 1976, I think it was, I received an invitation to the wedding of my old protector Neil Harvey. The invitation said he was to be married to a Miss Kathleen Jones. Harvey's background was poorer than mine, so I was quite impressed with the venue. It turned out Kathleen was the daughter of some East End get-rich-quick millionaire – a scrap merchant, I think. The wedding was to be held at a chapel in the Savoy, followed by a reception in the main hotel.

"Neil asked me to be best man. I was surprised he thought of me so long after school. Perhaps he didn't really have any other male friends, I don't know. He was always on the make, which didn't endear him to people."

"Did Harvey say what had happened to him after school?" Philippa asked.

"He became rich," Ward replied with a smile. "I remember him once saying that his mother had had to pay for his education at Heathfield School out of limited savings, which meant she had no spare money for luxuries. His school uniform was second-hand, and he always resented the way the richer boys at school laughed at it. Harvey told me that to pay his way, he had to go out on a paper round each morning before he went to school and he always dreaded the thought that one of his classmates might see him.

"He left school with the aim of making money as fast as he could, so that he would never be considered poor again. He had a natural gift for selling and decided he could make his money on the Stock Exchange. In those days the Exchange was still run by an exclusive group of moneyed graduates, but Harvey always had this superficially cultured veneer. This, together with a barrow-boy mentality made him a success as a stockbroker's clerk and then as a stockbroker himself."

Sipping his cup of coffee, Ward continued. "By the mid-1980s, I wanted to try something new. I was a good travel agent, well thought of by the company I worked for. I was still married to Annabel and still having affairs, which I usually managed to keep secret from her. It was probably only Annabel's Catholic upbringing, which stopped us from being divorced. But I enjoyed the structure of married life – it was a perfect excuse for not becoming too entangled with casual girlfriends."

Remembering where he was and whom he was talking to, Ward returned to his story. "The real reason I was feeling restless was I felt underpaid, compared with the large amounts of money being made on the Stock Exchange at that time. I thought about it a lot and I decided to take the risk of setting up my own travel agency. I realised I needed some additional capital and began to look around for possible sources."

"And you turned to Harvey?" Philippa prompted.

"That's right. Neil Harvey was the richest man I knew. I was a bit reluctant to approach him at first, as it might risk a friendship. But I studied lots of management textbooks, prepared my business plan and phoned Harvey up for an appointment. Oddly enough, he seemed pleased to hear from me and invited Annabel and me to dinner."

"What happened then?" Gould asked.

"While we were driving down to Harvey's home in Haslemere, I kept reminding Annabel how important the occasion was and as a result both of us were nervous when we arrived. However, Kathleen Harvey was always a good cook – it comes from the finishing school her father sent her to, I expect – and Neil could afford the most expensive wines, and the meal went off smoothly. As we agreed on the way down, Annabel offered to help Kathleen tidy up after the meal, while Neil and I discussed business."

"How did the meeting go?" Philippa asked.

"It was nerve-wracking. I remember being perched on the edge of a comfortable armchair and holding my business plan. I felt a bit like some Victorian character asking for a father's permission to marry his daughter. To show he was boss, Harvey kept me waiting while he poured both of us brandies. He then asked me what my proposition was.

'I'd like to set myself up in business on my own, Neil,' I said. 'I'm tired of working for other people and I've drawn up this business plan for a travel agency to be located in the City.' Harvey just stared at me and didn't say anything.

'Obviously, I need capital, Neil,' I went on 'and so I came to you. I have the contacts and experience of the business and you have the money. If you were looking for new business ventures, this might be ideal …' I remember my voice trailed away, as I handed over my carefully prepared business plan.

"Harvey looked at it as if it were dirty as he skimmed through it. 'I usually only invest in established companies,' he said, 'but I could do with a new hobby.' That's what he called it – a hobby. 'You said you were tired of working for other people, but if I put up the money you would be working for me.'

'I was planning that we could be equal partners, Neil,' I said – God, I was naive. 'You would just have to invest the money while I manage the business.'

Harvey stood up. 'Equal partners, Reg?' he bellowed – I was petrified by this time. 'When I'm taking all the financial risk? I don't think so. The best I could offer you is a quarter share.'

'A quarter? Is that all?' I asked.

'I am putting up the money, Reg,' he said. 'I'm probably being too generous just because we're old friends. Of course, you can always go to the banks, but they would charge some extortionate interest rate …'

"In the end I accepted, of course."

"'Fine, let's shake hands on it,' Harvey said, as we shook hands. 'To Harvey and Ward.' That was the first time I'd heard the words.

"And that was how your company started?" Gould asked.

"That's right. I remember that as we drove home, I told Annabel about the agreement.

'But that's terrible,' she told me. 'That means you'll still be working for someone else.'

'Not really,' I said. 'At least I will have some stake in the business – even if it's only a quarter.'

'You've let him walk all over you,' Annabel told me. I can still remember the look of contempt she gave me. 'I think you're making a big mistake.' She wouldn't talk to me for the rest of the journey home. That was the beginning of the end of our marriage." Ward paused, obviously recalling a painful memory. The two police officers kept silent, waiting for him to continue.

"In the event," Ward said, finishing his coffee, "our new business was a success. I brought over a lot of useful customers to the new agency and I worked long hours to make sure everything went smoothly.

"In the meantime, Neil Harvey was happy to be the silent partner in the agency. Over the next ten years, Harvey and Ward became one of the top travel agencies for City firms, and Harvey's investment was repaid many times over."

"But you were still just the junior partner?" Gould prompted.

"Yes, that's right. What's worse was that because of the amount of time I was spending in the office, my marriage to Annabel went downhill. I used to have regular affairs with other women, but I was still genuinely offended when Annabel announced she was leaving me. In our last argument, Annabel was angrier with Neil Harvey for forcing me to work long hours than with me.

"'Can't you see that man is exploiting you?' I remember her shouting. 'You think he's your friend, but I'd like to kill him.'"

Philippa interrupted at this point as she and Gould exchanged glances. "Are you still in touch with your ex-wife, Reg?"

"I haven't seen her for years, but I should know where she lives – I have to send her maintenance cheques every month. Why?" Reg asked, then realised the relevance of what he had just said. "Oh, I'm sure the threat wasn't real. You can't think she murdered Neil."

"We'd just like to talk to her, Reg," Philippa replied calmly. "Please leave her address with us when you go."

"Well, that's how the company was formed. You already know the structure of the firm as it is now. I've no idea who murdered Neil. We've always had tight security so I don't see how any intruder could have got in."

"We're fairly sure Mr Harvey must have let the attacker in. It was probably someone he knew," Philippa said. "Do you have any idea who could have killed him?"

"I've told you I was at home that night, but you'll have to take my word for that as I'm afraid I have no witnesses." Ward stood up as if to leave. "Well, I think I've told you everything."

"Stay a bit longer, Mr Ward," Gould intervened firmly. "You see, Mr Ward, we have evidence that at least one member of your company has been dealing in illicit drugs."

"Never." Ward shook his head vehemently. "We wouldn't stand for it. We'd dismiss anyone who did anything like that."

"We have your colleague, Charles Anson, under arrest now for trafficking in drugs." Gould's voice became less friendly. "What's more, he has said your late partner Neil Harvey was involved. What do you have to say to that?"

"I'm stunned," Ward replied. "We'll sack Anson straight away, of course. But I can't believe Harvey was involved – he was very straight in the way he did business."

"Tell me, Mr Ward, what can you tell me about a man called Hugh Marks?" Gould asked.

"Marks? Hugh Marks? I've never heard of him," Ward replied, after a moment's thought.

"His body was found in a canal in Mile End. He was an accountant who audited Harvey and Ward's books," Gould said, keeping a close eye on Ward's face.

"Oh, yes, I remember him. He started with us then disappeared. We got a new firm of auditors after that."

"Was it your decision to change the auditors?"

"Well, yes," Ward replied. "We were annoyed when he disappeared in the middle of an audit. We lost a lot of time, because his replacement had to start all over again."

"Had Marks found something incriminating about your company?"

"Not as far as I know. He wasn't with us for very long. He was with a firm of auditors – he visited lots of firms. If he was murdered it could be because of something he found about any of these other companies. Perhaps he just fell into the canal."

"We're sure someone murdered Marks, Mr Ward, and he was auditing Harvey and Ward's just before he died," Gould replied coldly. "Are you willing to allow the police access to your accounts?"

"I'm not sure. I will have to clear it with Kathleen."

"Please do that. Now, have you ever seen this man?" Gould showed Ward the mug shot of Jack Spendlove, which Anson had identified. Ward looked at it carefully and then looked stunned. "Oh, my God," he said. "It's Jack Spendlove. He hasn't changed much really. But I haven't seen him since school, so I can't help you very much."

"No, your identification's been very useful, Mr Ward," Gould said. "It's interesting Harvey and Spendlove were old schoolfriends."

"Not close friends, exactly," replied Ward. "As I said, Neil and I became friends because we both hated Spendlove."

"We have a witness who says he saw Harvey greeting Spendlove on the night of the murder."

"I don't know anything about that," Ward said, shaking his head. "Harvey never mentioned he had any contact with Spendlove since school."

"I got the impression Mr Harvey was very dominant in the company," Philippa interjected. "He didn't allow you to forget he had invested all the money."

"He was always in charge, yes," replied Ward "But we were still good friends." Philippa lapsed into dubious silence, as she continued to take notes.

"Detective Sergeant Cottrell tells me you were shredding a large number of documents yesterday. Could you tell me why?" Gould asked.

"Well, I suppose you're bound to find out eventually." Ward shifted uneasily in his chair. "I'd been claiming too much in personal allowances against tax. You know, claims for journeys I never made – that sort of thing. When Philippa told me she was an undercover police officer, I panicked."

"Is that all you were worried about?"

"Yes."

"Can you tell me again where you were between seven and midnight last night?" Gould asked.

"At home, I told you. I left the office at about six."

"And you say there's no one who can confirm that?"

"No, I live alone, now I'm divorced, and no one saw me last night."

"DS Cottrell gained the impression that Mr Harvey was difficult to work for. Is that how you found him?"

"Neil wanted always to be in control. I suppose it was fair enough as he put up most of the money."

"Did you ever want to set up on your own without Harvey around?"

"No, not really. I didn't kill him for that reason, if that's what you're thinking. Why should I? It wouldn't be logical." Ward was becoming angrier. "Neil's shares will probably go to Kathleen now and God knows what she will do with them. She could even sell them to a competitor who could decide to close us all down."

"Thank you, Mr Ward." Gould stood up. "You may go now. Don't forget to leave your ex-wife's address behind. Let me know if you remember anything that might be useful to us. I'm sure we'll be in touch."

Ward quietly left the office after signing the tape. When he had gone, Gould turned to his colleague.

"What do you think, Philippa?" he asked. "Ward has as much motive as anyone else. Just think of it – humiliated every day by someone he thought of as a friend. Ward said he was financially dependent on Harvey, and doesn't benefit from the murder, but he could have killed him in anger. Perhaps one insult too many and Ward finally cracked."

"I believe him, David." For some reason, Philippa felt herself blushing. "I know you're suspicious, but I've worked with him. I couldn't see him murdering anyone, and certainly not being involved in drugs."

"I know what you mean." Philippa was surprised to find Gould agreeing with her. "Ward's not really the criminal type. We don't know that anyone else in the company was involved in Anson's cocaine racket. I'd still like to find what Marks found out that was so incriminating it made someone murder him."

"Shall I arrange for us to see Spendlove now?"

"Yes, please, Philippa."

"Where does he live?"

"Oh, he's one of the untouchables. He's probably in his Mayfair office," Gould said, looking thoughtfully out of the window to the office workers walking along outside. "One thing's for sure. We're going to have a tough job pinning anything on Mr Spendlove."

Chapter 14

An hour later, Gould and Philippa were at the reception desk in the luxuriously appointed offices of Spendlove Associates. The pretty young receptionist told them, with just a touch of condescension, that Mr Spendlove would be free shortly. The two detectives sat next to each other on a leather-covered settee in the foyer.

"How does a drug trafficker end up with all this, David?" Philippa asked quietly, looking round at the plush offices.

"I was just asking myself the same question." Gould responded. "It beats our police station, doesn't it? You'll see lots of offices like this in the Serious Crimes Squad. They're generally based on some poor devil's misery."

"What business does Spendlove claim to be in?"

"Various services industries – office cleaning, catering, you name it. All perfectly legitimate apart from the original money which comes from drugs. It would be wonderful to put Spendlove behind bars. He's one of our chief targets. But don't be too worried about him. He'll be nailed eventually."

"He's doing pretty well in the meantime, though," Philippa said, largely to herself. Just then, a short well-dressed man with a sallow expression came into the foyer, with right hand outstretched. Philippa recognised him as Jack Spendlove from his mug shot. Gould pointedly refused to shake his hand.

"Mr Spendlove, as you know I'm Detective Chief Inspector Gould. This is my colleague, DS Cottrell. I have some rather serious questions to ask you," Gould said. "May we meet in your office?"

"Certainly, Chief Inspector," Spendlove replied, with impeccable courtesy. "Won't you both come in? It's always a pleasure to welcome the police." Spendlove's apparent civility was cloying, and Philippa could tell Gould was forcing himself not to lose his temper. They followed Spendlove to his plush office, where another man was waiting for them.

"This is Robert Rothenberg, my solicitor," Spendlove said. "I always like to have legal representation when I see the police."

"It hardly seems necessary, unless you have something to hide, Mr Spendlove." Gould replied. "Detective Sergeant Cottrell here will take notes." The four of them sat down round Spendlove's mahogany table. Spendlove opened a packet of Gauloises cigarettes and lit one.

"Can you first of all tell us if you have ever met a Mr Neil Harvey," Gould asked. Spendlove looked towards Rothenberg, shaking his head.

"My client has never met this man," replied Rothenberg. "I see from the newspaper that he has been murdered. I trust you are not suggesting my client was in any way involved."

"I presume Mr Spendlove can speak for himself, Mr Rothenberg," said Gould, as calmly as he could. "We have incontrovertible evidence that Mr Harvey and your client knew each other at school. Perhaps you could ask your client to refresh his memory. It shouldn't be difficult as you were at the school at the same time, Mr Rothenberg."

"I recall Neil Harvey from school, now you mention it, but I have not seen him for over thirty years," Spendlove replied. "So I am not sure how I can help you, Chief Inspector."

"We have a witness who saw your client visiting Neil Harvey on the night of his death," Gould said. "So, it is strange that your client denies meeting Mr Harvey recently. Can you explain the discrepancy?"

"What is the name of your witness, Chief Inspector?" Spendlove asked.

"I can't tell you that, Mr Spendlove, but he has been arrested on charges of trading in illicit drugs."

"Hardly a reliable witness, Chief Inspector," said Rothenberg. "The courts take a dim view of criminals turning Queen's evidence for lenient treatment. I am sure you would not be party to such a scheme."

"Can you tell me where you were between seven and midnight on Wednesday evening?" Gould asked Spendlove, starting on a different tack.

"Mr Spendlove was at a reception with several of his employees," Rothenberg said, a little too quickly.

"No doubt, they will testify to that effect?"

"No doubt. I will furnish their names, if you wish."

"That would be useful. I can remind them of the penalties for perjury," Gould replied in a weary tone. "Well, perhaps you would be good enough to report to the police station and make a formal statement, Mr Spendlove. I am sure Mr Rothenberg will go along to keep you company." Gould stood up ready to leave and Philippa followed suit.

While they were driving back to the station, Philippa turned to Gould.

"Did we learn much there?" she asked.

Gould shrugged his shoulders. "Not much, but at least it showed him we were serious. What evidence do we have after all? Rothenberg's right. No court would believe anything Anson said."

"Where does the investigation go now?" Philippa asked.

"I'm not sure, Philippa," Gould replied, thoughtfully. "We don't seem to have any definite leads at the moment. Still it's early days yet. It would be good to have Spendlove down at the station, even if it's only for a short time. We'll arrange an identification parade."

****

"If you see the man you saw in Harvey's office the night of his murder, just indicate his number."

It was the following day and Anson was standing in front of a two-way mirror at Snow Hill police station. The duty sergeant and Gould were preparing Anson for a carefully planned identity parade.

"It would be in your interest to be as helpful as possible, Mr Anson," Gould continued. "At the moment the only person we know who was definitely in the office with Harvey that night is yourself."

Anson replied with his characteristic insouciance. "I understand the position perfectly well, thank you, Chief Inspector. Shall we continue, Sergeant."

In accordance with official procedure, Gould left the room leaving Anson with the duty sergeant.

"Now, please take your time," the duty sergeant said. "Don't worry – the men in the parade can't see you. You needn't worry about your own safety. If anyone tries to intimidate you, just let us know."

Anson nodded. He looked at the five men before him all about Spendlove's age and appearance. He ignored the others and immediately spotted Spendlove as the man he had seen in Harvey's office that night. He wondered what he should do. Gould was probably right that identifying Spendlove would mean that he would be clear of any involvement in the murder. Then he thought of the amount of money he realised was behind Spendlove's operation. He also had a mental image of being beaten to a pulp by the man he knew as Nick, who he guessed was Spendlove's enforcer.

Anson sighed. "I'm sorry, Sergeant, I don't recognise any of these men. I'm sorry I can't be of more help."

The duty sergeant answered. "Very well, Mr Gould will take you back to your cells…"

Chapter 15

As requested, Kathleen Harvey turned up at the City police station the following morning and was ushered into the interview room. She looked with distaste at the worn furniture and the drab paintwork of the room. She was wearing an expensive looking grey suit and made it obvious she was worried about her clothes being soiled by contact with the chair she was about to sit on. Gould consciously made no effort to make her more comfortable. He had sent Philippa to interview the Harveys' au pair in Kathleen's absence. Apart from Gould and Kathleen, only a uniformed woman constable sat taking notes. After the initial form of words for the benefit of the tape recording, Gould opened the interview.

"I'm sorry for your loss, Mrs Harvey. Thank you for identifying your husband's body. The pathologist has confirmed your husband was killed unlawfully. Now, are you strong enough to answer some questions to help us find your husbands' killer?"

"I will answer as much as I can.

"I'm trying to go back as far as I can in this investigation, Mrs Harvey. Please tell me as much as you can about your husband's background and life."

Kathleen looked dubiously at Gould. "How far back do you want me to go?" she asked.

It struck Gould she had a curious accent, with cockney tones being overlaid by an upper-class veneer, obviously picked up at one of the top girls' public schools. Gould had gathered enough of her background to know that this reflected the fact that she had spent her early childhood at an East End primary school, before her father's money allowed him to send her to a more up-market establishment.

"Right from the time you first met," Gould replied. "The more we know about your husband's life, the better chance we have of finding his killer. Now, take your time, I'm not in a hurry to go anywhere."

"Very well, I'll start at the beginning. I first met Neil Harvey nearly thirty years ago when Daddy invited him to a dinner party in our family's house." Kathleen smiled to herself at the memory. "I should say my father was what you might call a self-made man; he made a lot of money in the war and was always trying to move up a social class or two. Anyway, Neil came into the room, dressed in a hired dinner jacket and black tie. He had done some City deals for my father and this invitation was by way of a reward. He made a point of circulating and giving his business card to as many people as he could.

"At the dinner, I found himself sitting next to Neil – I've never known how it happened. I'm sure he planned it in some way. I introduced myself as Mr Jones's daughter. Neil made it his business to be as charming as he could to me. I used to be rather plain in those days. Neil made it clear he had no objection to plain girls, as long as they had rich fathers." Kathleen at first smiled then dabbed her eyes.

"After establishing that I was unattached, he made his move. He invited me to a Young Conservatives' dinner the following week. I remember I was dubious.

"'You're not just interested in Daddy's money, are you, Neil?' I asked.

"'How do you mean?' he said, with a charming smile.

"'Because you wouldn't believe the no-hopers who think I'm an easy route to money,' I said. 'It's simpler all round if I stop anyone like that from the start. Daddy always says he's not going to leave me any money anyway, so I wouldn't want you to waste your time.'

"'No, I assure you, it's you I'm interested in,' he said. He was always a good liar. I've no doubt he was certain that, whatever happened, my father would make sure his only daughter was well provided for. He was right, of course.

"Neil's courtship of me started at that point and with his usual single-mindedness, he fairly soon got the result he wanted. For the lack of anyone better, I suppose, I agreed to marry him. It was a way of escaping from home, if nothing else. My father wanted a formal white wedding to show everyone how far he had come up in the world. Neil was willing enough to go along with Dad. Neil's only worry was about who to choose as best man. He spent most of his time pursuing his career, and he didn't have many male friends.

"You've already met one of the few friends he had. He'd gone to school with Reg Ward. Back at school, he had once stood up to the school bully and protected Reg. Neil knew that Reg had always been grateful and felt he would be a reasonable best man. He contacted Reg and it was all set up over dinner between Reg, Annabel – she was Reg's wife, but they've divorced since – Neil and me."

"What can you tell us about this school bully, Mrs Harvey?" Gould interrupted.

Kathleen looked surprised. "Neil once said his name was Spendlove – Jack Spendlove. But he's not important. I don't think Neil ever saw him after school. Why do you ask?"

"Please carry on, Mrs Harvey," Gould said, making a note that Spendlove's name had cropped up again in the investigation.

"Well, once we were married, Neil settled down to run one of my father's businesses. He kept in touch with people at the Stock Exchange. He had a knack of picking up rumours of take-overs before they were announced, and he was well on his way to becoming a very rich man by his mid-twenties.

"After we'd been married a year, I had twins. I studied Greek at school and we called the children Cassandra and Jason. Neil was genuinely pleased to be a father. He was especially happy when Daddy set up trust funds for both of them. Neil had the authority to manage the investments for the benefit of the children. Somehow, without doing anything obviously illegal, he ensured that a percentage of any deals made for the trusts came into his own pockets.

"Just after the children were born, I suppose we were in quite an enviable position. I don't think either of us ever really knew why our marriage went wrong after that. I don't think Neil even noticed that it had gone wrong. I think he felt that now I'd produced children and he had control of most of my money, he didn't need me anymore. Anyway, from then on, his affairs with women at the office became more frequent. I don't think Neil could even remember their names when the affairs finished, but he gave them generous handouts using my money, which kept them happy." Kathleen's eyes were full of tears at this point, and she pulled a handkerchief out of her expensive-looking handbag. She looked at Gould as if expecting some escape.

"Please carry on, Mrs Harvey," Gould said. "The sooner you tell me what you know, the sooner you can leave."

Kathleen shrugged with resignation. "As you wish. In 1980, my father died and left his large estate split three ways between myself and the two children. From this time, Neil felt little need to even be polite to me. He left me on my own in our large house in Haslemere, and we lived separate lives. Although he ignored me, he seemed quite close to our twins. As they grew up, he recognised them as being similar to himself. Cassandra, especially, showed some of the same ambition as her father, while Jason seemed closer to me.

"By the early 1980s, Neil was director of many of the companies my father had left me. While the shares were registered in my name, everyone knew that Neil controlled things. He liked to boast how he had come a long way from his poor background. He still occasionally saw Reg Ward – he was doing quite well in a travel agency."

"How did your husband set up Harvey and Ward?" Gould asked, keen to check Ward's story.

"One day, Reg came to dinner with Annabel. After the meal, Neil agreed to put up the money for a travel agency business that Reg wanted to set up. When Reg left, I asked Neil why he had done it.

"'It'll be fun having our own small business,' he said. 'I can always get rid of Ward when I need to. It might be a nice little business for Cassandra to cut her teeth on. He used to work in the Harvey and Ward office and run lots of other businesses from there.'

"'Does Reg know you'll be getting rid of him?' I asked Neil.

"'No, of course not,' he said. 'I want Reg to really work his guts out working this business up. That's what he's good at. Then when it's successful, I can pull the money out and make it all my own.'

"He was so pleased with himself that he poured himself another brandy. I was shocked really as Reg was as close to a friend as Neil ever had. In the event, as you know, the business has proved quite successful and Neil did very well out of it." Kathleen sipped water from a plastic beaker after inspecting it with distaste.

"Did your husband ever try to pull the money out from beneath Reg Ward?" Gould asked.

"No, there was no need. Reg worked so hard for so little reward that Neil must have thought it made more sense to keep him in post."

"Mr Ward told us he did all the work while your husband took three-quarters of the money," Gould said.

"Yes, I suppose it must look like that to him," Kathleen replied vaguely.

"How does it look to you?"

"Like that, I suppose," Kathleen replied, smiling slightly. "Still, my husband put up the money when Reg wanted it. If Reg wasn't happy, he could have gone somewhere else."

"Could we run through the events of the few days leading up to the murder, Mrs. Harvey?" Gould asked. "First of all, what sort of lives did you and your husband lead?"

"Your sergeant's seen our house in Haslemere, Chief Inspector," Kathleen Harvey replied. "We have a comfortable life-style. My husband is – or was – a very successful business man and he was away a lot."

"Did he take you on many business trips, Mrs. Harvey?" Gould asked.

"No, not very often. I don't like travelling much anyway and I was happy for him to go away on his own if he wanted. I have my circle of friends in Haslemere – all women, in case you're wondering."

"Did he go along with any colleagues on these trips?" Gould asked.

"Yes, by and large," Kathleen replied. "Oh, I know what you're going to ask. Did he go away with other women?" Gould nodded. "Oh, don't worry about my feelings. I'm not naïve enough to think that a man like Neil didn't have other women."

At that moment, a constable entered the room and spoke to Gould. "There's a call from DS Cottrell, sir," he said.

"Oh, damn it, Philippa's away investigating a suspect," Gould turned to the constable. "Tell them to put it through to this phone." Gould realised that Kathleen would soon find out that Philippa had been at the Harvey house at Haslemere but was happy enough for Kathleen to know how thorough the police investigation was. After speaking on the phone, Gould turned to Kathleen.

"Does the name Samantha mean anything to you?" Gould asked Kathleen.

"No, why?" Kathleen's response seemed genuine.

"I have information from two sources that your husband was seeing a woman with that name," Gould said. "It would be in your interest to be as forthcoming as you can." Kathleen shook her head. "For the benefit of the recording, Mrs. Harvey indicated a negative response. Now tell me again about the twenty-four hours leading up to your husband's murder."

"On Tuesday morning, that was the day before he died, he went to work normally."

"What time was that?" Gould asked.

"He took the 9:58 train from Haslemere up to Waterloo; he usually left his Jaguar in the station car park. That was the last time I saw him alive. I knew nothing more until the next morning when Cassandra phoned up to say he had been murdered."

"You're saying nothing unusual happened between the time he left and the time you received a call saying he was dead," Gould said as neutrally as possible, keeping a close eye on Kathleen's face.

"That's right, it was just a normal day until I received the news," Kathleen Harvey said, tears coming to her eyes again.

"Please tell us about your daughter's visit."

"Oh, you know about that, do you? I was annoyed when Neil didn't come home for dinner. If he had an evening appointment in town, he should have mentioned it to me. Then just when I was expecting Neil to arrive, Cassandra came in. She was in tears because Neil had just sacked her. I promised Cassandra to have a word with him and see if I could change his mind, but he was murdered before I got the chance."

"After the meal, what happened?"

"I tried to phone Neil but there was no reply. Cassandra had calmed down by this point and she drove back to London. I went to bed at about eleven o'clock – my usual time. By the next morning, I was getting worried that Neil had not come home, then I received the bad news from Cassandra. Soon after, your female sergeant came to see me. I don't think there's much more I can tell you, Chief Inspector."

Chapter 16

While Kathleen Harvey travelled to London to be interviewed by David Gould, Philippa had driven in the opposite direction to Haslemere to interview Tania, Mrs Harvey's au pair. Gould knew that this was the surest way of finding out how much Tania knew without her employer being present. When Philippa knocked on the door of the Harveys' house, Tania took a long time to reply.

"Mrs Harvey is away," Tania said in an Eastern European accent, when she came to the door. Her expression indicated she was seriously frightened.

"I know. It's you I want to see." Philippa pulled out her warrant card. "I'm Detective Sergeant Cottrell. You may remember I came to see Mrs Harvey when her husband was killed. May I come in?"

"I remember you, but I'm not sure I should…" the girl hesitated.

"It's up to you of course, but do you want me to ask the local police to check on your work permit?"

"Oh, very well, come in," the au pair conceded doubtfully after considering Philippa's threat. "I suppose it will be all right. Would you like a cup of coffee?" Tania stood aside and led Philippa into the kitchen. While Tania made two cups of coffee, Philippa pulled out her notepad.

"Could I have your full name for the record, please?" Philippa asked.

"Tania Kopic. I come from the Czech Republic," she said, pronouncing each word carefully.

"And how long have you worked for Mrs Harvey?"

"Three months," Tania replied. "I am here to improve my English. Now the Communists have gone, I am free to travel."

"There are no children, are there? It must be quite light work."

"Yes, I suppose," Tania conceded. "But Mr and Mrs Harvey sometimes have dinner parties, which need a lot of preparation."

"And what have they been like to work for?" Philippa asked. "Take Mr Harvey to start with."

"I did not like Mr Harvey," Tania said, blushing. "I did not trust him. I tried not to be alone with him."

"Why?" Philippa asked, looking up sharply. "Did he harass you at all?"

"Harass?"

"Did he make sexual advances at all?"

"Yes, he used to come too close to me sometimes and put his hand on my body. I did not like that. I told him he was too old for me and he should not do it," Tania replied, with a shudder.

"How did he react to that?"

"He did not like being called old, but he did not bother me after that. He said he had a girlfriend called Samantha who didn't think he was old."

"Did he say anything else about this Samantha?" Philippa asked.

"No."

"Did Mrs Harvey know about this?"

"No, I don't think so."

"And how does Mrs Harvey treat you?" Philippa asked.

"She can be very rude, especially about her dinner parties. She wanted everything perfect. I think she was trying to impress her husbands' friends too much."

"And what can you tell me about the night Mr Harvey was killed?"

Tania thought for a moment. "Mrs Harvey was annoyed that Mr Harvey didn't turn up for dinner. Then, Miss Harvey – Cassandra – visited at about seven o'clock, without any warning. It changed all my plans. Miss Harvey ate Mr Harvey's meal."

"Does Cassandra often come down to see her mother like that?" Philippa asked.

"She has never come down for an evening visit before."

"It's very important I find out how long she stayed."

Tania thought for a moment. "Cassandra left about nine," she said.

"Did Mrs Harvey stay home all evening?" Philippa asked.

"I don't know. She said I could have an evening out after Cassandra left."

"Was that unusual?"

"No, it was my normal evening off. I should have been off work at six. I was cross I had to serve dinner to Cassandra."

"What time did you come back after your evening out?" Philippa asked.

"About half past eleven. I didn't see Mrs Harvey then, but the light was on in her room and the radio was on, so she must have been there."

"But can you be sure? Be careful, this is crucial." Tania looked blank. "It is very important," Philippa reworded.

Tania thought for a while. "I see what you mean. You want to know if she could have gone to London and killed her husband. No, as I didn't see her when I came back. I suppose she could have left the light and radio on just to trick me."

"She has her own car, I suppose."

"Oh, yes," Tania replied.

"So, she would have had time to drive to London and then returned after you went to bed."

"Yes, I suppose so. I went straight to bed when I came back and slept until the morning, so I wouldn't have heard Mrs Harvey if she'd come back late." Tania paused. "I haven't been much use, have I?"

"No," Philippa said. "You have been very helpful. Thank you. I'll give you my card. Please phone this number if you can think of anything else." In the car afterwards, Philippa picked up her mobile phone and told Gould what she had learnt about Harvey's mysterious new girlfriend, Samantha.

****

When Philippa got back to the City police station, Kathleen Harvey had already left. Gould ran through Tania's statement.

"So, none of the main suspects we've seen so far – Harvey's wife, Cassandra, Reg Ward, Margaret Lane, Charles Anson – have strong alibis," Gould said thoughtfully. "From what Tania told us, either Cassandra or Kathleen Harvey could have come back to London and killed Harvey."

"The only one who claims to have an alibi is Spendlove," Philippa pointed out.

"And he's rich enough and has enough contacts to buy an alibi. All his staff will say he was with them whatever he was doing, so we would be wasting our time following that up," Gould replied. "One thing I'd like to know is why Harvey suddenly decided to ditch Margaret Lane and go with this Samantha."

"Perhaps he was just bored with Margaret?"

"Men don't ditch girlfriends out of boredom. They do it because they've found someone new. Do you think Tania was lying and she and Harvey were having an affair?"

"Possibly, but Tania was very convincing when she denied it. She said she told him to stop as soon as he got too close to her," Philippa said.

"Do you think Tania could be a suspect? She seems to have hated Neil Harvey."

"Anything's possible, but I can't see it. To travel all the way to London to murder a man who made a pass at her. It seems a bit excessive."

Gould was about to add something, when the phone rang. "Come along, Philippa, we've got the results of the autopsy."

Chapter 17

As Philippa drove through the traffic, Gould explained that all autopsies for Central London take place in a building in a remarkably run-down part of Westminster. As Gould and Philippa parked their car and walked up to the building, the acrid scent of death came out of the vents of the building. As Gould had reminded her earlier, this case was Philippa's first experience of a homicide investigation, and the truly repulsive odour of death mixed with formaldehyde stopped her in her tracks. She looked as if she might faint until David Gould put his arms around her.

"Are you feeling all right, Philippa?" he asked. "Don't worry – no one gets used to this smell."

"I'll be all right, thank you." Philippa blew her nose in a tissue and consciously recovered her composure. "Shall we go in?"

The two officers walked in and were directed into a large room with ancient tiles that had once been white but were now a mottled cream and dirty brown. A large, surprisingly youthful, man came to see Gould with out-stretched arms.

"Hello, David. You've got quite an interesting case for me here." He turned to Philippa. "We haven't met. My name's Robin Bruce."

"This is Philippa Cottrell," said Gould as they shook hands. "She's not really used to violent death yet. I think the smell's getting to her." Philippa felt annoyed that Gould should speak for her, but nodded politely at Bruce.

"What smell?" Bruce asked, sniffing the air. "Oh, yes, this autopsy smell, I don't notice it now."

"What have you got for us, Robin?" Gould asked, seeking to return to business.

"Well, the victim, Mr Harvey, was a man in his middle fifties. He seemed to take very little exercise – he was very overweight, but he seemed in reasonable health until the murder."

"I know. I used to work for him," Philippa said. Bruce looked surprised but continued.

"The victim was shot at short range. Death would have been instantaneous. The bullet went right into the centre of his forehead. The killer was either very lucky or very skillful. The bullet came out at the back of the head and should be near the scene of the murder."

"Yes, we found it. We've asked the experts to confirm it came from the gun we found near the body."

"What's interesting is that the bullet came from quite low down. It was rising when it entered his body."

"What does that tell us?" Philippa asked.

"It was probably someone sitting down."

"That's possible – there was a chair opposite the desk."

"There's one interesting possibility I wanted to raise, bearing in mind the narrow range and the rising trajectory, and that's suicide."

"You think he could have shot himself?" Philippa asked startled.

"Precisely."

"I don't think so," Gould replied thoughtfully. "We would have found his fingerprints on the gun if he had done that." Something stirred at the back of Philippa's mind.

"There was a tissue near the gun, sir," she said. "If he'd wanted to, he could have held the gun with that to cover up the suicide."

"That would be a lot of trouble," Gould said. "Why should he do it?"

"Insurance?" Philippa suggested. "That's what Rothenberg would say anyway if we charged Spendlove."

"Yes, he probably would. It would make it harder to get a conviction. Is there anything else, Robin?" Gould asked.

"No, that covers the main points. I can believe the original doctor's estimate of the time of death. I'll send you the full written report tomorrow," Bruce replied, showing his two visitors out. It was obvious he wanted to return to his full-time occupation among the dead.

Outside in the corridor something unexpected happened. The smell and heat of the autopsy room had finally overcome Philippa and she stood against the wall, drawing deep breaths of fresh air. David Gould put his arm around her to comfort her. Philippa broke away angrily.

"I'll be all right. It's just the stench in that place that overcame me." She stood away and breathed more deep gulps of air.

"I understand. Really, I do," Gould said.

Philippa moved closer to Gould, as he put his arms around her. They hugged wordlessly for about a minute before they stepped back. The two looked at each other, both apparently embarrassed about their sudden closeness.

"I'm sorry, I shouldn't have done that," Gould said after a while.

"No, it was my fault. It was just that awful stench. Let's forget about it, shall we?" Philippa smiled through her tears. They looked into each other's eyes. Despite Philippa's words, they both knew their relationship had changed. For the good of their careers they would have to keep appearances the same, but they both knew there was an undercurrent of attraction between them.

Chapter 18

"How should we interview Cassandra Harvey, Philippa?" Gould asked the following day, at their early morning meeting at Snow Hill police station.

"What do you mean?"

"Do you think our interview room is good enough for her or should we make an appointment at her office?"

"I think it would be fun to bring her down here," Philippa said, as she warmed to her subject. "Men are always rushing round trying to please her. Let her see how the rest of the world lives. It would show her we're serious as well."

"Don't worry. I was just joking, she's downstairs now. Can you bring her up and take the notes of the interview?"

Philippa went to the reception, feeling embarrassed at her outburst. She brought Cassandra through the crowded general office and into the interview room. Cassandra expressed no emotion at the seedy surroundings and the nude pin-ups on the wall.

"Thank you for coming, Miss Harvey," Gould said, standing up. "Please take a seat."

Cassandra sat down on the edge of her seat, somehow conveying the impression of granting a favour to the interviewing detectives.

"I realise you are still recovering from your father's death, Miss Harvey," Gould began, after making the routine identifications for the tape recording. "Thank you for agreeing to come and see us." Cassandra inclined her head. "As you know, Miss Harvey, DS Cottrell has been working undercover for a few days in Harvey and Ward and so she already knows some aspects of your work. But for the record, please tell me what your role is in your father's company."

"I have a selling role – I meet potential clients and try to sell our services."

"Do you still work at your father's company?" Gould asked.

"Yes, of course," Cassandra replied, apparently surprised at the question.

"I understood your father dismissed you the day before he was murdered."

"Oh, of course, obviously your spy has told you already," Cassandra said, glaring at Philippa. "Daddy made a great show of firing me the day before he was killed."

"How did you feel about that?"

"I was furious. I didn't know what he was thinking of."

"It could be said to give you a motive for murder, Cassandra," Philippa pointed out.

"Lots of people had motives. My father was a successful businessman – he upset quite a few people along the way. Why don't you interview some of them?"

"We're going quite far back in your father's history already, Miss Harvey, and we'll be interviewing everyone who's relevant," Gould replied. "Reg Ward has been very informative. But let's start with you, shall we? What did you do after your father sacked you?"

"I went to the local wine bar. I'm sure Philippa's told you all about that."

"You were with Charles Anson, I believe. Did you know that Mr Anson is in the cells below, charged with dealing in a controlled substance?"

"I was told that. I'm shocked – I didn't know anything about it. I never want to have anything to do with him again," Cassandra said with a convincing shudder.

"When did you first meet Mr Anson?"

"When he started work at the company – about a year ago."

"What was the nature of your relationship?"

"He was good looking," Cassandra replied. "It's useful to have a presentable man to go to places with – a bit of fluff, isn't that what men call attractive women? I was going to drop him soon. Don't look so horrified, Chief Inspector. Women are starting to treat men like they've always treated us."

"Did Anson know you were going to drop him as a bit of fluff?" Gould asked.

"I don't think so."

"Do you have a replacement in mind yet?"

"What do you mean?"

"Do you have another eligible man in mind as your next boyfriend?"

"Not yet, Chief Inspector. When I do, I'll make sure you're informed," Cassandra shot back.

Philippa intervened. "When I attended that meeting, I heard him say to you, 'We have to make your father see sense over this'. What did he mean by that?"

Cassandra thought. "Oh, he had some plan to reorganise the company. It was nothing important."

"We believe that Anson may have been involved with a professional criminal called Spendlove. Does that name mean anything to you?" Gould asked.

"Spendlove? No, I've never heard that name," Cassandra replied after a moment's thought.

"Your father mentioned he was seeing a woman called Samantha. Do you know who she is and how we can get in touch with her?"

Cassandra snorted elegantly. "No, I've never heard of her, but nothing would surprise me. My father was always going out with other women."

"Like Margaret Lane."

"Just like her."

"And did your mother know about these affairs?" Philippa asked.

"I don't know. She must have had suspicions, but I never talked about them with her. It was something between her and Dad."

"When was the last time you saw your father alive?" Philippa asked.

"When he sacked me."

"You didn't try to see him and persuade him to change his mind?"

"No," Cassandra replied, shaking her head. "My first reaction was to storm into his office and tell him what I thought of him, but I decided to wait until I had calmed down."

"Did you see him on Tuesday night at all?" Gould asked.

"No, I didn't."

"What did you do after leaving the wine bar?"

"I went home to my flat for a bit."

"Is that all?" Gould asked, in a sharp tone. "Before you reply, I should say we have already interviewed several other witnesses, who have been very co-operative."

"Well, I went down to my parents' house in Haslemere. I thought my mother could try to smooth things over between Dad and me."

"Were you expecting your father to be there?"

"No. I knew he was always working late. That's what he used to tell Mum anyway," Cassandra added with a bitter smile.

"But you didn't believe him?"

"Not really. Everyone in the office used to talk about Dad and Margaret Lane. I expect he had other women as well, but I didn't want to know about them."

"How did the meal with your mother go?" Gould asked.

"How did you know we had a meal?" Cassandra responded in a suspicious tone. "I suppose that au pair told you," she added after a moment's thought. "It went fine, thank you. Mum said she would speak to Dad about it as soon as she could."

"When was she expecting to see him next?" Philippa asked.

"When he came home, I suppose. She wasn't planning to come up to London to see him if that's what you mean."

"And what time did you leave Haslemere, Miss Harvey?" Gould asked.

"I suppose it would have been about nine."

"One thing puzzles me," Philippa said. "Why did you turn up for work at the usual time the next day if you had been sacked?"

"Oh, I thought if I came in as usual, Dad would have forgotten all about sacking me by the next morning. He could be very changeable like that."

"And what did you find when you arrived?"

"I was about to go in to Daddy's office, when I saw Philippa standing outside so I came away."

"But you didn't know I was a police officer at that time," Philippa pointed out.

"I did think it was odd, but I didn't realise Dad was dead. I went away for a coffee then came into my office and found you two there. You told me about Dad's murder and you know the rest."

"When did you phone your mother and tell her?" Gould asked.

"Oh, straight away."

"You told her by phone? I'm surprised you didn't ask us to tell her. We could have sent the local police round – probably a female officer. The uniformed police are trained to be tactful when they have to tell relatives about a sudden death."

"With all due respect, tactful is one thing police usually are not."

"I assume your mother will be taking over the running of the company now," Philippa said. "She might ask you to be in charge. It would be quite a step up in your responsibilities. Are you looking forward to it?"

"I don't know what my mother's plans are yet. If I were in charge, I would make quite a few changes."

"At the wine bar, your brother shouted across to you. You didn't seem pleased to see him."

Cassandra snorted. "I should think I wasn't. He works for one of our rivals who stole the Stock exchange contract from us. I hate him."

"Some people would say that's just fair competition."

"No, I made sure our profit margins in the bid were as low as they could be. The only way Jason could have won is by persuading his new company to make a loss."

"Why would he do that?"

"To get back at his father – and me, I suppose. I told you he hates all of us."

"If you are put in charge of the company now, you seem to have done quite well out of your father's death," Gould said. "It gives you a possible motive for having killed him."

141

"I didn't kill him, and I don't know who did," Cassandra replied, suddenly sounding like a sulky child.

"Thank you for coming in, Miss Harvey," Gould said, standing up to terminate the interview. Cassandra politely thanked Gould as she left, leaving a trail of perfume behind her.

After Cassandra had gone, Gould turned to Philippa. "What do you think? If Anson and Cassandra were trying to force Harvey into dealing in drugs, that might explain the conversation you overheard."

"But if I were defending her," Philippa replied, "I'd say her story hangs together. She could have come back after seeing her mother and killed her father in an argument or deliberately, but I can't imagine her getting her hands dirty with all that blood. I don't buy that stuff about Anson being a bit of fluff. It sounded phoney. The trouble is her whole life's a performance, so it's hard to know what's true and what isn't. I don't suppose she does much of the time."

Chapter 19

Gould was informed that Neil Harvey was to be buried at Saint Bartholomew's Church in Haslemere three days later. The investigations into the body had been completed and Gould had raised no objection to releasing the body for burial. In accordance with police custom, Gould was expected to attend the funeral and he invited Philippa as well.

Although in their brief acquaintance, Philippa had never liked Harvey, even she found it sad how few people turned up to his funeral. Only his widow, Cassandra, Reg Ward and a man in his twenties Philippa did not recognise were at the graveside. The funeral took place in pouring rain in front of the dark red Victorian church. Gould and Philippa remained at a respectful distance from the graveside allowing his family to stand nearby. A few bedraggled reporters stood on the street outside the churchyard.

As the chief mourners huddled together around the grave during the service, Philippa noticed a familiar figure standing nearby. Margaret Lane looked forlorn as the rain turned her hair into a sodden mess. Philippa went over to her. "What are you doing here, Margaret?" she asked in a sympathetic tone. "I'm surprised you were invited."

"Why shouldn't I be here?" Margaret snapped back, her eyes rimmed with tears. "I did everything for Neil for the last ten years. I've got as much right to be here as they have," she added, nodding at the small group of family mourners near the grave.

"I know the rest of them, but who's that man in the middle?"

"Don't you know him?" Margaret asked. "That's Jason, Cassandra's twin brother. They're both ancient Greek names. Kathleen always had a taste for classical names. I think her rich Daddy sent her to some posh public school or other. She's never had to work since."

"Did Mr Harvey see much of Jason?" Philippa asked, ignoring Margaret's invective against Harvey's widow.

"Oh, Jason used to work at the company, but he had some sort of argument with Neil a few years ago. They never saw each other since then."

"As far as you know," Philippa added. "Jason may have seen his father before his death."

"What do you mean?" Margaret asked sharply. "Oh, you think Jason could have been the one who visited Neil the night he died?" Philippa nodded, keeping her eyes on Margaret's face. "I suppose Jason could have killed his father. He certainly had a motive. He must have spent all the money he inherited when he was eighteen. He could have wanted money – and killed his father either deliberately or in a fit of temper." Margaret paused and then smiled slightly. "Does that give you something to investigate, Sergeant?"

"Very good, Margaret. Perhaps you should have my job, except we need evidence before we accuse people," Philippa said. "I think the service is ending now." The four mourners passed by. Gould and Philippa tried to look professionally respectful of the dead man. Just then, Kathleen saw Margaret.

"What's that woman doing here?" the widow shrieked. "Get her away."

"I've got as much right to be here as you," Margaret screamed back.

Philippa moved forward to stand between the two women arguing in the pouring rain. "I'm sure no one wants a

144

scene, Mrs Harvey. Miss Lane came to pay her respects to her former boss, that's all," Philippa said.

"I've laid on some refreshments at home. I can't keep her away, but she's not welcome," Kathleen added, as Cassandra tried to usher her mother away. "If she comes into my house, I'm going to hit her."

"I'm sure Miss Lane won't come to your house, Mrs Harvey," Gould said. "If she does, I will have her arrested for breaching the peace. Do you understand, Miss Lane?" he added, as the two women parted, and Margaret walked away from the other mourners.

"I wouldn't visit her house, if you paid me," Margaret hissed as she walked away to her car. Philippa stood behind to make sure Margaret left without any further scenes.

"That was quite dramatic, wasn't it?" Gould said to Philippa once Margaret had driven away. "I think we'll have to invite ourselves to Mrs Harvey's reception to make sure there's no more trouble, don't you?"

****

At the funeral tea, as Gould and Philippa kept a watchful eye, a few more people had joined the mourners. Gould and Philippa politely drank tea and ate sandwiches that Tania took around. Furniture had obviously been moved out of the Harveys' drawing room to accommodate a large number of mourners. The small number who turned up left the drawing room half-empty.

"Harvey's money may have bought him a big house but it didn't buy him many friends, judging by how few people have turned up here," Gould whispered to Philippa, out of earshot of the others.

"I wonder if the reason he was murdered lies somewhere in his past?" she asked.

"Possibly," Gould answered. "I'd love to know if he was really involved in the drug-selling as Anson said. There might be some clues here. Let's circulate, shall we?"

As Gould suggested, Philippa tried to mingle with the other guests. She walked over to Reg Ward, who was standing on his own. He nodded politely when he saw Philippa.

"How are things going at Harvey and Ward's?" she asked.

"Harvey's death has been a shock, as you can imagine," Ward said. "I'm worried we'll lose quite a few contracts because of the bad publicity. I hope you can solve it all quietly so our customers forget about it soon. Are you making any progress?"

"We are pursuing various lines of inquiry," Philippa replied, careful not to commit herself. "Have you thought any more about whether Harvey was involved in drugs?"

"Yes, and I'm still convinced he didn't know anything."

"I know he was a hard man," Philippa said. "But did he have any soft spots? Did he ever really love anyone or anything?"

"That's a difficult question," Ward continued, turning round to make sure he was not being overheard. "He married Kathleen, of course, but I think that was because she had a rich father – Kathleen inherited a fortune from his scrap metal business. Neil had lots of women beside Kathleen. You've met Margaret and there have been many others, but I don't think he ever loved any of them. I think Cassandra was the only person he loved – apart from himself of course. He loved money and power as well – power more than the money, I think."

"Do you know why he broke up with Margaret Lane just before he died? He told her he'd found someone else. He mentioned the name Samantha to her. Does that mean anything to you?"

"No, Neil and I never talked about that sort of thing." Ward replied, with an embarrassed shrug. "Everyone knew he had mistresses, but he only ever spoke to me about work, all the time I knew him."

"Who do you think Harvey left his money to?"

"I've no idea, but we're about to find out. His solicitor's just arrived," Ward replied, nodding to a middle-aged man carrying a briefcase, who had just been showed in by Tania.

Just then, Mrs Harvey called for silence. "I've asked Mr Davies here to read Neil's will. It's a bit old-fashioned, but I thought this would be the best way to get it over."

"Are you happy for Detective Sergeant Cottrell and I to stay?" Gould asked. Mrs Harvey looked to Mr Davies.

"It won't take very long," the solicitor said. "As long as Mrs Harvey is content, the officers can stay." Kathleen Harvey nodded agreement, and Mr Davies took his papers out of his briefcase. "Tania," Kathleen addressed the au pair, "Don't just stand there. Get the chairs ready." Tania glared at Kathleen, with eyes full of hate, and rearranged the chairs in a semicircle. The other guests took their places while Gould and Philippa stood at the back of the room.

"It's really very simple," Mr Davies announced in an understated fashion, once his audience fell silent. "Mrs Kathleen Harvey has the sole use of all the late Mr Harvey's assets for as long as she lives. When she dies, all the assets are transferred equally to Miss Cassandra Harvey and Mr Jason Harvey. That is all there is to the late Mr Harvey's will. Are there any questions?"

Silence greeted Mr Davies's announcement of the will. The conditions were fairly standard, but Philippa was sure there was relief in Kathleen Harvey's face as she realised that while she might not be able to sell her late husband's property, she had their sole use and would be able to continue to live the life of a very rich woman. Reg Ward went up to Kathleen Harvey and put his hand on her shoulder. Philippa made sure she moved close enough to overhear their conversation.

"If there is any way I can help, Kathleen, let me know," Ward said. Cassandra, who was also standing nearby, came up to her mother's side.

"I am sure my mother can manage," Cassandra said, glaring at Ward. "After all, I am in a good position to look after her shares in the company."

"Yes, thank you, dear," Kathleen replied. "I'm sure Reg was only trying to help. After all, he and Neil were friends a long time."

Reg Ward walked away under Cassandra's hostile stare. He said no more but took his coat from the cloakroom and left the house. Since the funeral tea was obviously over, Gould and Philippa thanked Kathleen and followed Ward out to his car.

"How does that leave you, Reg?" Philippa asked as he unlocked the key to his mid-range saloon.

"Oh, it doesn't really matter to me. I just hope Kathleen will prove to be a congenial major shareholder. I only hope she doesn't allow Cassandra to take control." Ward nodded to Philippa as he got into his car and drove away. Gould and Philippa walked over to their own official car.

"Did you learn much from the funeral, sir?" Philippa asked.

"The only one who would speak to me was Tania. She was still upset she had to prepare a meal for Kathleen and Cassandra when she was supposed to be having an evening off. I told her to contact the phone number you left with her in case she learns anything. She couldn't stand Harvey and hates his widow even more. She should be a useful informant inside their household," Gould said. "As you said, if Tania was having an affair with Harvey she was keeping it very quiet. I'd like to know who this Samantha was that he was ditching Margaret for."

"What did you make of the funeral altogether?" Philippa asked.

"Grim is the best word to describe it. I don't know why they make us go through the ritual of attending these things. This one was more interesting than most. We must interview Jason, even though Margaret thinks he hadn't spoken to his father for a while. He had as good a motive as anybody – from what we know of him, I wouldn't be surprised if he hated his father. Mind you, I think Ward might have been right that Harvey's only real love was his daughter," David Gould replied. "Perhaps there was nothing he wouldn't do for her."

"Even deal in drugs?" Philippa suggested.

Gould did not reply but looked thoughtfully out of the window as Philippa drove the car back from the Surrey countryside through the suburbs and to their City of London police station.

****

At the end of the funeral reception, when the visitors had left, only Kathleen, Cassandra and Jason remained. Tania was silently tidying up at the far end of the long sitting room. Jason tried to chat to Tania, but only received a glare in response. Jason shrugged his shoulders, untied his black tie and dropped his suit jacket onto the nearest settee.

"Thank God that's over," he said, sitting down. "We can stop pretending now."

"What do you mean?" Kathleen said, looking at him.

"For pity's sake, let's stop pretending we're going to miss my father," Jason said, with a sneer. "I hated him and I'm sure we all did."

"Don't talk like that about your father," Kathleen replied in a tearful voice.

"Be careful, Jason, can't you see Mum's upset?" Cassandra said.

Jason gave a scornful laugh. "Oh, shut up, Cassie. You hated Dad – more than I did if anything."

"At least I worked for him," Cassandra spat back. "You went to work for one of our competitors. It was your fault we lost that Stock Exchange contract."

"We beat you fair and square. You and Dad shouldn't be in business if you can't stand competition," Jason shouted.

"Stop this squabbling at once," Kathleen called out, raising her voice. "We've all got to decide what to do next."

"How do you mean?" Jason asked, sitting up.

"The business has to go on," Kathleen replied. "According to Neil's will, I inherit while I'm alive, then it's split between the two of you. As far as I can see, that means all three of us need to run things as well as we can and hope that you two have something left to inherit after me."

"Yes, I suppose you're right, Mum," Jason said, as Cassandra nodded. "What do you propose?"

"I don't want to run the business myself," Kathleen said. "That means I need to appoint someone else. Someone who knows the business."

"I've had lots of experience in the industry," Jason said. "I would make a good job of running the company."

"How about Reg Ward?" asked Cassandra. "He knows more than anyone else about the business."

"No, Reg has always been a loser. He'll only ever be a deputy. There's only one person I can think of to run it." Kathleen paused. "I'm sorry, Jason, but I'm going to ask Cassandra to take over."

"You can't be serious, Mum," Jason shouted after a moment's pause. "Not after all I've done."

"What do you mean?" Kathleen asked. "What have you done to help the business?"

"Oh, for God's sake, let's not spell it out," Jason said.

"We have to accept Mum's decision, Jason," Cassandra said in a calm voice. "I will be happy to take over. I know I can do a good job."

"Oh, it's OK for you, isn't it, Cassie. You get all the money without getting your hands dirty," Jason screamed.

"What are you talking about?" Cassandra asked.

"Oh, I've had enough of this," Jason said, picking up his tie and jacket. "But I'm not going quietly."

"You're always part of my family, whatever happens," Kathleen pleaded.

"Oh, no, I'm not," Jason said stamping to the door. "Goodbye." The door slammed shut and Kathleen and Cassandra heard Jason stamp away down the gravel drive. The two women looked at each other without speaking.

Unnoticed, Tania took the card Gould had left and picked up the kitchen phone. She thought over the insults that she had been forced to put up with since she had been working at the Harveys' house. She was surprised to be helping the police – her family's experience during the Communist days in Prague had made her scared of them – but she hated the wealthy Harvey family who employed her even more. She still shuddered when she remembered Neil Harvey putting his hand up her skirt while his wife was away. The way Kathleen spoke to her was even worse.

After a moment's thought, Tania left a summary of the Harveys' conversation on Philippa's voicemail, then replaced the receiver. She was glad she had phoned Philippa and hoped the information was useful to the police. Tania smiled to herself as she washed the crockery after the funeral tea.

****

After Jason Harvey left his family home in a furious temper, he climbed into the bright yellow Lotus Elan his father had given him as a twenty-first birthday present a few years before. As he relaxed in the leather seats he looked around at the well-tended lawns of the family home around him. It dawned on him he had a choice – he could either try to make his own way in his career or somehow benefit from his father's money. He thought of his contemporaries in the firm he worked for with contempt – all of them cutting corners to meet the mortgage payments on their small houses. Then he thought of the stylish women that he enjoyed dating – he was realistic enough to accept that they were after his money more than the pleasure of his company.

The choice seemed obvious. While it was comforting to know that half his father's estate would come to him on his mother's death, there was no reason why she should not live for twenty or thirty years. But how was he to get back into his mother's good books? Instead of driving off in a hurry, Jason started the car and drove away, deep in thought. He told himself he was really no better off with his father dead than before. The opulent detached houses of stockbroker belt Surrey moved past his car windows as he pondered his next career move.

Chapter 20

It was a surprise for Gould and Philippa to hear at Harvey's funeral that as much as half of his estate would in due course go to Cassandra's twin, Jason, as according to Margaret Lane and others, Jason had quarrelled with his father some years before and as far as she knew they had not spoken since then. For some reason, despite their disagreement, Harvey had not changed his will to exclude Jason.

Jason was there at his father's funeral, chatting pleasantly enough to the other guests. Philippa would have recognised him as Cassandra's brother – they both shared the same good looks and air of superiority. David Gould asked him to come to the station the next day and he agreed to be interviewed. When he arrived, even in the dingy surroundings of the interview room, his air of condescending superiority was undimmed. The police decided to keep the information that Tania had provided secret for the time being.

"When did you last see your father alive, Mr Harvey?" Gould began, and the police officers were startled to hear him laugh out loud. Both Gould and Philippa waited until he stopped.

"Oh, I'm sorry, Chief Inspector." Jason apologised. "Your question just reminded me of a famous picture. It's just nerves, I suppose. I last saw my father some two years ago. I was working at the company's offices, but I found it too claustrophobic working so close to my father and decided to leave."

"Did your father object to you leaving the company?" Gould asked.

"Yes, Dad certainly did object," Jason said. "Mind you, while I was working for his company, he used to imply I was sponging off him and I should make my own way in the world. There was no way of winning with my father."

"Where do you work now, Mr Harvey?" Gould asked.

"I'm still in the travel agency business, working for one of Dad's rivals."

"How did your father feel about that?" Philippa asked.

"I don't know. Cassandra said he was pretty annoyed, but I felt it was a useful way of gaining experience."

"Did you expect to come back and run Harvey and Ward's – perhaps when your father died?" Gould asked.

"I suppose it was at the back of my mind, but I wasn't expecting him to die so soon. In the long term, I would like to take over the family business. I'm sure I could make a good job of it," Jason said absently, but continued with more force, as Gould deliberately said nothing. "But I didn't kill Dad. Why should I?" he protested.

"You've just told us you'll probably be financially better off with your father dead, Mr Harvey," Gould replied. "You could have expected to inherit the firm as soon as your father died. It was probably a shock that you didn't inherit immediately your father died. Mind you, your mother received a great deal of money, and I have the impression you got on better with her than your father."

"I suppose so, but I know nothing about my father's murder," Jason replied like a sulky child.

"Where were you on the night of his murder?" Gould asked.

"Quietly at home. I'm afraid I don't have any witnesses."

"Do you know many of the people who work for Harvey and Ward's now?"

"No, most of them have changed since I worked here. Reg Ward I've known all my life, of course, and Margaret Lane I know as well."

"Do you see much of your mother and sister?" Philippa asked.

"Cassandra and I have always had a strange relationship – being twins, I suppose. I think I've always been my mother's favourite, but she was too much under my father's thumb to help me much. I tried not to phone home when he was there in case we quarrelled."

"Did you have any money problems before your father died, Mr Harvey?" Gould asked.

"No, not especially. As I told you, I have a good job."

"You live in a small flat at the moment. It must be a step down from being at the family home. That must be worth at least a million," Gould observed. "You can't be living the same lifestyle that you were used to."

"I'll manage, thank you, Chief Inspector," Jason said, sullenly. "I earn a reasonable living."

"As a Junior Executive?" Gould asked. "Struggling for enough to pay the mortgage? After your parents' house in Haslemere, you must miss all that luxury. Do you have a young family to look after, Mr Harvey?"

"No, I don't have a family," Jason began to turn aggressive. "Look what is this, Chief Inspector? I've told you I don't know anything about my father's murder. Do you have any evidence against me?"

"No, Mr Harvey, I'm just trying to ascertain the facts," Gould said. "A remarkable number of people involved in this case seem to have been safely tucked up in bed when your father was murdered. Tell me, what do you know about Margaret Lane?" he asked, suddenly changing tack.

"Margaret's been my father's PA for years. People say she was having an affair with Dad."

"Would you be surprised if she was?"

"No, not really. My father was always having affairs with other women," Jason answered.

"How did your mother feel about that?"

"I don't know. I think she was prepared to overlook his affairs as long as he kept them away from home."

"Did you get angry about it?" Gould asked.

"Me? No, why should I?"

"You seem to be very close to your mother. Perhaps you were hurt on her behalf when your father had affairs."

"Very Freudian, I am sure," Jason sneered. "No, if my mother wasn't worried, why should I be?"

"We believe your sister has been seeing a man called Charles Anson. Do you know him at all?"

"No, I've never heard of him," Jason replied, after a pause.

"He's currently under arrest for dealing in cocaine."

"I've still never heard of him."

"We are trying to find out if anyone else in Harvey and Ward was involved in drug dealing. Did your father mention the matter at all?" Gould asked.

"Never, though as I said, I have not spoken to him for several years."

"Did you ever suspect that your father might be involved in drug trafficking himself?"

"Dad? A drug dealer?" Jason laughed out loud. "Hardly! He was the most conservative person I've ever known. No one who knew him would imagine him going to drugs parties or smuggling anything through Customs."

"The really big dealers don't mix with the teenagers themselves; they employ middle-men to do that," Gould said.

"I don't know anything about that, but I still say no. I know my father had his faults, but he would never do anything like that."

"Can you explain why your father had a small amount of cocaine in his pocket when he died?" Gould asked.

"I can't believe that," Jason said, then paused. "If that's true, I assume the murderer planted it out of mischief."

"Have you ever been involved in drugs yourself, Mr Harvey?"

"No, never," Jason replied.

"I find that a little strange, Mr Harvey. You see I checked the police computer, and it showed that you had been given a six-month suspended sentence eight years ago for dealing in cannabis."

"You can't hold that against me." For the first time in the interview, Jason grew angry. "It was years ago and that was only pot."

"You won't mind if we search your house, Mr Harvey, then."

"Do what you like. I have nothing to hide."

"Thank you, Mr Harvey. I suggest we stop this interview there."

Chapter 21

"How are we going to find out if Harvey was really a drug smuggler, David?" Philippa asked as she discussed the case with Gould next day at the station. They had developed the habit of having coffee together every morning.

"Yes, that's one question we've got to answer," Gould replied, deep in thought. "Anson says Harvey was involved but there's no way of checking if Anson's telling the truth, of course. He could be just spinning us a line to get a light sentence. We've looked through all Harvey's papers here and there's nothing incriminating."

"It's interesting that Spendlove, Harvey and Ward were all at school, together." Philippa said.

"Together with that crooked solicitor, Rothenberg." Gould added. "I've been wondering if we could play on that in some way."

"How do you mean?" Philippa asked.

"Spendlove would never tell us what was happening, but he might tell an old school friend who went to see him." Gould paused. "An old school friend like your Mr Ward, for instance."

Philippa stared at Gould. "You want Reg to go and see Spendlove?" she asked, aghast. "But Spendlove is a serious criminal. He could even be a murderer. As far as we know, Reg Ward could be too."

"I think you've managed to convince me that Ward's too harmless to be a killer." Gould replied. "In fact, he's too harmless to be much of a threat to anyone. That's why I think he could be so useful to us. Just imagine you're Spendlove, and

Harvey was under his thumb in some way. Either Spendlove killed him or someone else did for an unknown reason. In any event, Spendlove will want to know what's been going on since his death. At the very least, even if Anson is the only one involved in selling drugs, Spendlove will want someone to replace Anson within the company."

"And you're going to let an innocent man get involved with a dangerous drug trafficker?" Philippa asked, her voice raised with incredulity.

"Don't get so worried, Philippa." Gould replied. "It'll only be one meeting. Ward will report back to us and that'll be the end of it."

"I suppose you'll want him to carry hidden microphones and all that."

"God, no," Gould said. "Spendlove will be bound to spot anything like that."

"And for all we know, eliminate Reg Ward."

"Don't be so melodramatic," Gould replied. "Spendlove doesn't like blood on his hands – not from someone who could be tied back to him."

"So how are you going to ask Reg to co-operate?" Philippa asked, then paused as she caught the look in Gould's eyes. "Oh, no, you want me to ask him? Because I worked undercover with him?" Tears came to Philippa's eyes. "I can't keep treating the poor man like this."

"All you're asking him to do is co-operate with the police and find out who killed his old friend and business partner. What's wrong with that?" Gould asked. Philippa could think of no reply. "I've called Ward in. You go and talk to him."

Philippa left Gould's room and walked down to the interview room where Reg Ward was waiting nervously. He stood up when she came in.

"I'm glad to see you, Philippa," Ward replied. "It's a relief. What's going on? They won't tell me anything. They've just asked me to come in for another interview."

"Don't worry, Reg," Philippa said, reaching out her hand to reassure him. "You can go soon. Your earlier statement has been very helpful." She paused. "But there is something you can do for us."

Ward, who had looked relieved at first, asked "What's that?"

"You see, Reg," Philippa began. "We're convinced the truth behind Harvey's murder lies somewhere in the past. You've known him longer than anyone else. That means you're in an ideal position to find out the truth. You know you mentioned someone who was at your school called Spendlove."

"Jack Spendlove, yes, but I haven't seen him for years."

"Well, we believe he's now one of the biggest drug smugglers in London. We think he may be involved in the murders of both Neil Harvey and Hugh Marks, your auditor. We believe he's paid for another of your old acquaintances – Robert Rothenberg – he's a solicitor now – to defend Charles Anson on the drug running charge. You have to be seriously rich to afford Rothenberg, and Spendlove must be paying him. There's no other explanation. It's pretty conclusive that Anson has been smuggling for Spendlove, even though Anson may not know it."

"So, what do you want me to do?" Ward asked.

"We'd like you to make contact with Spendlove. We're sure he will be willing to see you," Philippa said. "He'll be curious to know what's going on in Harvey and Ward's, since Harvey's death."

"I'm not sure he will see me," Ward interrupted. "As I told you, even at school, we weren't exactly friends."

"We're sure he'll be very interested in anything you have to say about your company," Philippa continued. "Now, can you think of a plausible reason to go and see him?"

"I don't know." Ward thought for a while. "I suppose it could be like that time I went to see Neil Harvey."

"When you needed capital to start up your company," Philippa continued the thought. "How would it be if you needed money to buy up Harvey's shareholding?"

"But that's all gone to Kathleen," Ward protested. "She won't sell anyway."

"But Spendlove won't know that. And if he does, it would be interesting to know how he found out. It would show how close he is to the Harvey family."

"I suppose I could tell Spendlove I need money to buy out Kathleen," Ward said. "But if what you say is true, he won't take kindly to having the wool pulled over his eyes."

"You won't have to lie to Spendlove, Reg. I'm sure Kathleen would sell you the firm for enough money," Philippa reassured him. "Just tell the truth and say if you had the money, you could buy out Kathleen, then see what he says."

"Very well, for your sake I'll try it." Ward smiled to himself. "We've come a long way since you were my secretary, haven't we?"

Philippa nodded. "That'll be very helpful. I'll see you out, Reg. We'll be interested to hear how you get on."

When they walked out of the police station it was raining, and Ward looked gloomily at the bad weather. Philippa touched his arm in farewell and stood at the door watching him as he drove off. As she went back into the station, she was filled with a vague concern at what she had persuaded Reg Ward to do.

The following day, Ward drove to Mayfair and soon found the offices of Spendlove Associates. He gave his name to the receptionist and waited nervously in the plush lobby. He thought over the brief phone call he had made to Spendlove. It was interesting Spendlove had not seemed particularly surprised to hear from an old school acquaintance whom he had not seen for more than thirty years. Eventually, the pretty receptionist summoned him into Spendlove's office. Ward walked along the plush carpeted corridor, imagining what he would say.

Spendlove stood up as Ward walked in. Ward instantly recognised the teenage thug he had once known, thirty-five years older. Spendlove's Armani suit and diamond cufflinks spelt money as he walked across the thick pile of the carpet to greet his visitor.

"Reg Ward, as I live and breathe!" Spendlove advanced with his hand outstretched. "What a long time! We've both come a long way since Heathfield School, haven't we?"

Ward shook his hand politely, though he realised both of them knew how false Spendlove's bonhomie was. "Hello, Jack," Ward said. "It was good of you to agree to see me."

"Well, no doubt, you haven't come to talk about old times. Take a seat and tell me what I can do for you." Spendlove pointed to a leather armchair as he took up a seat opposite. Spendlove lit a Gauloises cigarette while Ward spoke.

"I've really come to ask a favour, Jack," Ward began. "I don't know if you remember Neil Harvey – he was at school with us." Ward looked for some sign of recognition which he could relay back to Philippa but Spendlove's face was impassive. "Well, we set up our own travel agency business. We've been doing quite well, but Harvey was murdered recently. You may have seen it in the papers." There was still no reaction from Spendlove. "I've been given the option to buy some shares and I wondered if you could help me come up with the money," Ward concluded nervously. "I could pay you back over time, of course."

There was a long pause while Ward waited for Spendlove to speak. "So, after all these years you've come to ask me for money," he said, his voice filled with contempt.

"That's what I'm saying, Jack," Ward said. He flinched as he felt the power of Spendlove's glare.

"Tell me about this company of yours," Spendlove said.

"We started it about twenty years ago – it's a pretty successful business. Neil Harvey was more of a sleeping partner, while I work full time, but he had most of the shares. His wife – his widow, that is – has control of them now but she's offered them to me at a good price as long as I can come up with the money straight away." Ward recited the fiction he had concocted with Philippa.

"And you seriously expect me to invest in your company now?" Any customers are going to be scared of all this publicity. Tell me, who do the police suspect of Harvey's murder?"

"God knows, they're interviewing everyone at the moment. There's one thing, it may be just a coincidence, but one of our staff has just been arrested for drug smuggling. They've been asking me if I think there's anyone else involved but I don't think so. They even seem to think that Harvey was involved in some way, but I told them that was ridiculous."

"I suppose visiting dealing rooms like Anson did is a good opportunity to deal in drugs. Do the police know how he got the drugs?" Spendlove asked.

"I've no idea, Jack," Ward replied. He made a mental note that Spendlove was the first to mention Anson's name.

Spendlove got to his feet. "Well, Reg, it's been good to see you after all these years. It's an interesting proposition. I'm always looking for new investments. I don't know if you remember Robert Rothenberg." Reg nodded, with a mental image of the crawling little boy who used to run errands for Spendlove when they were at school. "He handles my legal affairs now. I'll ask him to call round to your office and find out some more details. He'll be there at ten o'clock the day after tomorrow. He'll find the way."

Ward eagerly jumped to his feet, happy to escape from the air of menace in Spendlove's luxurious office. "Thank you, Jack, I'll expect to hear from Robert, then." Ward took a deep breath of fresh air when he was out in the street. He felt he had a fair amount of news to tell Philippa.

****

The next day, Ward visited the City police station to tell Gould and Philippa of his visit to Spendlove.

"It doesn't sound as if you've taken us any further forward, Mr Ward," Gould said after Ward had finished.

"Well, it's fairly conclusive in tying Spendlove with Anson," Philippa replied. "You've done very well, Reg."

"Thank you, Philippa." Ward said. "I did my best, but I'm not as used as you to dealing with people like Spendlove." Ward gave Gould a reproachful look.

"Well, it's better than nothing." Gould replied, grudgingly. "Now let's see what we can get from that crooked shyster, Rothenberg, when he comes to see you. Give us a ring when he gets into contact and we'll have Philippa listen in. Will you do that for us, Mr Ward?"

"I'll do it for Philippa. I'll let you know when I hear from Rothenberg. Now, if you'll excuse me, I do have my own work to do, Chief Inspector." Ward stood up ready to leave.

"I'll show you out, Reg," Philippa said. As they walked down the corridor with its peeling paint, Philippa thanked him again.

"That Chief Inspector of yours seems hard to please," Ward complained. "Still, I'll give you a ring when Rothenberg calls. I'll look forward to seeing him put away somewhere."

"I knew we could rely on you, Reg," Philippa reassured him as they parted. She touched his arm as he left. She watched Ward depart through the dingy lobby with its fading posters appealing for information on a variety of past crimes. She told herself she hoped the murder of Neil Harvey would not end up another unsolved mystery.

****

The next day, Ward waited impatiently for Rothenberg to keep his promised appointment. Philippa was hiding in an adjacent room with equipment geared up to tape any incriminating remark Rothenberg might make.

Eventually, Rothenberg was announced. When he came in, Ward immediately felt the loathing for the man that he had had for the teenager he had known at school. Covering up his feelings, Ward held out his hand and greeted his visitor. "It's good to see you again, Robert," Ward said trying to sound sincere. Rothenberg merely grunted as he took a seat. "How many years has it been?"

"I think you know why I am here," Rothenberg said, looking around impatiently. "I am not here to talk about schooldays."

Rothenberg's abruptness had the perverse effect of making Ward more confident. Ward could suddenly see the fifteen-year-old boy he remembered; he had got the better of Rothenberg then and felt he could do the same again.

"How interested is Spendlove in helping me buy these shares?" Ward asked. "I seem to remember you were always close to his thoughts at school and I presume you still are. He must be a very lucrative client for you, isn't he, Rothenberg?"

"Please call me Mr Rothenberg, Mr Ward," Rothenberg hissed. "We're not at that wretched public school now and my relationships with my clients are none of your business."

"Very well, what can I tell you about Harvey and Ward's, Mr Rothenberg?"

"From what I can gather from the press, your partner was murdered in unfortunate circumstances, Mr Ward," Rothenberg said. "Obviously that is nothing to do with my client directly, but I gather you visited him to request a loan to buy shares from the bereaved's family."

"That's correct," Ward replied. He was about to say more when he remembered that his remit was to see how much information Rothenberg already had rather than to tell him anything. Ward waited for the other man to continue.

"You will appreciate that this publicity does not make Harvey and Ward attractive for a respected investor like my client," Rothenberg continued. "But in view of the long acquaintance between my client and yourself, he is willing to investigate the possibility of investing in your company. But he must first be assured that there are no further scandals."

Ward looked as innocent as he could. "How do you mean 'further scandals'?"

"Well, apart from the obvious murder of Neil Harvey, there are rumours that one of your staff members – his name's Anson – has been arrested for dealing in drugs."

"How do you know about that?" Ward asked. "There hasn't been much publicity about it."

"I'm sure there was some mention in one paper." Rothenberg shook his head impatiently. "Anyway, no matter how I heard it, I want to be sure that it was an isolated incident."

"I believe so, but perhaps you can tell me," Ward said. Suddenly his anger at the damage done to his company rose inside him.

"How do you mean?"

"Come off it, Rothenberg, everyone knows you are still what you were at school – a slimy scumbag who does Spendlove's dirty work for him," Ward said, his voice rising out of control. "At least, Spendlove is an honest crook – you pretend to be a lawyer."

Rothenberg stood up. "I don't have to listen to any more of this. Goodbye, Mr Ward." He turned to go, then looked back, and at once Ward recognised the schoolboy Rothenberg had once been. "You don't have Harvey around to protect you now, do you, Ward?"

"I saw you off before and I can see you off again," Ward snarled as Rothenberg went out through the door.

When Philippa came out of the next-door room from where she had been listening to the two men's conversation, she was surprised to find Ward smiling to himself.

"I've been waiting for thirty years to tell that man what I think of him," Ward told Philippa. "I don't know when I've enjoyed myself so much."

"Maybe so, but we haven't learnt very much." Philippa complained. "But I wish we could tell that slimy scumbag of a solicitor what we think of him as you just did. Police rules wouldn't allow it." She paused as she considered what Rothenberg had said. "It is strange that Rothenberg knew so much about Anson's arrest. He wanted to be sure there weren't any other scandals about to come out." Philippa told herself that while it would not stand up in court, it convinced her that Spendlove and his solicitor were involved in the drug running. "I wonder if they've got someone else working inside your company and want to make sure their cover isn't about to be blown. Keep us in touch with any developments, won't you, Reg?"

Chapter 22

That afternoon, Gould and Philippa walked up to the semi-detached house in the run-down suburb of Walthamstow in the extreme northeast of London. This was the address they had been given for Annabel Ward, Reg's ex-wife.

"This is very different from Kathleen Harvey's house," Philippa remarked.

"There must have been some jealousy between the two partners. Harvey with all the money and Ward doing all the work."

"Can I help you?" asked the woman who came to the door. She had an accent that would have sounded more at home in Somerset. She had a dark buxom appearance and heavy arms. Philippa had a mental image of her as a farmer's wife with many children. From Ward's interview, Philippa could imagine how badly the lack of children in her marriage would have affected her.

"Mrs Ward?" Gould asked, showing his warrant card. "I'm Detective Chief Inspector Gould and this is Detective Sergeant Philippa Cottrell. May we come in?"

"Yes, I'm Annabel Ward," the woman replied, in a surprised tone. "Please come in, but I'm not sure how I can help you."

Gould and Philippa followed her into the small over-furnished drawing room, which seemed to be saved for visitors. There was a large picture of the Virgin Mary above the mantelpiece and Philippa noted that there was a wedding photograph of the young Reg Ward and Annabel on the sideboard. Annabel indicated that her two visitors should be seated. Philippa sat on the edge of a sofa and took notes in her notebook.

"Thank you for seeing us, Mrs Ward," Gould began. "You may have read about the murder of Mr Neil Harvey last week."

"That man!" Annabel replied, her voice full of scorn. "Yes, I read about his death."

"You don't sound sorry that he died, Mrs Ward," Gould suggested.

"I should think not," Annabel said. "He made Reg work all the hours God sent while he did nothing and took all the money." She crossed her ample bosom, which was heaving with indignation.

"We're trying to look at Mr Harvey's business history. We understand originally your husband asked Mr Harvey to put up the money for the travel agency, Mrs Ward," Gould asked.

"Yes, against my advice, Reg went to see him and agreed to Neil becoming the majority stake-holder in the firm. It was the biggest mistake Reg ever made. That was nearly twenty years ago, and Neil has had Reg under his thumb ever since," Annabel replied.

"Until now, Mrs Ward," Philippa prompted. "Things may be different now Neil Harvey's dead."

"Even now, whoever takes over Neil's estate has total control over Reg," Annabel replied, addressing herself to Gould. "He should never have agreed to join that partnership."

"Mr Harvey's estate has been left to his wife until she dies," Gould said. "I understand Cassandra Ward will be taking over day-to-day control for the time being."

Annabel snorted. "She's as bad as her father. And to think I was her godmother. Still am, I suppose."

"Can you think of anyone who would want to kill Mr Harvey?" Gould asked.

Annabel laughed. "Everyone who knew him, I should think. And that includes me."

"Where were you last Tuesday night, Mrs Ward?" Gould asked.

"Here, of course," Annabel replied, her voice betraying her unhappiness at her position. "Now my marriage has broken up thanks to that man, I've no money and nowhere to go."

"And when did you last see Mr Harvey?" Philippa followed up.

"I haven't seen Neil Harvey for three years at least," Annabel said, blushing. It struck Philippa it was in the manner of a lie told by someone unused to lying.

"And what about your ex-husband, Mrs Ward," Gould asked with his eyes fixed firmly on Annabel's. "Do you still see him at all?"

"No, my husband never sees me," Annabel replied. Philippa noticed there seemed to be unshed tears in her eyes. "I think he was seeing someone called Sally when we divorced, but I don't know who he's with now. He pays me a maintenance cheque every month and he thinks that's the end of his duty to me. It was his work that broke up our marriage – Neil Harvey made him work too hard. It was nothing to do with his other women. Men are so susceptible; you have to expect them to stray sometimes."

There was an embarrassed silence as the two police officers caught each other's eyes. "Well, if you haven't seen Mr Harvey or your husband for a few years as you say, then I have no more questions. You will be sure and contact me if there is anything you think of," Gould said, as he passed her his visiting card.

Annabel stood up. "Thank you, Chief Inspector, I will be sure to give you a ring." She gave Gould a polite smile but glared at Philippa as she ushered her visitors out through the hall with several religious icons on the walls. As Philippa followed Gould down the garden path, she could feel Annabel's eyes staring at her from the open door with something close to hatred.

"Why was she looking at me like that?" Philippa asked, after the two detectives got into their car. "She didn't speak to me during the whole interview."

"How would you feel if a beautiful woman came to your door and asked questions about your husband?" Gould asked in return. "But I've never met anyone who shows their true feelings as much as that. It makes her a bad liar. It makes a change in our line of work, doesn't it?" he said. "I'm prepared to bet that she's seen Neil Harvey more recently than she said. I wonder why. She certainly hated Harvey enough to kill him. We'll have to add her to our list of suspects." Just then, Gould's mobile phone rang.

"I see … That's very interesting … Yes, I'll be there now." Gould put the phone back in his pocket and turned to Philippa. "I'm afraid we've got to release Charles Anson on bail."

"Oh, well, I suppose it had to happen. We've only booked him on a small-scale trafficking charge. The bail money would be a lot of money for someone to pay."

"There's no problem over money. Anson now has the same solicitor as Jack Spendlove – Robert Rothenberg. It looks like Spendlove has decided to bail one of his own staff out of jail. I want to be there when Rothenberg signs him out."

Chapter 23

After a journey across London, with frequent use of his siren to clear his way through traffic, David Gould ran up the stairs of the City of London police station as fast as he could, while Philippa trailed after him. He arrived at the foyer as Anson was signing for his possessions, with Rothenberg, dressed in a three-piece pinstripe suit, standing beside him.

"Hello, Mr Rothenberg," Gould said. "I didn't expect us to meet again so soon. How do you come to be representing Anson?"

"I am not obliged to give you any information, Chief Inspector," Rothenberg replied coldly. "Mr Anson has agreed for me to represent him. Any relationship I may have with Mr Anson is now protected from police questioning, as you very well know."

"It does seem strange that yesterday you claimed to know nothing about this drug-peddling case and yet today you are representing our only suspect."

"Mr Anson has not been found guilty in any court of law, Mr Gould," Rothenberg replied. "Until then he is entitled to bail as long as the money is forthcoming. And before you ask, I am not proposing to tell you where the bail money is coming from."

"Obviously, Jack Spendlove," Gould replied. "He is your main client."

"I leave you to speculate as much as you like, Chief Inspector," Rothenberg said, as he accompanied Anson out of the station. "In the meantime, I am taking my client home." Rothenberg turned to face Gould. "Good bye, Chief Inspector, no doubt we will meet again in court."

Gould said no more as he watched Rothenberg and Anson walk out of the building and into Rothenberg's top of the range Jaguar.

"Should we have them followed?" Philippa asked, adding 'sir' for the benefit of the nearby desk sergeant.

"Yes, please, Philippa. Follow them in the unmarked car. They won't recognise that."

Philippa ran down to the officers' garage in the basement and revved the car as fast as it would go. She reached street level in time to see Rothenberg's distinctive British racing green Jaguar disappear around the corner. However, the traffic lights around the corner slowed their progress and she was in an ideal position two cars behind. A few hundred yards later, they went into Rothenberg's offices and Philippa waited outside.

"They've gone into Rothenberg's offices, David," she briefed Gould when she managed to get through on her mobile phone. "What shall I do?"

"That's bad news, Philippa," Gould's reply came back, "but stay outside. There's just a chance Spendlove might go in to see Anson."

"Sure thing," Philippa replied as she hung up the mobile. She prepared herself for a long wait, and there was no sign of anyone suspicious arriving for the rest of the day. Eventually at about half past five, Anson left and got into a chauffeur-driven Mercedes. Philippa followed and found the car dropped Anson back at his own Dockside flat. When she phoned back to base, Gould told her to give up the surveillance and she went home.

****

When she arrived back at the station the following day, she asked Gould what he had hoped to find through her surveillance.

"In fiction, the villain always has a pang of conscience and leads the police straight to the murder weapon," Gould replied with a wry smile. "It doesn't usually work in real life."

"Not in this case, anyway."

"One thing I'd really like to know is the nature of the relationship between Cassandra and Charles Anson. If they're still a couple, that might mean she's involved in the drug running. It would be an extra motive for her to have wanted her father dead."

"When I was undercover, I formed the impression that she was very keen on him, but not so much the other way round," Philippa said.

"Can you disguise your appearance, Philippa?"

"Yes, I suppose so."

"Would you like to follow either Charles Anson or Cassandra and see if they have lunch together?" Gould asked.

"Wouldn't it be better if it was an officer they didn't know?"

Gould shook his head. "No, I'm sure they wouldn't recognise you in disguise."

Philippa pursed her lips but agreed to continue with the surveillance.

****

Philippa resumed her vigil outside Anson's dockside flat next morning. It was only a hunch that he would try to see Cassandra as soon as he came out of prison, and as Philippa waited in her blond wig for several hours, she wondered if it might be a waste of time.

Soon after midday, however, Anson came out of his flat into his garage and started his bright red Porsche. As the engine warmed up, he checked his hair in the driving mirror – Philippa, watching from the other side of the road, felt certain that whoever he was seeing was female and someone he wished to impress. Philippa followed Anson through the busy lunchtime traffic, to a fashionable restaurant in the new Broadgate development and watched as he went inside.

She got out of her car and carefully tried to get a view of his lunch date through the stained-glass window. He waited for a few minutes then Cassandra came in and joined him. The change in their demeanour since that meeting at Harvey and Ward's office, the day Philippa joined, was startling. While before, Cassandra seemed to be paying court to Anson, this time round the roles were reversed.

Although Philippa could not hear any words from her position, the pair's body language made it clear how the conversation was going. Anson was justifying his position while Cassandra was not accepting anything he said. Within a few minutes and before any food was delivered, the lunch came to a dramatic end. Cassandra poured the contents of an ice bucket down Anson's trousers and walked out, coming very close to Philippa as she left. When she brushed past Philippa, Cassandra's expression was so furious that the few passers-by instinctively moved out of her way. Philippa was sure she had not seen been seen, and also convinced that whatever relationship Cassandra once had with Charles Anson was at an end.

Chapter 24

The following day, Charles Anson looked nervously around the expensively decorated Mayfair office into which he had been ushered. He subconsciously touched a padded envelope in his pocket. He noticed a man standing silently in the far corner. "Mr Spendlove, isn't it? I saw you in the identity parade. I gather I have you to thank for getting me out of prison," Anson said, tentatively extending his hand to the man opposite. Spendlove stood up and walked across the plush pile carpet and stood directly in front of Anson. Although Anson was a much taller man, faced with the force of Spendlove's personality, Anson instinctively looked away.

"I did not get you out of prison," Spendlove declared. "You did not see me in Neil Harvey's office the day he was killed. If the police ask you any more questions, you have never seen me in your life. Do you understand?"

"I'm not sure I can do that, Mr Spendlove," Anson said. "I'm very honest – sometimes. I saw Harvey let you into his office, the night he was killed. I lied about recognising you in the identity parade, but I could always tell the police I had changed my mind. I'm sure they would be pleased – they might put in a good word for me at any trial."

"I advise you not to be honest with the police, Mr Anson," Spendlove replied. "Telling them too much would endanger your health. Anyway, whatever you think, I didn't kill Neil Harvey."

"I know that. I was there. I also know who did kill him. I'm sure you and I can come to some sort of financial arrangement."

Anson continued. "The police have been asking me what I know about Neil Harvey's murder. I made out I didn't know anything, of course." Anson pulled the small padded envelope from his pocket. "That's not strictly true. I saw exactly what went on. There's something here that the police would love to get hold of. Also, the person who put their fingerprints on this item would give a great deal of money for it. So, it would be useful for a spot of blackmail, but unfortunately, I don't have the resources that you do." Anson broke off and indicated the plush surroundings of Spendlove's office. "Alternatively, you could give it to the police – it might get you off a murder rap."

Anson emptied the contents of the envelope onto Spendlove's desk. Anson enjoyed the stunned reaction of the older man as he stared at what fell in front of him.

"Is this what I think it is?" Spendlove croaked. "How did you get hold of it?"

Anson smiled with increasing confidence. "Do we have a deal, Mr Spendlove?"

****

For the next few days, Gould continued to keep an eye on Anson. Two detectives spent every evening trailing him around a series of nightclubs and casinos. They were baffled by his behaviour – he entered clubs, had one drink looking around as if he was seeking someone or something then left. Nothing came of their surveillance for several days and Gould ordered an end to the trailing of Anson.

The day after the police trail ended, Anson seemed to have found what he was looking for. In a corner of one club, he saw Jason Harvey clutching a bottle of beer, which he occasionally sipped from. Like most of the people crushed around him, Jason found it safer to drink from a bottle than to risk his drink being spiked in an open glass. He gazed vaguely at his current girlfriend, who was blond and beautiful, like his last half-dozen girlfriends, but he could only vaguely remember her name. No doubt, she would be expecting another chunk of his inherited money in due course. He took another sip and looked around. Through the haze of a mixture of tobacco and marijuana smoke, he became aware of a man he vaguely recognised talking to him.

"Jason, do you remember me? We met once in your father's office," Charles Anson said.

Jason tried to focus through the fumes. "You're Charles Anson, aren't you? You were going out with my sister. I thought you'd been locked up."

"I'm out on bail," Anson replied. "There's something I want to talk to you about. It will be in your interest to listen."

Jason shook his head. "I've got nothing to say to you. You're trouble. You're the reason that Chief Inspector Gould keeps giving me a hard time." Jason turned to walk away. Just then he felt Anson's arms firmly gripping his own.

"As I said, Jason," Anson repeated, as he pushed Jason's arms further up his back. "It would be in your interest to listen to what I have to say. We'll step outside for a moment."

Jason resisted at first, but Anson's arm lock was too strong for him and he meekly nodded and followed Anson. "What the hell's all this about?" Jason asked when they were outside.

"There's something your family will want to know about," Anson said. He pulled a polythene bag containing a small revolver out of his pocket. "The police would be interested in this," he added.

Jason stared. "It's a gun. Are you saying it's the gun that killed my father? How did you get hold of it?"

"Never mind that. Fortunately, I have no wish to help the police any more than I can. The bad news for you is that I now work for someone you will like even less than the police."

"What are you talking about?" Jason asked and then stared open-mouthed as Anson outlined his proposal.

****

The following day, Cassandra picked up the phone in her new office. "Cassandra Harvey," she said, in a voice of authority.

"Cassandra, it's Jason here," came the voice on the phone. "Did you hear me?" Jason repeated, when Cassandra uttered a weary sigh.

"Yes, I heard you, Jason, but I've got a company to run. Is this important?"

"Yes, it sodding well is important. I can't talk over the phone. Where can we meet?"

Cassandra uttered a deep sigh. "When have you had anything important to say, Jason? If it's about how many birds you pulled last night, I'm not interested."

"You'll be interested in this. I'll see you in that courtyard outside Liverpool Street Station at 1 o'clock. We can go for lunch."

"Oh, very well, I suppose the company can wait for an hour. But it had better be good. If this is some ploy to borrow money from me, I will be seriously annoyed."

****

Two hours later, Cassandra met Jason at the appointed place. Jason was pacing impatiently outside a wine bar. "Why are you late? Has anyone been following you?" he asked as soon as Cassandra arrived.

"What's the matter with you? No one's been following me, why should they?" Cassandra asked. Her expression indicated that she was worried about her brother's sanity.

"We must go somewhere we won't be recognised," Jason said, grabbing his sister's arm. He walked past the wine bar that Cassandra was about to enter. "That's no good. There might be people from Harvey and Ward there … That should be all right," he added, dragging her off to a dark-looking noisy pub. "No one will hear us there." Jason led her through the throng of mostly male drinkers over to a corner table. Cassandra was conscious of the lascivious glances of the men and sat sulkily on her own while Jason got their drinks. She glared at one man who tried to join her table until he took the hint and staggered drunkenly away. Eventually, Jason brought the drinks over and put one in front of Cassandra.

"Why did you bring me to a place like this?" she hissed. "Half of these men seem to think I'm looking for a pick-up."

"Never mind about them," Jason replied. "I met an old boyfriend of yours yesterday."

"Who's that?"

"Charles Anson."

"Him," Cassandra spat out. "I ditched him when the police said he was dealing with drugs," Cassandra said, her eyes sparkling with hatred.

"Yes, well, he's not going to disappear quietly." Jason looked around to make sure no one was listening. "He showed me the gun that killed our father."

"He's got the murder weapon?" Cassandra echoed, her voice raised in horror. "You've got to tell the police. He could be the murderer."

"It's not as simple as that, Cassie. He's got some extra information I think you should know about."

Cassandra leaned forward to hear what her brother had to say.

****

Later that day, Anson returned to Spendlove's office.

"I've made contact with the killer, Mr Spendlove," Anson said. "The deal we talked about has been arranged."

Spendlove smiled. "You have done everything I asked, Charles. I can take over now. The money I promised has been deposited in your bank account. It won't stop you going to prison for drug dealing, but it should make your life much more comfortable when you come out."

"Thank you, Mr Spendlove. It's been a pleasure doing business with you. I will say goodbye now."

Chapter 25

The next day, Gould and Philippa went to the ballistics section deep in the basement of Scotland Yard. Gould explained that since the City of London force was so small, it used the Metropolitan Police's central scientific facilities. A few guns were being fired in the corner of the room. Philippa had never been to this section before and found the sound of weapons being fired deafening. A sandy-haired man came up to the two officers. Although no more than forty years old, he walked painfully slowly, as if he was a much older man.

"This is Chris Marshall," Gould introduced them as they shook hands. "Chris saved my life once."

"That's right. I stopped a bullet aimed at your boss." Marshall winced at the painful memory. "Shall I tell you everything you want to know about firearms in one sentence?"

"What do you mean?" Philippa asked.

"Whatever you do make sure they're pointing at someone else," Marshall replied, with a smile failing to hide the painful truth in what he said.

"What have you got for us in the Harvey case?" Gould asked, anxious to return to the purpose of their visit.

"You're not going to like this, David," Marshall began. "But the bullet you pulled out of the wall and which had a particle of Harvey's blood attached was not fired by the gun you told me you had found in the room."

"What?" Gould and Philippa asked at the same time.

"There is no doubt about it," Marshall continued. "The grooves made on the bullet which passed through and killed Harvey were not made by the gun you gave me."

"That's absurd!" Gould exclaimed. Philippa could see the blood drain out of his face.

"I'm sorry, David, if it's bad news, but I'm quite certain the bullet came from a different gun – one with the same calibre but definitely not the same one," Marshall said, as he turned to walk away.

"Can you tell me the make of the gun that killed Harvey?" Gould asked, calling Marshall back.

"You know I can't do that, David," Marshall replied surprisingly gently. "You bring me the gun and I can tell you if it's the right one, but not otherwise."

Gould was still too stunned to reply, but Philippa managed to thank Marshall on their behalf.

"Come on, let's have a coffee," she said to Gould.

****

A little later in the Yard canteen, Philippa brought two coffees over to where Gould was waiting. She touched his hand to try to grab his attention.

"What does this mean for the case, David?" she asked, as she passed him his coffee.

"It means I'm not sure what we're dealing with here, Philippa," Gould replied, still subdued. "One moment I feel we're dealing with an ordinary domestic crime – a wife, a daughter or a colleague who killed Harvey on the spur of the moment. Now we seem to be dealing with a professional hitman who kills Harvey with perfect precision. Then whoever it was seems to carry a spare gun to drop at the scene of the crime just to confuse us and delay things for a few days. Who could get hold of a hitman like that?"

"Jack Spendlove, for a start," Philippa suggested.

"That's a possibility. But how do we prove it?" Gould said. "And perhaps someone apart from Anson was involved with Spendlove's cocaine racket. But who? Could it have been Harvey? Or was that cocaine a blind left by the murderer?"

"At least there's one piece of good news," Philippa suggested, trying to cheer Gould up. "It's going to be pretty difficult for any defence lawyer to argue it was suicide."

"No," Gould said, with a forced smile. "I can't see how Harvey could have shot himself and then swapped the guns."

Philippa and Gould finished their coffee in the Yard canteen. Philippa had an urge to put her arm around Gould and try to distract him from the depression he was obviously feeling about the way in which the Harvey investigation was going, but she kept silent. Gould squeezed her hand by way of thanks for keeping him company. They sat together in companionable silence.

****

On the way back to Snow Hill police station, Philippa asked Gould a question that she had been pondering for some time. "What do you think will happen to Anson's customers now?"

Gould's eyes lit up. "That's a damn good question, Philippa. One thing's for sure. Someone else will come in to meet the demand. They always do. That's the trouble with fighting against the drugs barons. They always win in the end."

"Do you think all Anson's customers know he's been arrested?"

"Most probably will, but there's bound to be some who don't know," Gould replied, then turned to her when they came to a red traffic light. "What are you suggesting?"

"I've been working on an idea. I'll bet Anson's phone will be ringing with customers deprived of their regular fix."

"Go on."

"Well, why don't I deal with them? I could say I've taken over the drugs franchise."

"That would be dangerous, Philippa," Gould said. "You know the rules against entrapment. Can you manage it?"

"I think so," Philippa replied, as she looked out on the rush hour traffic, "but I'm going to need a lot of support."

Chapter 26

The next day Philippa found herself sitting at Charles Anson's old desk and taking his calls. Cassandra, the new boss of the company, raised no objection to Philippa working in the office. Philippa thought hard about the most appropriate line to take. No doubt, Anson had been spending some time working genuinely for Harvey and Ward but Philippa realised she had to know exactly how much drug dealing he had been doing. After some considerable time searching Anson's office, all Philippa had to go on was a list in the drawers of his desk of contacts in the various City firms. She planned how to see how many of the names listed were Anson's drug customers. Her typical tactic was to phone up the contact listed, with the conversation going along the following lines:

"Hello, my name's Philippa Maxwell of Harvey and Ward's. I've taken over from Charles Anson who used to deal with your account. I've just called to ask you to phone me if you need any of the services that Charles used to supply." Philippa tried to make the word 'service' as full of innuendo as she could, but, in most cases, there was simply a non-committal acknowledgement from the person she was phoning. Whether this was because Anson's business with them was above board, or because they had heard of his arrest and decided to keep out of trouble, it was impossible to say.

Only one call, to a Mr Ringer, sounded promising. After Philippa's opening speech, the man at the other end asked if she really meant all of Anson's services. She assured him she did and, after some hesitation, he asked her to come around to his office near Liverpool Street station. She reported this to David Gould, and it was agreed she would attend with a radio microphone and small tape recorder hidden in her handbag.

The next day, Philippa was ushered into a small interview room at Mr Ringer's office. As he politely invited her to sit down, she noticed his suit – it looked expensive.

"Well, Mr Ringer, I hope you will be able to put some of your company's business my way now I've taken over from Charles Anson," Philippa said in a bright tone of voice.

"How much do you know about Charles's business arrangements?" Ringer asked, tapping his fingers nervously on his desk.

"How do you mean?" Philippa asked as innocently as she could.

"Charles used to supply high quality stuff to some of the people here," he explained.

"What stuff?"

"For God's sake, love," Ringer shouted, his cultured accent slipping, "I mean cocaine, the white stuff. Don't you understand?"

"Are you asking me to supply cocaine?" Philippa asked deliberately obtusely for the benefit of the hidden tape recorder.

"Yes, I am. If you can't, I'll make the firm's travel arrangements through someone else."

Philippa stood up and pulled a warrant card out of her handbag. "You should know that I'm a police officer investigating the supply of controlled drugs. Do you want to answer questions here or down at the station?"

Ringer's face turned white when he saw the warrant card. He opened his mouth as if to say something, but then simply nodded.

"How long have you been buying drugs from Anson?" Philippa asked.

"About two years," he replied, his voice trembling with nerves.

"How did it start?"

"It was an ordinary business contract at the start. Charles just handled the company's travel arrangements. Then he started dropping hints about having contacts in the airlines who made regular trips to Colombia. I suppose he could see I was interested and after a while he used to supply some drugs each week."

"Was it just for your own consumption or did you supply other people?"

"What do you take me for? It was just for my benefit." Ringer stopped and Philippa looked at him disbelievingly for several seconds. "Well, all right then," he continued. "I sometimes sold it on to a few friends, but I'm not a trafficker. You're not going to do me for that, are you?"

"Charles Anson is under arrest. At the moment, I'm investigating a murder."

"Who's been murdered?" Ringer's voice contained a nervous tremour as his hands started to shake.

"A man called Neil Harvey. He was head of Harvey and Ward – Anson's travel firm. I'm trying to find out how many people in the firm knew about Anson's sideline."

"I can't help you there," Ringer replied.

"Did Anson ever mention any of his colleagues?" Philippa asked.

Ringer shook his head. "No, we didn't chat much. There was no need to involve anyone else in his company. Whenever Charles went on holiday, he stocked me up with the stuff before he left, so I never had to deal with anyone else."

"Did you get the impression he was dealing on his own or were other people at the company working with him?"

Ringer thought for a moment. "I don't think he could have been working on his own. He used to talk about having the stuff flown in – he couldn't have organised all that by himself," he replied.

"As I said, I am investigating the murder of Mr Neil Harvey – chairman of Harvey and Ward. I need to find out if he was involved in Anson's drug dealing. Do you know anything that might help me with my inquiries?"

"No, I've never heard of Harvey," Ringer replied, baffled. His lack of knowledge sounded genuine.

"Does the name of Jack Spendlove mean anything to you?"

"No, nothing," Ringer answered after a pause.

Philippa stood up ready to go. "Well, you will be hearing from us soon. Thank you for your help, Mr Ringer."

Ringer's face lit up. "Does this mean I won't be charged?"

"We'll have to see about that, Mr Ringer," Philippa replied as she walked out of the room. In fact, she doubted she would be able to charge Ringer on the basis of their interview, but she reflected it would do no harm to scare him a bit.

****

Philippa returned to Harvey and Ward's and waited by the telephone. As she expected, it was not long before it rang.

"I want to speak to Philippa Maxwell." A gruff male voice came down the phone. When she acknowledged her name, the man continued. "This is to let you know we don't tolerate intruders on our patch. If you don't want your pretty little face damaged, you'd better stop." The phone went dead before she could say anything.

Philippa pondered the call after she put the phone down. It all happened too suddenly for her to be scared. Her first thought was to put a trace on it, but it merely confirmed it was made from a public phone box near Leicester Square. She had enough police experience to know that this sort of threat was to be expected by any officer investigating drug dealing, but she wondered who could have made it. Presumably neither Ringer nor any of his associates made the phone call as they would know that she was an undercover policewoman and so not a competitor. The nightmare scenario was that they felt sufficiently confident of their power to consider threatening a police officer. Alternatively, one or more of the other people from Anson's list must have realised the significance of her call and warned people higher up the criminal tree that she was apparently setting up in competition. Philippa decided to wait until she arrived home before phoning Gould about the threat she had received.

Chapter 27

At the end of her day taking the role of Charles Anson, Philippa started to tidy up the desk and went to switch her computer terminal off. Anson had left no photographs of his family and friends, and Philippa still had little handle on his friends, many of them probably involved in drugs as well. She reflected that although she had taken her post as a secretary at Harvey and Ward as part of an undercover police operation, she had in fact started her career working in an office. The drudgery of it had eventually led her to join the police force, but something about office work still appealed to her and she felt quite at home tidying up the office at the end of a day's work.

She wondered how it would be if she had stayed working in an office. Philippa's childhood friends always told her she was the most unlikely policewoman they had ever known. Sometimes she thought they were right – she did not feel at home in the essentially male world of the police force. The hard-drinking camaraderie among both male and female police officers was alien to her and she tended not to socialise among her colleagues outside of work time.

Having satisfied herself that everything had been put away, Philippa put her coat on as protection from the January weather outside. She had always hated this time of year, when it became dark early in the afternoon. She reflected to herself that she had never entirely overcome her childhood fears of the night, but smiled to herself at the incongruity of a trained detective sergeant being afraid of the dark.

As Philippa left the City skyscraper, she went past the same concierge who had been so unwelcoming when she had first reported for work. He was still reading the sports page in some tabloid newspaper, and she smiled to herself as she wondered if he was reading the same issue as two weeks before. Then she started to walk towards the Bank station. She always caught the Docklands Light Railway to her flat in Greenwich. Like most of her colleagues, Philippa was not a resident of the City. She had grown up in a nondescript suburb called Sydenham. She stayed there with her mother, until she felt sufficiently flush with funds to buy her present flat.

Although, Philippa enjoyed the City and being part of its historically distinct police force, she always enjoyed coming home to her Greenwich. On this particular evening, her train journey home was uneventful and she passed her time, trying to sort out her feelings about David Gould. Somehow, she had lost touch with her old friends, of both sexes, when she joined the police, as she gradually found less and less in common with them. She had a reputation of being a loner among her female colleagues and she made her low opinion of her male colleagues rather too obvious.

Walking through the darkened streets from Cutty Sark station, she wondered if it was because they were both loners that Gould and she had become friends. He was a good deal older than her and with much more experience of the police. The problems with his marriage were common knowledge at the station, and Philippa asked herself how seriously she wanted to become involved with him, knowing how disapproving the force was of fraternisation between different ranks.

It was while Philippa's thoughts were running along these lines that she became aware that someone was walking along behind her. This was not surprising for a commuter area at this time of the evening, but bearing in mind the threatening phone call she had received earlier in the day, she asked herself if she could have been followed from when she left the office. However, with the large mass of commuters all going home at about the same time, it was impossible to tell. Had there been anyone on the train? Again, it was impossible to say, as Philippa had been too preoccupied in her own thoughts when she boarded the train to take any notice of her fellow passengers.

She asked herself if she was imagining being followed? She had done enough undercover following of suspects to know the tricks. She stopped and looked in a newsagent's window. The footsteps following her stopped immediately. When she looked behind her, she could see nothing. The man, whoever he was, was obviously an expert. Then suddenly she saw the man's face – small and rather weaselly, reflected in a shop window.

Philippa knew her mobile phone was at the bottom of her handbag. It would take too long and be too conspicuous to rummage around for it. The only sensible step for her to take was to walk home as fast as she could. Like all police officers, she had some self-defence training, but she knew that was no defence against an assailant armed with a gun or carrying a knife. She told herself that running from an assailant, like running away from a dog, can simply provoke an attack. 'Keep calm, be confident, don't look round, don't look scared,' she told herself as she walked quickly home towards her flat.

It was with a great sense of relief that Philippa reached the door of her ground floor flat and with trembling hands turned the key in the lock. After bolting the door, she had time to collect her thoughts. When she had calmed down, she decided she was the subject of a vivid imagination scared by the threatening phone call she had received. She vowed to put the incident out of her mind and started to cook her evening meal. She told herself she needed to take her mind off things. Cooking was a hobby of hers and she happily began to measure the ingredients for a new pasta dish, following the instructions in the glossy cookery book that her mother had bought her for Christmas. Philippa happily blended the ingredients for the sauce and the scent of the basil and oregano wafted through the kitchen.

Philippa was reflecting that there was something wonderfully therapeutic in simply following the written orders of a recipe. Having placed the dish in her oven, Philippa relaxed then suddenly noticed smoke. It took her a while to realise that something was seriously wrong. In her pleasant daydreams about cooking, her first thought was that she must have left something burning on the hotplate of her cooker by mistake. When she realised that she had not, she rushed into the corridor and noticed smoke coming from underneath the front door. At the same time, she noticed the shape of a man through the glass in the door and the letterbox opening was pushed ajar.

"I told you to keep out of our business," snarled the man through the letterbox. Philippa instantly recognised the voice as that of the man who had threatened her on the phone. Her first thought was to push open the front door and confront him. However, all the advice she herself had given to members of the public not to confront dangerous men came back to her.

Philippa knew the logical approach would be to phone the local police straight away. She felt however, that phoning

David Gould would get help more quickly. With trembling fingers, she phoned Snow Hill police station only to find he had gone home earlier than usual. She next looked up Gould's home phone number in her secret book of senior police officers' out of work contact numbers.

The phone seemed to ring for ages, but eventually Philippa heard Gould's voice on the line.

"David, it's Philippa. There's someone attacking my flat." Philippa was unable to keep the panic out of her voice.

"OK, I have the address here. I'll come right away. But call 999 as well to get the local cops round."

"Yes, but please be quick." Philippa dialled 999. "Police," she said without thinking when the emergency operator came on the line. "My name's Cottrell, DS Cottrell ... Yes, DS ... I'm in the City police ... My flat's being attacked. Come quickly ..." She managed to read out her address before being promised an immediate police response. Realising she could do no more, she again took stock of her position. She checked that all her doors and windows were secure; she remembered from her training that a locked door holds fire back for up to an hour and so she should have no fear of the fire itself.

Philippa's only worry was the smoke. It was now billowing strongly from underneath the front door. She started to cough and calculated that she could survive no more than ten minutes or so. If there was only one man attacking the flat, it might be safe to leave by the back door. However, if this was a well-planned attack, as it seemed to be, there may well be an accomplice positioned there. Philippa wondered if her neighbours would notice anything, but remembered they were often out. She looked at the minutes on the clock and calculated that in ten minutes whatever happened, she would try to escape from the back door and face any attacker that might be there.

Just then she heard the reassuring siren of a police car and the sound of someone running away. Still feeling shaken, Philippa waited for the knock on the door and the shouts of the policemen outside before she opened the front door. She stood choking in front of the uniformed constable.

"Detective Sergeant Cottrell?" the policeman said. "We got your call. Are you all right?"

"I think so," Philippa replied, through her coughs. "Did you see anyone running way?"

"No, he must have heard the siren. It looks as if someone had been burning cloths and newspapers outside your door. I can smell the paraffin. Do you know who it could have been?"

"No, it may be part of an enquiry I'm working on, but I don't know who it was."

Just then they saw a car drive up at high speed and Gould come out. He ran up the steps and held Philippa's hands.

"Are you all right? Did you see who it was?"

"I recognised the man's voice," Philippa replied. "He threatened me on the phone at the office today. I think I saw his face when he was following me home."

Gould turned to the uniformed constable. "How about you?"

"No, whoever it was had already gone, sir," the constable replied.

"Probably heard your siren, I expect," Gould said. "If you'd been more discreet, we might have caught him."

"I'm sure he did his best," Philippa protested. "It was a great relief to hear him."

"Oh, very well," Gould said. "Thank you for coming round."

"Yes, sir," the constable replied. "Glad to be of service. You've had a shock, miss. Come to the station tomorrow and have a look at some mug shots to see if you recognise him. Goodnight," he said, leaving.

"Will you be all right tonight, Philippa?" Gould asked. Philippa nodded, but something in her manner made him hesitate to leave her. "Why don't we go inside. We could both do with a strong drink. Have you got any brandy, Philippa? It'll be good for the shock."

"Yes, it's in that cupboard over there. I'm sorry about this," Philippa said, starting to shake.

"Don't worry about it," Gould replied, pouring out two brandies and passing one to Philippa.

"I thought the brandy was just for me," Philippa said, struggling to smile.

"I think we both need one," Gould said. "I don't know if it works, but it makes you feel better." He sat awkwardly at the opposite end of Philippa's sofa. "Let's hope the intruder doesn't come back. Perhaps I should get the local police to put a man outside all night. Or I could stay here to keep an eye on things. I'll stay on the sofa, of course," he ended lamely.

"I would feel safer to have someone here," Philippa replied. "This sofa pulls out. I'll get some sheets." She left Gould in the living room while she went to fetch some bed linen. He stood up while she pulled the bed out and the two put a sheet on the bed. While they were doing this, their hands touched and Gould put his arms around her. She held him close while he kissed her. After a moment, he moved his hands inside her blouse. Their two bodies fell onto the newly made bed.

Chapter 28

It was strange for Philippa to wake up next to David Gould the following morning. After a session of lovemaking which should have been passionate but in fact was rather tentative, they had fallen asleep in each other's arms.

When Philippa awoke, the sheet had fallen down to expose her breasts. Gould's arm lay across them. She blushed as she remembered how they had made love the night before then she managed to climb out of bed without waking him. She grabbed her robe and walked towards the bathroom. As she stood in the shower, she tried to make sense of her feelings. Would this be a one-night stand, which they would both try to forget? Would Gould think she was sleeping her way to promotion? Perhaps he would think her call to him was a stunt to drag him into bed with her? She shuddered at the turn her thoughts were taking as she dried herself and put on her robe again. She walked downstairs and made herself some coffee.

A little later, David Gould opened his eyes after a long sleep and looked up at a ceiling he did not recognise. His momentary sense of disorientation vanished when he remembered where he was. He realised that since breaking up with his wife, Gould had forgotten how satisfying lovemaking could be. He felt some remorse for having taken advantage of Philippa's panic at being followed and was unsure of what he would say to her this morning. He looked across and noticed he was alone in the bed.

So, where is she? Gould asked himself as he dressed then walked downstairs. He found Philippa drinking coffee at the small table in the kitchen. They both hesitated before they spoke.

"I don't know if you want breakfast," Philippa said. "I don't have much food in the flat. I wasn't expecting anyone to stay."

Gould felt embarrassed by the implied reproof in Philippa's voice. "I'm sorry. I got carried away. I was wrong to spend the night with you."

"I suppose you sleep with all your female colleagues," Philippa replied, her eyes brimming with tears.

"No, of course not. You know that's not true," Gould said. "Since I've broken up with my wife, I haven't been seeing anyone."

"What happens now?" Philippa asked after a pause.

"We carry on working together, just as before," Gould replied. "Then, if you like, we can see each other in our own time."

"What do you mean, 'If I like'?"

"I mean I'd like to see you after hours, please, if I may," replied Gould. "But if you're seeing someone else, it's your privilege to say no."

"I'll think about it," said Philippa. "But no one at the station must know. We'll still call each other 'sir' and 'sergeant' when there's anyone around." She made them both breakfast and when Gould had left, she phoned the local police station.

Chapter 29

"Do you think you'll be able to identify the man who followed you?" the sergeant at Greenwich police station asked Philippa later that day. She had told David Gould she would visit the station on her own. It was strange being treated as a member of the public by the local police, but Philippa was co-operating as fully as she could.

"I'll try, but I only saw him for a moment," Philippa replied. She smiled to herself as she recalled how many times she had heard those words when interviewing witnesses as a policewoman.

"Now, I'd like you to look through these mug shots and see if there's anyone you recognise," Sergeant Anderson said. He looked to be approaching retirement and seemed content to play everything by the book. "I will leave you now but let me know if there are any faces that look familiar. Is that all right?" Philippa was about to say she knew the drill better than he did and objected to being treated as a helpless female, when she realised that was exactly how she felt at present. She obediently leafed through the mug shots on the desk in front of her, trying to recall the face she had seen the previous evening.

After around half an hour, when Anderson came back, Philippa had narrowed the choice to three suspects. There was one face that seemed very like that of the man who followed her, while two others were possibilities. Anderson nodded in recognition as Philippa pointed out the most likely one.

"Do you know him?" she asked.

"Yes. We'll take care of it," Anderson replied, then realised that Philippa would want more information than the normal member of the public would. "His name's Miller – Nicholas Miller. He's an enforcer for a drug dealer called Jack Spendlove."

"Spendlove's a suspect in an investigation I'm involved in," Philippa said, nodding with recognition.

"We'll call Miller in for an identity parade. I expect your Chief Inspector Gould will want to be involved."

A few hours later, Philippa stood in the lobby of Greenwich police station with Gould and Anderson. She had been told the drill, even though she had arranged many identity parades herself. There was a parade of six men who she could observe through one-way glass so she could not be seen. After some thought, she had no hesitation in picking the fourth one as the man who had followed her home and attacked her flat.

"It's number four, I'm sure it is."

Anderson nodded. "Thank you, miss … er, Sergeant, you've done your duty. We'll take over now."

"But I still want to be involved in the case," Philippa protested.

Gould shook his head. "Sergeant Anderson's right, Philippa, we'll go by the book. You can't be both victim and investigating officer. The sergeant and I will take over. Take the rest of the day off. You've had enough for one day."

Philippa opened her mouth to protest, but a look at the faces of Gould and Anderson told her it would be useless. She thought about how important it was not to give a defence lawyer any ammunition by breaking police rules and decided she would leave without protest.

****

Within a couple of hours, the local police had brought in the suspect whose face Philippa had identified. Gould and Anderson interviewed the man. Nicholas Miller, a wiry man aged about forty, dressed in jeans and leather jacket, sat back in the chair and looked at the walls of the interview room with studied unconcern.

"Can you tell us where you were between five and seven p.m. last night?" "We know you're working for Spendlove, why don't you just come clean and tell us. He wouldn't do anything for you." "Do you know the maximum sentence for arson?" The questions coming from alternate interviewers were met with dead silence.

Finally, after ten minutes of silence from the suspect, Gould terminated the interview. "Very well, Nicholas Miller, you are to be charged with attempted arson last night. You are not obliged to say anything, but it may harm your defence if you fail to reveal information that you subsequently rely on in court." Miller was led away, still in gum-chewing silence.

Afterwards, Gould and Anderson talked among themselves.

"What do you make of him?" the sergeant asked Gould.

"He's tough, all right," Gould replied. "He's worked for Spendlove for years. Was he hard to find?"

"No, that's the oddest thing," Anderson answered. "He was at home at the most recent address he gave his probation officer and came without any trouble. It's almost as if he was expecting us. We went to his flat in Mile End and there he was."

"Did you say Mile End?" Gould asked, standing up. "Call him back, will you. I have a few more questions to ask him."

After a few moments, Miller was escorted back into the interview room.

"We're investigating the murder of a man whose body was found in the canal at Mile End a month ago on the twelfth of March," Gould said, keeping his eyes fixed on Miller's face. For the first time, the suspect looked scared.

"I don't know anything about any body in any canal," Miller whined.

"We're looking for someone with local knowledge of the area. Someone just like you. Was Spendlove behind it?"

"No," Miller replied, his confidence returning. "Never heard of him."

"You're lying," Gould said. "Everyone knows you work for him."

Miller again folded his arms and looked out of the window.

"You realise you're facing a long prison sentence. With your record, threatening a police officer will not go down well with any judge," Gould said, but Miller's silence was total. Gould realised he had no evidence to charge Miller with either of the two murders he was investigating. He would have to be content with a charge of attempted arson of Philippa's flat.

Chapter 30

A few days later, Reg Ward stood in his living room and closed the curtains. It was raining heavily and he was looking forward to a quiet evening at home. He walked back to his armchair, looked at his TV dinner on the tray on the table and shuddered. He told himself a man of his status should be doing better for himself than this, but then shrugged his shoulders. At least, unlike his old school friend, Neil Harvey, he was still alive. He closed his eyes and took another mouthful of his reheated meal. He could not remember the description on the packet, but whatever it was, it bore no resemblance to the reality in front of him.

To try to take his mind off things, Ward looked at the situation comedy on the television in front of him. Although the canned laughter blared out, he found nothing remotely amusing in the programme. He stood up and walked to switch the set off – he was proud that he never resorted to the remote control and so gained the exercise of stretching his legs. Suddenly, the doorbell rang. "Damn," he said to himself, preparing himself for an unwelcome visit from a double-glazing salesman or a Jehovah's Witness. Switching the set off, Ward went to open the front door, preparing to send the unwelcome intruders away.

"Hello, Reg, how are you?" Possibly the last person Ward expected to see was in front of him. Annabel, his ex-wife, stood on the doorstep. "Aren't you going to invite me in?" she asked, water dripping from her raincoat. She had done her hair differently from the way he remembered – it was longer and less stylish – and her eyes looked strained.

"Er, yes, come in, Annabel," Ward replied, ushering her into the hall and helping her to take off her coat. "I wasn't expecting to see you. Come into the front room. There's no one here." Annabel walked uncertainly into the untidy bachelor front room. "I'm afraid it's not as tidy as you used to keep it," Ward called from the hall. "Take a seat, if you can find a clear space."

Annabel gingerly picked up some dirty socks from the settee, deposited them at arm's length onto the floor and sat down. "Can I get you a drink?" Ward said, coming into the hall. "I have a bottle of red wine open. You used to like that." Annabel nodded her acceptance and took the glass Ward offered her.

"You don't seem to have done very well for yourself, Reg. Do you call this home?" Annabel asked, looking around dubiously.

"Well, it'll do for the time being," Ward said, becoming defensive under Annabel's questioning. "It's not as tidy as you used to keep it. It must have been three years, hasn't it, Annabel? How have you been?"

"Bloody awful since you ask," Annabel replied. "How's what's her name?"

"It was Sally, as you very well know, and I haven't seen her for years," Ward answered. "Have you come here to talk about old times, Annabel? I thought our bickering days were over."

"No," Annabel replied, sipping her wine, "it's about the change in your position."

"What do you mean?" Ward asked, after a pause.

"I had a visit from two City of London policemen the other day," Annabel said. "When I say 'policemen', one of them was female and extremely pretty, as you probably noticed."

"That'll be Philippa."

"I'm glad you're on first terms already," Annabel continued. "They asked me about Neil Harvey's murder. I told them I didn't know who killed him but whoever it was did you one hell of a favour."

"It doesn't look like much of a favour from my point of view," Ward complained. "I've spent ages with the police while they've gone over my life story. I don't think that Chief Inspector Gould believed a word I was saying."

"Well, as long as you're innocent you haven't anything to worry about," Annabel said. "The question is, what you are going to do now you don't have Harvey taking all the money from your business."

"What can I do?" Ward asked. "Kathleen now owns three-quarters of the shares. Legally, there's no difference now Neil's dead, just a different name on the share certificates."

"Don't be stupid, Reg," replied Annabel. "You know you're the backbone of that company. You don't need any of the Harveys' money now. They need you more than you need them. I'm sick of Neil sitting in that office with his phoney abstract painting and creaming off all the money."

"Have you just come back to argue, Annabel?" Ward asked. "Because I thought we finished all our arguments three years ago when we divorced."

Annabel finished her wine and stood up. "You're just the same as you always were, Reg. You won't stand up for our rights."

"We're divorced, remember. The rights are mine not ours anymore," Ward said.

"We'll always be a couple, Reg, no matter what piece of paper you have," Annabel retorted. "I'm going to see Kathleen and that daughter of hers to get what belongs to us, even if you're not. Thank you for the wine, Reg. I'll see myself out."

Before Ward could get to his feet, Annabel had taken her coat, opened the front door and slammed it behind her. Ward stood in the hall, open-mouthed. He thought over their conversation and one thing in particular puzzled him. Neil Harvey had bought an abstract painting for the first time only a week before his death. He could think of no way his ex-wife would have known of it, unless she had seen Harvey shortly before his murder. He was in no doubt that would make Gould consider Annabel a suspect. Ward told himself that everything he knew about his ex-wife made it impossible to believe she could kill anyone. Then, he told himself that the mood in which she left his house made him less certain.

Chapter 31

The following day, Annabel Ward handed in her ticket at the barrier and walked out of Haslemere station. She held a small piece of paper with Kathleen Harvey's address in her hand and looked about her. A taxi driver held open his door, hoping for a fare, but Annabel ignored him. The days of taking taxis belonged to the time when she could rely on her husband's expense account, and they were long gone.

Annabel recalled that the last time she had been to Haslemere was the fateful day when her then husband had signed the partnership contract with Neil Harvey. Although in money terms, Reg's career had taken off then, Annabel could never forgive Harvey for the workload he had imposed on Reg which she was sure had destroyed her marriage. Fortunately, that time, Reg had driven to the station looking for directions and Annabel could remember the way they had gone to find Harvey's house.

Annabel cast her mind back to the meeting she had with Neil Harvey shortly before he was killed. She blushed with embarrassment as she recalled her hope that Harvey would meekly increase the share of the profits that went to Ward. Instead, she had to endure the humiliation of waiting many minutes underneath the abstract painting outside his office, until she was finally admitted to see Harvey. Within a couple of minutes, he had thrown Annabel out of his office, without any pretence of politeness. She felt sure that there must be some guilty secrets that Harvey had that she could use against him, though she did not know what they were.

But with his death, that chance had evaporated. Instead she had come to visit Kathleen, with some vague hope that the two women could reach an understanding.

After around half an hour walking uphill, with one or two wrong turnings, Annabel reached the end of Kathleen Harvey's drive. It was a hot day and she had received strange looks from people driving by; it was evident that walking was very much a minority exercise in this part of Surrey. As she stood at the end of the drive, she gasped as she saw the large detached Tudor-style house with its big garden. She realised that in fact, the house was little changed from when she had last seen it, but compared with the crowded part of London in which she now lived, it seemed even bigger than she remembered. After a further walk up the drive, Annabel rang the doorbell. A young woman dressed in jeans answered the door. "Can I help you?" she asked in an Eastern European accent.

"I've come to see Mrs Harvey. Who are you?" Annabel asked.

"My name's Tania," the girl replied. "You're not from the press, are you? I've been told to call the police if any more press people come to the door."

"I am nothing to do with the press. Please tell Mrs Harvey that Annabel Ward is here to see her."

"I've been told to say that Mrs Harvey is not receiving visitors at present," Tania said. Annabel suddenly burst into tears, faced with the prospect of a long wasted journey. Tania seemed to take sympathy on her. "You wait there. I'll fetch Mrs Harvey." Tania shut the door and went away.

After a couple of moments, Tania returned and opened the door again. "Mrs Harvey will see you now," she said, ushering Annabel into the drawing room. While waiting for Kathleen to join her, Annabel looked around at the luxurious furnishings and thought of the contrast with both her own and her ex-husband's properties. She reflected that both their houses would fit comfortably into this room.

"Annabel, what a surprise." Kathleen came into the room. She was dressed in tasteful grey, obviously a compromise between funeral black and too bright a colour. She came forward and kissed Annabel on her cheek. "Won't you take a seat? Has Tania offered you anything? Let's have some tea," Kathleen said without waiting for a response. While waiting for tea to be served, Annabel gathered her thoughts together.

"Do you remember the first time Reg and I came here?" Annabel asked. "Reg wanted money for the business."

"Yes, of course I do," Kathleen replied coldly. "We've all come a long way since then."

"Reg worked really hard for Harvey and Ward. A lot of all this," Annabel indicated the luxurious surrounding, "is due to Reg's hard work."

"Reg put in the labour, Neil put in the risk capital," Kathleen replied in a superior tone. "Neil got most of the financial return. That's the way these things go. Life's not always fair."

"I was sorry to hear of Neil's death," Annabel continued with her prepared speech. "You must be devastated."

"Yes, it was a sad loss," Kathleen agreed, in a voice devoid of emotion. "But I have to plan for the future now."

"It's really the future I've come to see you about, Kathleen," Annabel said.

"What do you mean?"

"Now Reg is taking over most of the work, I feel he is entitled to a greater percentage of the company shares. He has asked me to see if something can be arranged amicably," Annabel continued.

"Forgive me, Annabel," Kathleen said. "But I thought you were divorced from Reg now."

"We are getting back together again," Annabel said, blushing slightly as she lied. "We are prepared to offer a good price for your shares."

"I'm afraid I've decided to keep all Neil's shares in Harvey and Ward, and I've asked Cassandra to take over Neil's chairmanship at the company," Kathleen replied.

Annabel put down her teacup and her voice became harsher. "To be frank, Kathleen," Annabel said. "I visited Neil the day he died. He had a lot on his mind and he told me some things he was worried about. I am sure the police would be very interested in what I could tell them."

"What are you talking about?" Kathleen asked, studying Annabel's expression with suspicion. "Why don't you just tell the police whatever it is?"

"I think you know what I mean. I won't say anything else now." Annabel stood up, leaving a piece of paper on the coffee table. "This is the address where I can be reached. Good bye, Kathleen. I hope, when you have thought about it, we can come to some compromise."

Annabel walked out of the house, leaving Kathleen staring open-mouthed behind her. She wondered what information Annabel had, or thought she had. After a few moments' thought, Kathleen picked up the phone and dialled a number. "You'll never guess who's just been to see me ... Annabel Ward ... Yes, I thought they were divorced too, but she says they're getting together again ... She says she went to see Neil just before he died ... I don't know what she saw but she's trying to blackmail me ... I'm very worried, so should you be... OK, thank you." For the first time in her life, Kathleen picked up one of the cigarettes her husband kept for visitors and lit it.

****

Later the same day, Kathleen looked across at Jason and Cassandra across her dinner table. It was the first time the three of them had been together since the day of the funeral. With Tania's help, Kathleen had organised a gourmet meal and she was pleased that her two children had not quarrelled so far.

"It's great to be together as a family again," Kathleen said. "We shouldn't argue all the time."

"We have enjoyed the meal, Mother," Jason replied. "But let's not press things too far. We're not a happy family yet."

"I'm happy to put our differences aside, for Mother's sake," Cassandra said.

"It's all very well for you, Cassie," Jason shouted. "You run Dad's company, while I'm scrimping and saving like a pleb."

"Carry on doing well at that company you work for, and I might give you a job in the future," Cassandra replied.

"Oh, thank you, Lady Bountiful. You might generously give your own brother a job. I should be running that company, not you."

"Now, children, let's not spoil the evening," Kathleen interrupted. "There is something I wanted to talk about. Annabel Ward came to see me this afternoon."

"Reg's wife, or his ex-wife," Cassandra said. "What did she want?"

"She had some idea that I should give Reg more of the company now that Neil's dead."

"What's it got to do with her? They've been divorced for years, haven't they?"

"She said they're getting together again. I don't know if that's true, but she's a Catholic and doesn't accept they're divorced."

"I hope you told her to get lost," Jason said. "We don't owe her – or Reg – anything."

"Yes, I did, but then she came over all mysterious and said she knew some secrets that could bring me down."

"What secrets?"

"She wouldn't say, but she had been to see Neil before he died and claimed to know something. What could it be?"

Jason snorted with derision. "She's bluffing. How could she know anything? Certainly not the one thing that matters."

"Do you think so?" Kathleen asked. "I've been worried all day about it."

"If you're worried," Jason replied, "I'll go and tackle her. I'll see what she knows."

"That would be great if you could, Jason," Cassandra added, looking at her brother with a new respect.

In the kitchen, Tania moved away from the door to the dining room and made a mental note of what she had heard.

Chapter 32

Cassandra walked into her father's old office and looked around. It was a week since she had taken control of the company. She smiled to herself as she recalled how her father had sacked her just a few weeks before. She decided she was in the mood to make some changes straightaway.

She was about to press a button to summon a member of staff when she thought better of it. She felt she would enjoy the look of fear on their faces as she asked them to come into her office. Cassandra walked out through the door and straight to the desk where Margaret Lane sat typing at a keyboard.

"Come into my office, please, Margaret," Cassandra said.

"Yes, Cassandra," Margaret replied as she followed Cassandra into her new office.

"Take a seat, Margaret," Cassandra said, as she closed the door behind her. "I've decided to make a few changes here," she continued, as she sat on the edge of her desk. "I won't go into the details of what services you provided to my father but for obvious reasons, I won't be needing them. In fact, I won't be needing you at all. You are dismissed. Please clear out your desk and leave the building."

Margaret rose unsteadily to her feet. Tears came to her eyes as she tried to speak. "I'll have my revenge for this," she began. She saw the gloating in Cassandra's eyes before she broke down in tears and left the room.

Cassandra was starting to enjoy herself and wondered what her next step should be. After some thought, she pressed the intercom and asked Reg Ward to come in.

When he entered the room, Ward looked nervous. "You asked to see me, Cassandra?" he asked.

"Yes, I did. Please sit down." Cassandra leaned forward threateningly as she had seen her father do so often. "I'm planning on making a few changes. I've already got rid of Margaret Lane, but there's no reason why you can't carry on working here." She paused for effect.

"Thank you, Cassandra," Ward said. His demeanour was that of a frightened rabbit and his whole body seemed to be shaking with nerves.

"But in future, I will be insisting on seeing a detailed explanation of all your receipts before they are approved. There will be no more fact-finding trips to exotic countries with female colleagues. Do you understand?" Ward nodded. "Very well, as long as that is understood I am sure we can carry on working together. Now I am sure you have work to be getting on with." Ward left the office, murmuring his thanks and Cassandra leant back on her father's old swivel chair. She felt she was getting the hang of management and looked forward to her future career.

****

Later that day, there was a knock on Cassandra's office door. She looked up angrily as Annabel came in.

"Annabel, it's been a long time since I've seen you. I've been looking forward to having a word. What are you doing here?" she asked.

"I've come to see you about Reg's position, Cassandra. I'll sit down, if I may?"

"What do you mean, Reg's position?"

Annabel sat down and looked around the office. "We all know Reg has been the mainstay of this office for years. I've come to see if there is some way he can be put in charge of the firm. You know he'd do a good job. It would be in the interest of the firm as a whole."

Cassandra gave a long theatrical sigh. "I realise you've known me all my life, Annabel."

"I'm your godmother. I went to your parents' wedding. I remember you as a baby."

"I was going to say, Annabel," Cassandra continued as if Annabel had not spoken, "that things are different now. As you may have noticed, I'm a grown-up woman and you are no longer married to Reg."

"Reg will always be my husband," Annabel said with tears in her eyes.

"In short, I have nothing to say to you. I know you've been to see my mother with the same pathetic claptrap. First, I make the decisions for the company now, not my mother. Second, I don't appreciate your attempting to blackmail our family. I don't believe you really know any secrets about us. Unless you want to tell me what they are." Annabel shook her head. "I thought not. I think this conversation is at an end. Please close the door on the way out." Cassandra returned to reading some papers on her desk. Annabel opened her mouth as if to say something, then swallowed and walked out of the room.

Once she was sure Annabel had left the offices, Cassandra picked up her phone, and dialled.

"Mother, you'll never guess what. Annabel's been to see me. I'm sure she doesn't know anything ... Perhaps you could let Jason know he needn't bother going to see her … Well, keep trying his mobile … Yes, I'll try as well. Bye."

Cassandra hung up and dialled Jason's number and tutted to herself when she received no reply.

Chapter 33

Annabel Ward looked at the busy traffic outside her Walthamstow house with annoyance. She needed some last-minute shopping and wanted to go to the corner shop on the other side of the road. She realised it was more expensive than a supermarket but told herself this was an emergency.

While waiting for a gap in the traffic, Annabel shuddered as she recalled again the humiliation she had felt when Harvey had thrown her out of his office. She told herself she was determined to get some money from the Harvey family now that Neil was dead. Bluffing about what she knew about the company was risky but there was not much else to do. She was confident she would be hearing from Kathleen or Cassandra soon.

As Annabel was about to cross the road, she noticed a large black car coming too fast on her side of the road. She stepped back from the curb but, as if in a nightmare, it mounted the pavement and came straight towards her. She moved further back but she could not escape. She tried to see the driver but it was impossible through the tinted glass. She opened her mouth to scream, but before she could make a sound, the car had run straight into her. The last thing she heard was the noisy exhaust as the car sped away around the corner. Blood came out of her mouth that could no longer speak.

****

The next day, Gould looked at the battered body of Annabel Ward in the council morgue in Tottenham. She was lying in one of many body drawers. The others had crudely written names shown on labels, but Annabel was still officially anonymous. Although he was used to the sight of corpses, Gould hated visiting morgues and reflected that each body told a different tragedy. He could feel Philippa shudder beside him.

"We found your card in her handbag and decided to phone you," Detective Sergeant Barry from the Walthamstow station said. "It seems like a normal hit and run case. We haven't found any witnesses to the incident yet, except one person who claims they saw an expensive black car driving too fast away from the scene. Probably someone was driving too fast and the car spun out of control. It happens all the time, as we all know."

"Not in this case it didn't," Gould replied, with a grim expression. "I'm investigating two murders already. This one's the third."

"I'm happy to help, of course. What do you know about the victim, sir?" Barry asked.

"Her name's Annabel Ward. We interviewed her last week and I'm sure there was more she could tell us. Her ex-husband's involved in a murder case we're investigating. The senior partner in his travel agency business was killed."

"She's wearing a wedding ring as well as an engagement ring. Isn't that odd if she's divorced?" Barry asked. "Unless she remarried, of course."

"No, she's a Catholic," Philippa replied. "As far as she was concerned, marriage was for life."

"Well, we need someone to identify the body," Barry said. "Would her ex-husband be willing to do that? We haven't found any other relatives so far. Shall I send someone round to pick him up?"

"No, I'll tell him," Philippa said. "He knows me. I don't want him to hear the news from a stranger."

Gould nodded agreement. "Yes, you tell him, but don't forget he's a suspect until we know otherwise."

****

A few hours later, Philippa knocked on Reg Ward's office door. Ward stood up with a smile when he saw her come in, but a glance at her face showed that the call was serious and official.

"What's happened, Philippa?" Ward asked.

"I have some serious news for you, Reg. I don't want to tell you here. Could you come to the station with me?" she asked.

"What is it? Have you found who murdered Neil yet?"

"I'll tell you at the station, Reg," Philippa said. "I think it would be better that way. We're not sure if it's to do with the Harvey murder or not," Philippa replied, "but come with me, please."

Ward gaped at her, apparently bemused, then locked his desk and followed her out. While Philippa was driving them through the outskirts of the City, Reg Ward turned to her and said, "This isn't the way to your station. Where are we going?"

"I'll tell you more when we're there," Philippa said.

Ward looked baffled but said no more until Philippa parked outside Walthamstow police station. She turned the ignition off and turned to look at Ward. "I'm sorry to have to tell you this, but a woman was killed near here by a hit and run driver yesterday morning. We're fairly sure it was your ex-wife."

"Annabel? Killed?" Ward echoed, his voice faltering.

"I'm afraid so, Reg," Philippa said, watching his reaction carefully.

"But are you sure?"

"The local police will ask you to identify the body. They originally called us because she had our visiting card in her handbag. We gave it to her when we went to see her last week. When did you see her last?"

"I hadn't seen her for three years, then she turned up last week. She said you'd been to see her." Ward looked tearfully out of the car window. "This is terrible. It must be a drunk driver. I hope they catch whoever did it." A sudden thought crossed Ward's mind. "Why did they send you to tell me? Wouldn't the local police normally do that? You don't think I had anything to do with it, do you?"

"We don't suspect anyone yet, Reg," Philippa said, instinctively reaching out to reassure him. "I just thought you would prefer to be told by someone you know. I'll take you in to see the local police. Would you like me to take you home afterwards?"

"No, thank you," Ward answered, with tears in his eyes. "Tell Chief Inspector Gould you don't need to spy on me anymore."

Ward turned sharply to go into the police station, before Philippa could reply. She looked sadly after him as he left. She told herself that telling relatives of a death is a basic part of every police officer's job and in a murder investigation everyone had to be a suspect. It did not prevent the tears in her eyes, as she felt how her job stood in the way of making friends outside the force. She told herself the police was a worthwhile job but she wished it did not ruin so many other parts of her life.

****

An hour later, after a short trip from the police station, Barry, as the local investigating officer, led Ward into the morgue. The mortuary assistant pulled a refrigerated drawer out for inspection. After a moment to steady himself, Ward looked down at the body of his former wife. He shuddered with recognition.

"For the record, do you identify the deceased as Mrs Annabel Ward, sir?" Barry asked.

"Yes, that's Annabel, my ex-wife," Ward announced.

"Thank you, sir. Please come back to the station and make a statement to that effect," Barry said, as the drawer was closed.

****

After a short drive, Gould, Barry and Philippa looked across at the dispirited form of Reg Ward across the interview desk in Walthamstow station. He listlessly stirred the cup of tea he had been offered.

"I'm sorry to have brought you here to learn such sad news, Mr Ward," Gould began.

"We married when I was twenty-two, you know. We were together for a long time," Ward replied, his eyes filled with tears. "What I don't understand is why you're involved. What's the City of London police got to do with a road accident in Walthamstow?"

Philippa and Gould exchanged glances. "We're worried that this wasn't a hit and run accident. It's possible that whoever killed Neil Harvey also killed Annabel," Philippa said. "In fact, we think it's likely. We realise that you've had a severe shock, but it would help us find your ex-wife's killers, if you could answer questions now."

"Is that why you asked when I'd last seen her?" Ward asked. "Am I a suspect?"

"We have to ask these questions just for the record. Everyone who knew Annabel must be treated as a suspect. We haven't ruled anyone in or out at this stage," Gould answered. "Could you confirm that you are willing to answer questions now?" Ward nodded. "For the record, Mr Ward indicated agreement. Please tell me when you last saw your ex-wife, Mr Ward."

"Annabel came to see me last week. I hadn't seen her for about three years before then. It was after you'd been to see her. She had an idea that I could take over the company now Neil Harvey's dead."

"And can you?"

"No, not really. As I told her, the shares go to Kathleen and she's given them to Cassandra to manage. If anything, it could be worse than when Neil was alive. I don't know what Cassandra's plans for the company are at all."

"And did Annabel accept that?" Philippa asked.

"No, she told me I had to stick up for myself," Ward answered. "She said she was going to see Kathleen and Cassandra, but I don't know if she did or not."

"We'll follow that up. Was there anything else you can tell us about Annabel's visit, Mr Ward?"

"Well, there was one odd thing. She mentioned an abstract painting in Neil's office – he'd only had that for a week before he died. I can't think how she would have known about it, unless she'd been to see him in that last week."

"She told us she hadn't seen Harvey for three years," Philippa said. "You're saying she was lying about that?"

"Yes, unless someone told her about the painting – but I can't think who. She didn't have any connection with the firm since we divorced."

"Can you think of a reason why she would have gone to Harvey's office during the week before he was killed?" Gould asked.

"No, she had no reason at all to see Harvey."

"Mrs Ward was killed at around eleven o'clock this morning. Can you tell us where you were then?"

Ward thought for a moment. "At a meeting at work, lots of people there will be able to confirm it."

"Thank you, Reg," Philippa said, after a nod from Gould. "DS Barry will arrange a lift home for you, if you wish."

"I'm sorry I was short with you earlier, Philippa. I'd be happy for a lift from anybody."

"I'll give you a lift home, Reg," Philippa said, picking up her bag to lead Ward to the police car park.

****

"We're here to see Mrs Harvey." It was the following day and Gould and Philippa had knocked on the door of Kathleen

Harvey's home. Gould had decided to adopt a more aggressive stance. Tania looked scared at Gould's tone.

"Yes, sir, I will show you in," Tania replied, as she directed the two detectives into the stylish sitting room.

"Good morning, Mrs Harvey. We have some questions to ask you. We understand Annabel Ward visited you during the last week."

"How did you know that?" she asked. Receiving no response from the two detectives, she continued. "Oh, very well, I suppose there's no harm in telling you. She came to see me a few days ago. It was quite a surprise – I hadn't seen her since she and Reg were divorced three years ago."

"I must know what you discussed," Gould said in a firm voice.

Kathleen looked startled at Gould's sharp tone, then continued with a nervous laugh. "She had some idea that Reg should take over the company now Neil's dead. Complete nonsense, of course. I'm the major shareholder now and I've asked my daughter to take over. Annabel seemed to think she was still married to Reg – I think she's gone off her head. She can't accept they're divorced."

"What else did you talk about, Mrs Harvey?" Philippa asked.

Kathleen continued nervously. "Annabel said she'd been to see Neil before he died and she knew something about his murder. She wouldn't say what it was – she just said there were criminal activities." Kathleen suddenly became angry. "That's what this is about, isn't it? She's gone to you with some story or other. I tell you, I wouldn't believe a word she said."

"I have some sad news for you, Mrs Harvey," Gould said, his eyes fixed on the woman's face. "Annabel Ward was killed by a hit and run driver yesterday morning."

Kathleen looked shocked. "That's terrible. Some drunk killed her, I suppose. The poor woman! I wouldn't have said those things about her if I'd known."

"We don't think it was an accident, Mrs Harvey," Gould replied. "We're pretty sure Mrs Ward was murdered. The tyre marks indicated the car accelerated just before it hit her."

For the first time, Kathleen Harvey looked scared. "Do you think it's anything to do with Neil's murder?"

"We're almost certain it is, Mrs Harvey," Philippa said. "Whoever murdered your husband could also have been involved in killing Annabel Ward. It's hard to believe it's a coincidence. Either the same person killed both – or we're dealing with a conspiracy."

Kathleen Harvey's eyes looked from one police officer to the other, like a cornered rat. Suddenly, before either detective could reach her, Kathleen fell in a faint to the floor.

"Quick, pick her up," Gould told Philippa. The two picked the unconscious woman up and laid her on the settee.

Philippa checked her pulse. "There's nothing to worry about. She's just fainted. Annabel's death must have been a hell of a shock."

"You look after her, I'll make a cup of sweet tea." As Gould entered the luxuriously appointed kitchen, he switched on the kettle. He realised this was a perfect opportunity to see if he could pick up any clues to help the murder investigation. The first thing he noticed was that the kitchen was so spotless there was no indication of its owner's personality at all. He read through the scraps of paper on the notice board, with details of coffee mornings and other local events, but they contained nothing suspicious.

As Gould looked out of the window, he noticed two cars on the drive – a blue Jaguar, which he knew used to belong to Neil Harvey and a small white Toyota, which was most likely Kathleen's. Gould went outside and examined the bodywork of both cars carefully but neither showed signs of being in a recent collision.

Gould returned into the hall. "Miss Kopic, Tania," he called. The Czech au pair came up from the basement.

"Mrs Harvey's fainted, but first I need to know if she has been acting unusually recently."

Tania thought. "Well, last night, she had the two children – Mr and Miss Harvey for dinner – that hasn't happened for a long time. Jason hasn't been around since the funeral."

"Do you know why there was this change?"

"I don't know, but a lady called Annabel Ward came around yesterday. Mrs Harvey seemed upset after that and I heard her phoning someone soon afterwards. I couldn't hear it all, but I think she must have been talking to one of her two children and then they were both here last night."

"Did you hear what they talked about over dinner?"

"Well, I'm sure Annabel – Mrs Ward's – name came up. Mrs Harvey said she was worried Annabel had some secret. I think Jason said he was going to look into it."

"Thank you, Tania. That's helpful. Could you make a cup of tea for Mrs Harvey now?" Once Tania had made the tea, Gould took it into the living room. Philippa took it from him and placed it in front of the still unconscious Kathleen.

"I heard you talking to Tania," Philippa said. "Did she see anything suspicious?"

"Cassandra and Jason were both round last night – straight after Annabel visited. Kathleen may have been spooked by the visit and decided to do away with Annabel. Mind you, I had a look at both of the Harveys' cars, but there's not a scratch on them."

"You didn't seriously think this woman would drive up to Walthamstow and run over Annabel Ward, did you?"

"Maybe not, but why's she reacting like this?" Gould asked. "Would the average person faint when they're told someone they've only seen once in three years is killed?"

"It could be delayed stress from her husband having been killed. Perhaps she thinks she might be next."

"Or else she knows more than she's telling. Mind you, I'm sure when we told her about Annabel's death, she did look genuinely surprised. I doubt if even a professional could act that well."

Just then Kathleen began to stir. As she sat up, she focussed on Gould and Philippa. "Oh, I'm sorry. I must have fainted. It was a shock. I've known Annabel for ages, you see."

"That's all right, Mrs Harvey. Have this sweet tea and take your time," Gould said. "Was Mrs Ward a close friend of yours? Only you said you'd only seen her once in the last three years."

Kathleen continued in a voice close to hysteria. "Yes, I suppose it's strange to react like this, but it's always a shock when someone you know dies unexpectedly. We used to be such good friends."

"Do you have any idea who might have killed Annabel, Mrs Harvey?"

"No, not really," Kathleen answered in a vague fashion. Suddenly her mood changed as she sat up sharply. "I'm sorry, but I don't think I can help you any more now. I must ask you to leave. I'd like to lie down for a while."

Gould and Philippa stood up, with obvious reluctance. "As you wish, Mrs Harvey. Please let us know if you can think of anything else that would help us," Philippa said.

"Would you like me to ask someone to come round – your daughter, perhaps, or your son?"

Kathleen stood up and walked toward the front door. "No, I don't want to disturb Cassandra or Jason, they're both very busy. Thank you for letting me know about poor Annabel," she continued as Gould and Philippa walked outside to their car. Kathleen looked out of the window and made sure they had gone down the long drive and off her property.

Then she went to the phone and dialled. After a few seconds, she spoke rapidly into the mouthpiece. "The police have just been round ... Someone's killed Annabel ... It was you, wasn't it ...?" Kathleen started to sob. "No, it's not what I wanted ... I've a good mind to tell the police what I know ... I don't care what happens to me now." Kathleen slammed the phone down and sat on the sofa, crying uncontrollably.

Chapter 34

"We have three murders to investigate now. First Hugh Marks, then Neil Harvey and now Annabel Ward. Shall we go through the main suspects?" Gould asked the next day, looking at the audience in front of him. It was an unseasonably hot day for October. All the detectives involved in investigating the Harvey murder and the related killings were gathered for a case conference. They were crammed together in Gould's office either sitting in chairs or leaning uncomfortably against office furniture. Philippa was amongst them and waited for Gould to start to speak. She and Gould were scrupulous in keeping their relationship secret, but they both knew it was only a matter of time before the whisperings started. Gould paused for effect, as he gathered his thoughts together. He was not expecting any response to his rhetorical question.

"Let's start with the Harvey murder. We'll go through people who were closest to the victim. His junior partner was Reg Ward. They knew each other since schooldays. From what we know of the late Mr Harvey, he didn't have friends, but Ward was the closest to one he had. Ward had the opportunity and he may have become tired of playing second fiddle. Philippa – DS Cottrell – can tell us how much Harvey used to humiliate him." He turned to Philippa. "DS Cottrell thinks he's innocent but you'd agree, we have no hard evidence to clear him, wouldn't you, Philippa?"

"Yes, David," Philippa said, standing up. "Reg Ward might have suddenly decided to stand up for himself. He must have resented doing all the work while Harvey took most of the profits. Reg must be treated as a suspect." She could not keep the regret from her voice.

"Thank you. Then there's Annabel, Ward's wife. She's now been killed herself, but she could still have murdered Harvey. She had a good motive."

"She was Ward's ex-wife, sir, they were divorced," one of the detectives – DC Fox – called out.

"She was a good Catholic," Gould continued. "As far as she was concerned, she would always be his wife. We know she also resented Harvey making Ward do all the work for only a quarter of the money. She said she hadn't seen Harvey for three years, but I don't believe her. Could she have come back and had some fatal argument with Harvey? She knew about the abstract painting he bought just before he died."

"How did she get on with Reg Ward?" Fox called out.

"She didn't say a word against him in our interview – it was all how much she hated Harvey," Philippa replied.

"It's just that Annabel could have murdered Harvey and tried to frame Ward for the murder. Kill two birds with one stone, if you like. Then Ward killed her in revenge," Fox countered.

Gould looked exasperated. "I doubt it. Let's try and be realistic, shall we? Next, there's Margaret Lane, Harvey's secretary, office manager, or whatever she calls herself. She was the dead man's mistress, but she'd been ditched the day before he was murdered. She certainly had a motive, didn't she, Philippa?"

"The day before the murder, I found her crying in the ladies'. She said she wasn't going to take it lying down."

"I thought she'd been doing that for years," came the cockney voice of a recently recruited detective constable from the side of the room.

Gould waited for the ribald laughter to die down. "Let's be serious," he said. "Lane said she knew lots of secrets which she was going to use against Harvey. We haven't followed that up enough. It seems Harvey had a new mistress called Samantha, but we haven't found any record of such a person in any of Harvey's effects. She could be a suspect, if she exists. Any ideas would be welcome."

"Lane was the person who found Harvey's body in the morning. That's always suspicious," the recent recruit suggested, anxious to redeem himself in his Chief Inspector's eyes.

"Yes, but we know Harvey was murdered the previous night, not that morning, so that doesn't prove anything. Unless Lane came in early the next morning to cover up something or other." Gould suddenly became excited. "You might have something. She could have killed Harvey the previous night and either planted the wrong bullet or the wrong gun the following morning. As far as we know, she's the only one with the opportunity to have planted it before we arrived. She was in before nine because she was in the office when you arrived, wasn't she, Philippa?"

"Yes, but that doesn't prove anything. She was a workaholic. She was always in early," Philippa pointed out.

"She's one to bear in mind, anyway," Gould said. "The next suspect is Charles Anson, who's been charged with drug pushing, based on DS Cottrell's undercover work. He says Harvey was involved, but we don't know for sure if that was the case. He says Harvey had a meeting with a character called Jack Spendlove the night he died. Spendlove's a man we're all familiar with and he went to school with both Harvey and Ward. Anson was bailed by Spendlove's lawyer – a slimeball shyster called Rothenberg – and went to his offices. He'd already failed to pick Spendlove up in the identity parade, but I'm sure he was leant on. I don't doubt that next time we talk to Anson he will have been persuaded to deny ever seeing Harvey and Spendlove together.

"Anson could have murdered Harvey – either they were both involved in the drugs or the deceased found out about them and threatened to go to the police. That would fit nicely with the facts, as we know them. It's just we need more proof." Gould looked around at his assembled officers. He could tell he had their attention.

"Next, we come to Harvey's family," Gould continued. "First, there's his wife, Kathleen, who inherits the use of the money as long as she lives, but then it passes on to the two children – Cassandra and Jason – when she dies. She has no particular motive as far as we know. She had all the money she needed anyway. She must have known about his mistresses already but she has no real alibi. Her au pair saw the light on in her room when she went to bed, but that doesn't prove anything. She could have gone to London later that night. Perhaps Harvey ditching Margaret for a new model was just a step too far for his wife."

"Have you found any evidence that Kathleen had found another man? That could be a motive," Fox called out.

"None at all, the au pair has seen no sign of one and she would have enjoyed telling us if Kathleen had anyone," Philippa said.

"Cassandra's next," Gould continued. "She worked in her Daddy's company, until she was sacked the day before the murder. That could be a motive. It can't have been much fun being sacked in front of all your colleagues." Gould turned to Philippa. "You thought there was something phoney about her reaction to her father's murder when she came in the next day, didn't you, Philippa?"

"Yes, but she's artificial at the best of times, so it's hard to tell," Philippa said. "But she had no clear explanation for coming into the office when she had been sacked the previous day," she added. "She says she didn't know anything about Anson's drug dealing, even though they were a couple. I saw her walking out on him in a restaurant, so she could have been genuinely shocked when she found out, but I wouldn't accept anything she says or does at face value."

"Jason, Cassandra's twin brother, was at the funeral, but he'd quarrelled with his father years before," Gould continued. "Could he have come back and murdered his father after some sort of argument about money? Jason was working at a rival company and had just beaten Harvey and Ward to a big contract. He says he hadn't spoken to his father for two years, but that's hard to believe. I don't think Jason's the type who wants to make his own way – he'd be lost without his Dad's money. Jason was busted for cannabis use when he was a student, but he's got no convictions since then. He had a row with his mother and sister after the funeral, and as far as we know, he's having to support himself. It'll be quite a shock to him living without his family's money."

"He seems to live above his income, so it'll be interesting to see what happens when his funds run out," Philippa said.

"The au pair is called Tania," Gould continued. "Like everyone else, she hated Harvey. She says he made a pass at her, but she turned him down – that's when he mentioned Samantha. She could be lying but she was very convincing. Another point we've found out is that Tania's here illegally. Maybe she made her way to London and killed Harvey to cover that up or for some grievance or other. Mind you, that seems to be clutching at straws.

"Now we come to what the policeman in Casablanca called the usual suspects." Gould looked around, pleased with his knowledge of films, to find blank expressions on the faces of his young colleagues. "That's Jack Spendlove and Robert Rothenberg. We all know Spendlove's behind half the drugs circulating in London and Rothenberg's in his pocket. They could have had Harvey killed for any number of reasons. He could have been innocent and threatened to expose what was going on. He could have been working for Spendlove and wanted too big a slice of the action. Or he could have been working for another gang and this is a turf war. It certainly looks like a professional hit – one shot through the head – and misleading evidence planted to confuse us."

"Don't we think the murderer was sitting down? That could mean Harvey knew him and invited him in," Philippa asked.

"He could be a stranger who made an appointment to see him. That security lock should have kept uninvited people out anyway. That's what we have to date – lots of suspects but no evidence. In short, we are no further forward than when we started this murder investigation." Gould paused and looked around the assembled detectives. "We have two other murders that might be related – Hugh Marks and Annabel Ward.

"Let's cover Marks next. His was the first murder, which started Philippa's undercover work in the firm in the first place. He was an auditor with a company that deals with lots of companies. It's only a guess that his death related to Harvey and Ward's, but it would be a hell of a coincidence if it wasn't. We've checked the accounts and there's nothing unusual. So, Marks may have heard or seen something unusual in the corridors of Harvey and Ward that made someone want to murder him. I think we'll have to put that case to one side for the time being."

"Shall I go through the Annabel Ward case?" Philippa asked and continued with her prepared speech as Gould nodded. "Annabel Ward was run over in what looks like a hit and run case. No witnesses have come forward to the collision, but someone saw a large black car speeding away shortly afterwards. There's no CCTV on that particular stretch of road. The local police think it's a road accident unless we can prove otherwise.

"Most of the suspects have alibis for the time of Annabel's murder. Ward, Margaret Lane and Cassandra were all in the same meeting. Jason was at work. Spendlove and Rothenburg were both in their offices with witnesses – their own staff, so they could have been bought. The only suspect with a large black car is Spendlove, but we've checked and there are no marks on it. We know Annabel went to see Kathleen and Cassandra, wanting more money for Reg Ward. When we told Kathleen about Annabel's murder, she fainted. She seemed genuinely frightened, more than guilty. According to Tania, Kathleen invited Casandra and Jason for dinner. That was very unusual, and it seems to have been to dis-cuss what to do about Annabel's threats. We interviewed Cassandra the other day. She admits sending Annabel away with a flea in her ear when she visited the Harvey and Ward's offices. Cassandra claims to know nothing about Annabel's death.

"One odd thing is that Ward thinks Annabel must have been to Harvey's office because she mentioned a new paint-ing he'd only had for a week. Our theory at the moment is she tried to blackmail the killer by claiming to know something about the murder. We don't know whether she was bluffing or really did know something.

"Then, Jason Harvey has to be a suspect. He could have killed his father – either to inherit his money or simply because of an argument. He heard that Annabel had visited his mother and claimed to know something suspicious. Suppose he then panicked and ran Annabel over to keep her quiet. He seems to have a strong alibi, but he could have paid someone else to do it That theory all hangs together." Philippa sat down at the end of her presentation.

Gould looked around to the assembled detectives. "Well, ladies and gentlemen, those are the facts as we know them. Does anyone have any ideas on what the hell we do now?"

Chapter 35

The death of Annabel complicated the police investigation, seeming so out of place compared with the other killings. Gould and Philippa read and reread the interviews the police had undertaken, but no new events arose as the autumn months passed by. They were sure that one of the suspects that they had in their sights was the perpetrator, but their alibis could not be broken. One day at the end of November came the moment David Gould had been dreading. He had an appointment with the Commissioner to discuss his progress investigating the murder of Neil Harvey. Philippa accompanied him for support.

Gould turned to her as they climbed into the official car to go to the Commissioner's office in the Guildhall. "I hate to admit defeat, Philippa, but it's necessary sometimes," he said, wistfully. Philippa touched his hand to reassure him, making sure the official driver could not see them.

As they travelled through the clogged streets, she reflected that it was through her friendship with David Gould that she had begun to love the strange anomaly of the City of London. The Guildhall they were driving to was a symbol of its archaic electoral system based on the handful of people who actually lived in the City. She remembered waiting in ceremonial uniform on the Lord Mayor in her early days in the force and wondering what relevance this office had to the present day.

Later, she enjoyed watching the Lord Mayor's parade with people from all over London and began to enjoy having a direct link with historical figures such as Dick Whittington. She began to like the curious contrast between the City's Wren churches and its skyscrapers. Its curious toy-like Docklands Light Railway seemed to her to add to its charms.

As she was involved in these thoughts, the car arrived at the Guildhall and she followed Gould upstairs to the Commissioner's office. As they waited silently in the ante-room, it occurred to her that she had never seen Gould so despondent. Eventually, they were called in. The Commissioner, a tall ascetic man who had spent the early days of his career in the Glasgow force, opened the talk.

"I wanted to have a word, David. I'm worried about the lack of progress. You still haven't solved the murders of Hugh Marks and then Neil Harvey yet, David," the Commissioner began. "There are lots of other cases that need resources. I can't justify keeping detectives on this case that's not going anywhere."

"We have found out a lot, sir, and it has helped having DS Cottrell on the case. She was working undercover in the company at the time of the murder," Gould answered.

"So how near are you to making an arrest?" the Commissioner asked.

"We're investigating three murders here. Annabel Ward's death seems part of the same pattern. I'm sure they're connected in some way, but I don't think the same person killed all of them," Gould said.

"Is there any point in keeping the full number of staff on the enquiry, Gould?"

"To be honest, no, sir. I can't see any new lines of enquiry to follow. But we can't let these murders go unsolved."

"Do you have any viable lines of inquiry?"

"No, sir," Gould replied. "But can I have another month? There's something I'd like to try."

"Very well, a month, but no longer. Then it'll go onto a lower priority. I'll have to take most of the detectives off this case. Do you understand? A year from now, we'll close it down altogether unless anything comes up. We can't keep devoting resources to one case if we're not getting anywhere."

Gould and Philippa stood to attention. "Thank you, sir," he said. He opened his mouth as if he wanted to say more but decided against it and led Philippa out of the room.

****

Half an hour later, Gould and Philippa were in the canteen back in the Snow Hill police station. Gould seemed a broken man as he listlessly stirred his coffee. Philippa knew about some of his successes and felt it would have broken the heart of anyone to see him like this. She reached out and held his hand.

"You heard what the Commissioner said, David," she said. "You can't always get a result under our system." Gould nodded but did not say anything. "Think of all those other cases you were successful on."

"It's very kind of you, Philippa, but you don't have to encourage me. An actor's only as good as his last performance. When you're a detective, you're only as good as your last case." Gould looked at Philippa. She could see the same thought had occurred to both of them. "We've been working too hard on this case. Shall we take an afternoon off? You could come round to my flat."

Philippa nodded without saying anything. Half an hour later they were in bed together. Just as he had raised Philippa's spirits when she was feeling faint back at the autopsy room, she felt it was her turn to give him support. As they lay side by side after making love, she felt that they were now a couple and that nothing could separate them. She could not predict the dramatic future course of the Harvey murder case.

Chapter 36

Charles Anson's case came up at the City Crown Court two months later. His solicitor had made sure Anson wore his Armani suit again and he resembled the suave executive he had once been. Philippa was called to give evidence for the prosecution. Gould was in the well of the court to offer moral support when she took the stand. She gave a brief account of how she had seen Anson trading in cocaine. Then Anson's expensive barrister rose to his feet.

"Were you in uniform when you were observing my client, Detective Sergeant Cottrell?" the barrister asked, in a deceptively friendly voice.

"No, sir. I was undercover in plain clothes," Philippa replied. Her mind was trying to anticipate the barrister's supplementary.

"Is it fair to describe you as an attractive young woman, Detective Sergeant?"

"I wouldn't know, sir," Philippa replied. Some spectators in the public gallery giggled as the judge glared at them.

"Well, take it from me that you are." The barrister looked at the men on the jury to show he was on their side. "When you were dressed in attractive clothes, do you think it was possible my client was trying to impress you?"

"I don't think so, sir," Philippa replied. She felt herself becoming annoyed but recalled everything her training had taught her to keep calm under defence cross-examination.

The barrister waited a precisely timed few moments for some doubt to be raised in the jury's minds. "Thank you,

Detective Sergeant, that will be all," he said, smiling patronisingly at Philippa.

The prosecuting barrister rose to his feet. "While you were interviewing the accused, Detective Sergeant, was he helpful to the police at all?" he asked.

"Well," Philippa replied, "he said his employer – a Mr Harvey – had told him to deal in the drugs."

"Did you interview this Mr Harvey at all?"

"We were not able to do so, sir. He was murdered shortly afterwards." Philippa could not resist a smile of triumph at Anson's barrister.

"How soon was this after you saw the accused trafficking in drugs?"

"The next day, sir."

"And did the accused supply any helpful information about the murder?" the barrister asked.

"No, sir, he said he was in the office and saw a man arrive but wasn't able to identify a suspect we had in an identity parade we arranged."

"He said he was in the office on the evening of the murder," the prosecuting barrister repeated for the benefit of the jury. "Thank you, Detective Sergeant, that will be all." Philippa walked out of the witness box, conscious of the eyes of all the male spectators. She sat next to Gould in the well of the court. He gave her hand an encouraging touch.

During the lunch interval, the two sat in the court canteen sipping coffee. "That barrister made me sound like some sort of tart, as if I was trying to seduce Anson," she complained, under her voice, to avoid being overheard.

"Don't worry," Gould replied. "Once the defence starts insulting the police, it means they know they've lost. I could tell the jury were on our side, when you mentioned the murder. Let's treat ourselves to somewhere special tonight if we win." Philippa nodded agreement.

The trial was over quickly, in the afternoon. Philippa was the only prosecution witness. Anson called his old headmaster and an elderly uncle as character references but it was obvious he had no reasonable defence. In his summing up, the judge told the jury only to consider the charge on the warrant sheet. In particular, he warned them not to take any account of the murder for which Anson had not been charged. Nevertheless, the jury only took a few minutes to record a verdict of guilty. Taking the defendant's previous drugs-related convictions into account, the judge said he was minded to sentence him for a lengthy imprisonment, subject to any mitigating case made by the defence.

After eating out at an expensive restaurant near Gould's Barbican flat that night, Gould turned to Philippa. "Why don't you move into my flat?" he asked. "It's silly living apart like this. It's too big for just me, now my wife's moved out."

"What if Audrey suddenly came back?" Philippa asked in return, moving her hand away.

"No, she's not coming back," Gould replied. "I got a letter from her solicitor today. She wants a divorce."

"I'm sorry … I suppose," Philippa said, unsure what to say.

"Don't be," Gould said, reaching out to hold her hand. "It's not your fault. Audrey and I weren't talking long before you came on the scene."

"We'll give it a try and see how it works out," Philippa replied. "But I'll still keep my own flat as well."

Gould stood up. "Let's pay the bill and go home," he said.

Chapter 37

One morning three weeks later, in Gould's flat, Philippa was pouring them both coffee during breakfast. The kitchen was modern, but without character as Philippa did not feel sufficiently at home to impose her own personality on it. Gould and Philippa were living together, apparently happily, though Gould was never sure if Philippa was happy with the uncertain state of his divorce. He often told himself he ought to tidy things up, but the time never seemed quite right. He was always planning to look for somewhere to live without any old associations, but, in the meantime, this flat was convenient, as was his relationship with Philippa.

"We've got to jumpstart the Harvey case, Philippa," Gould said. "I'm not going to have a failure like that on my record. We only have a week before the Commissioner takes most of our staff away."

"Don't feel badly, David, everyone knows you can't solve every case. Think of the other cases you've solved."

"I'm not interested in failure," Gould said, slamming his cup down. "Isn't that what Harvey once said to you? I'm going to stir things up a bit. Phone Rothenberg to come and see me, will you? He can pass a message on to Spendlove for me."

"What have you got planned?" Philippa asked. "We don't have any new evidence."

"Just trust me," Gould replied. "I'm going to make Rothenberg squirm. My job is to put criminals like Spendlove behind bars. Some rules are made to be broken." Gould's tone did not encourage Philippa to ask further questions.

"Be careful, won't you, David." She looked worried as they left the flat to go to work.

****

That afternoon, Rothenberg sat with his briefcase in front of him in Gould's office. He waited with perfect calm to hear what Gould had to say to him.

"I was surprised to receive your summons, Chief Inspector," said Rothenberg. "I assume this has some connection with the Harvey murder earlier this year. I believe I made it clear that my client had never heard of the late Mr Harvey until you visited him and is not able to assist in your enquiries."

"Except when they were at school together."

"Childhood days are hardly relevant to our discussion, are they, Chief Inspector?"

"We'll see. You denied that Mr Spendlove knew Neil Harvey," Gould replied. "But now we have a new witness who saw Mr Spendlove talking to Mr Harvey not long before the murder. I would strongly suggest that it would be in your client's interests to come in and make a fuller statement."

"Thank you for your free advice, Chief Inspector," Rothenberg said, picking up his briefcase. "Now, unless this new witness has a name, it seems unlikely that there is any point in continuing this conversation…"

"No, that will be all." Gould stood up. "Don't forget to charge your client for your valuable time spent travelling from Mayfair to the City, will you, Mr Rothenberg. I expect you'll charge for several hours' travel expenses," he added, with unconcealed sarcasm.

Gould escorted Rothenberg down to the Snow Hill reception. As they passed the front desk, the uniformed sergeant called to Gould, "Chief Inspector, that interview with Charles Anson has been typed up." Gould looked angry and embarrassed. "Not now, I'm busy," he snapped.

Philippa could tell Rothenberg had heard the sergeant's remark though he left without comment. As they watched the lawyer leave, Philippa turned to Gould. "I'm sure Rothenberg heard that message," she said. "Have we really heard from Anson?"

"I told the desk sergeant not to tell me anything while Rothenberg was here, but," he added, with a satisfied smile, "you can't get the staff these days, can you?" Philippa could not tell what Gould was thinking and was about to speak when he interrupted. "Are you free to interview the rest of the suspects, Philippa?" he asked. "Let's rattle a few cages."

****

And so, a few months after her first encounter with Harvey and Ward's, Philippa was standing outside the same City skyscraper where she had started her undercover assignment. The corridors seemed virtually unchanged as she was ushered into the offices of the new managing director. The surname on the door was the same, but everything else had changed as Cassandra Harvey greeted her in her father's old redecorated office. Her long elegant legs stretched out below her tailored mini-skirted suit.

"What a pleasant surprise to see you again, Philippa." Cassandra stretched out her hand, her expression immediately belying her words. As always, her manner reminded Philippa of a queen graciously receiving one of her subjects.

"Hello, Cassandra, thank you for seeing me," Philippa said, sitting opposite her. "The reason I am here is to keep open the file on the death of your father."

"Yes, it was a great loss," Cassandra said, in a voice devoid of expression. "I am only just starting to get over it." She waited politely for Philippa to ask her next question.

"Don't you feel awkward working in the room where your father was murdered?" Philippa asked, looking around. She remembered the day earlier in the year when Margaret Lane stopped her in the hall to tell her about Harvey's murder.

"No, it's not awkward really," Cassandra replied. "I try to put it into the back of my mind. I'm always so busy running the company these days, I don't get a chance to become depressed." She looked around at the trappings of power around her with evident satisfaction.

"And the decorations are very different too," Philippa said. This was an understatement – all trace of Neil Harvey's leather surroundings had disappeared, and it was now decorated like a picture in a Laura Ashley catalogue. Philippa was sure most male visitors would find the feminine atmosphere overpowering. Knowing Cassandra, Philippa imagined the intention was to make them feel ill at ease. Cassandra was evidently happy to use any means to enforce her authority.

"Could you tell me if you have had any more thoughts on who could have murdered your father?" Philippa asked, anxious to return to the purpose of her visit.

"No, not really," Cassandra said, after a few moments' thought. "It might have been someone involved in drugs – that's all I can think of. I read all about Charles's activities at the trial, but we haven't had any more trouble since he left. I would look in that direction if I were you."

"Are you still in touch with Anson?"

"No, why should I be?" Cassandra asked, in an offended tone. Philippa said nothing. "Oh, I know I might have been keen on him once," Cassandra continued "but now I know all about him, I'd like to kill him."

"Can you tell me what has happened to the other people who were working here a year ago?" Philippa asked.

"Well, you probably know more about Charles Anson than I do," Cassandra began. "I believe he's still in prison somewhere. Then there's Reg Ward – he still works in the building. I sacked Margaret Lane. I can give you her home phone number – I don't think she's got another job yet," Cassandra added with obvious satisfaction.

"How about your mother?"

"Oh, she still lives in the same house, as always," Cassandra said. "She owns all of Daddy's shares, but she's just a sleeping partner. I do all the work nowadays."

"Does she have the same au pair?" Philippa asked. She had Tania's new address in Prague but decided to feign ignorance.

"No, the last girl went home. She wasn't loyal enough for us. Mum has a new one but I can't remember her name."

"Was your father's life insured at all?"

"Oh, yes, I inherited that money." Cassandra smiled with satisfaction. "It was quite useful – I'm financially independent now."

"What's happened to your brother?"

"His main hobby is still chatting up birds, as far as I know," Cassandra replied, her lips curling with distaste "but we haven't spoken for a while, so I can't tell you very much."

"So, there's nothing you would like to add to the statement you made at the time of the murder?" Philippa prompted.

"No, nothing," replied Cassandra, after some thought.

"Thank you, Cassandra," Philippa said with exaggerated politeness, trying to hide her dislike of Harvey's daughter. "I won't bother you anymore. I would like to interview all the people I saw last year. I'll start with Reg Ward, as he is here."

"Are you sure that's necessary?" Cassandra asked, in a startled tone. "I don't think any of them will know any more than they did last year."

"Murder enquiries are never closed, Cassandra. We owe it to the families of the victims to keep investigating," Philippa replied, standing up. "I'll find my own way to Reg's office, thank you." She left Cassandra staring at her, open-mouthed. For once Philippa felt she had the better of one of their encounters.

It did not take Philippa long to find the office of the man she had once pretended to work for. She knocked on the door and went in. She noticed Ward was in a smaller office and no longer had his own secretary – she wondered if Cassandra's hand was behind this.

"Hello, Reg," Philippa said, as she went in. Ward stood up, initially puzzled and then genuinely pleased as he recognised her. He walked over to the door and ushered her in.

"Philippa, what are you doing here?" he asked. "Come in, take a seat. It's great to see you again. You're looking good."

"I'm afraid I'm here on police business, Reg," she said, sitting opposite him. "I've just been to see Cassandra. Chief Inspector Gould and I are looking into Neil Harvey's death again."

"Why now?" Reg asked, his manner becoming more serious. "Has something come up?"

"No, there's nothing specific to tell you," Philippa replied. "It's three months since he died, and it's always good to check if people remember anything new." Ward nodded, with what seemed no more than polite interest. "Do you have anything to add to your earlier statement?"

"No, nothing new. I've thought about it a lot since – especially since Annabel was killed, but there's nothing new. Nothing at all."

"Can you tell me what's happened in the last year here?"

"Well, as you've seen, Cassandra has taken over," Ward said. "It's quite a change. I used to think Neil Harvey was overbearing, but he was nothing compared to his daughter."

"Her mother was left everything in the will," Philippa said. "But Cassandra was left the insurance money, I understand."

"Yes, that's right." Ward said. "Her mother doesn't take much interest in the company now. She leaves it all to Cassandra."

"And how's the company doing now?"

"Well, there was some loss of business after the murder. I suppose customers were worried about any scandal. But one sight of Cassandra in her short skirt and most of the male punters came back to us."

"And you're still in the same position in the company?"

"Yes, still junior partner," Ward replied. "It's disappointing, of course, and I'd really like to get out and start up somewhere else. But as it's a partnership, the only person I could sell to would be Cassandra, but she would only offer me a pittance. She's got me over a barrel, really."

"Cassandra said you hadn't had any more instances of drug dealing since Anson was arrested?" Philippa prompted.

"No," Ward said. "I really feel that was a one-off case. We've been extra careful when taking on new people since then."

"Do you think Harvey was involved in drugs at all?"

"No, as I told you last year, I'm sure Harvey would never have taken part in anything like that."

"I wonder if you're right," Philippa said more to herself than to Ward. "Has Jack Spendlove been in touch since we last spoke?" she asked. "He might have tried to take over the company with Harvey out of the way."

"No, I've not heard from Spendlove since you sent me to talk to him. If I never see him again, I'll be happy."

Philippa stood up. "Thank you, Reg, for seeing me. I won't take any more of your time."

"What shall I do if I remember anything else?"

"Phone me at the station, Reg. You know the number. I must be going now."

Ward stood up to see Philippa to the door. "It's been very nice seeing you again, Philippa. I wondered if we could have a meal some time," he asked, with what he hoped was a winning smile. He waited expectantly for Philippa's response.

"Reg," Philippa replied in as gentle a fashion as she could. "I am a police officer on an investigation. Besides which I am fully accounted for at present." Ward's face fell, and on an impulse, Philippa leant forward and kissed him on his cheek. "Thank you, anyway," she said, as she turned to leave. She supposed she ought to be offended that Ward had asked her for a date at such an inappropriate time but she could not be. She told herself that all women have a slight fondness for men who have fallen for them, no matter how unsuitable they are. She hummed happily to herself as she left the travel agency's office to go back to the Barbican flat she shared with David Gould.

****

Jason Harvey stood outside his flat and looked forlornly at the seven-year-old Fiesta outside his door. The Lotus that he used to drive was now a distant memory, along with the blonds he used to go to clubs with. Still, he told himself, he had a day off work and fancied going somewhere. In the past, his favourite hobby was driving along Knightsbridge and through the West End. With the roof of his convertible down, there was nothing he used to like more than to watch the admiring glances of the women and the jealous looks from the men who were walking along the road.

This enjoyable pastime was now beyond his means, and he reflected that he would have to economise, but he was determined still to enjoy himself. An hour later, he was walking out of Knightsbridge underground station, enjoying the ambience of the fashion-conscious crowds around him. He looked wistfully at the prices of the men's jackets in the shop windows and realised that the only clothes he could afford now were from a charity shop.

However, he was sure his limited means could run to a coffee and he felt he knew the right spot. The coffee shop on the top floor of Harvey Nichols was a social magnet for beautiful young women with rich fathers and Jason took the lift there with a feeling of cheerful anticipation. Buying a cappuccino from the bar, he found a table on his own. A year ago, he had enough money and charm to have had at least a chance of picking up one of the girls with model looks who were taking a break from shopping. He tried to make eye contact with them, but the way in which they looked straight through him showed how far his stock had fallen in the past year.

The café, which was only half full, was laid out with tables for four around the edge. Jason was making an imaginary choice between two young women, who looked like models, chatting at the opposite corner. Suddenly, a tall blond man appeared before him. Jason was trying to place his face when the man spoke.

"Mr Harvey, could I have a word with you?" he said.

"Chief Inspector Gould, isn't it?" Jason replied after a baffled pause. "How did you find me here?"

"I make it my business to know where you are at any time. I hope you don't mind if I join you." Gould sat down next to Jason without waiting for permission and looked around at the plush surroundings. "This makes a pleasant change from my police station, doesn't it?"

"What can I do for you, Chief Inspector? I told you all I can three months ago. You should be finding my father's murderer – not drinking coffee in Harvey Nichols."

"You'll be pleased to know I'm continuing to investigate your father's death. Have you anything new to tell me?"

"No, I don't think so," Jason replied in a careful tone.

"What's happened to the Lotus, Mr Harvey? It's not like you to take the tube."

"Have you been following me? The tube's more convenient – I still have the Lotus, thank you," Jason said.

"The police computer says you sold it several months ago. You have a seven-year-old Ford now," Gould replied in a flat voice.

"Oh, very well, you obviously know already," Jason replied in a sulky voice. "The finance company took the Lotus back – the repayments were becoming too expensive."

"Why's that?" Gould asked in an unsympathetic tone. "Isn't your family giving you any money?"

"No, we had a bit of a row," Jason replied in a tired voice. "Mum asked Cassandra to run the company for her and froze me out of things."

"Just after the funeral, wasn't it, Mr Harvey?"

"How do you know that?" Jason asked suspiciously.

"Never mind how I know, but I bet it must cramp your style."

Jason nodded wistfully at the group of attractive young women he had been ogling. "A year ago I would have invited one of them out in my Lotus, and they'd have accepted. Now I'm reduced to window shopping." Jason looked at Gould curiously. "Still, you haven't come to listen to my troubles."

"No, Mr Harvey, I've got enough worries of my own. Like trying to find your father's killer. Some people might say there's a poetic justice in your being poor now. Perhaps murdering your father didn't pay as well as you expected."

Jason stared at Gould. "I didn't kill my father. What evidence do you think you have against me?"

"Motive, means, opportunity. It all fits. You have no alibi. You could have called round to see your father that night. When he invited you in for a drink, you either had an argument then killed him or murdered him straightaway. It all sounds very convincing to me," Gould said, with his eyes on Jason's face.

"But I didn't do it," Jason protested, looking around vainly for help.

"Maybe not, but I've seen people go to prison for life on weaker cases. Do you want to go to prison, and only be freed on probation when you're old and grey? Those girls won't even let you look at them. You'll probably have forgotten how to do it then, anyway." Gould chuckled happily.

"You're threatening me. You could lose your job over this."

"Oh, don't worry," Gould said, with what he hoped was an annoying smile. "This interview isn't being recorded. That's why I said it makes such a nice change from the station. Of course, if you want to become a miscarriage of justice… What will they call you – the Knightsbridge One? Do you think anyone will march to get you out of prison?"

"You bastard."

"Of course, it might be easier all round if you tell me who the real murderer is. If it's who I think it is, telling them about our conversation might just bring them round to make a confession. Think about it – you know where you can find me." Gould finished his coffee and stood up. "Enjoy your window shopping," he added, nodding at the young women on the other tables, before he walked out of the coffee bar.

For a few minutes, Jason looked thoughtfully after Gould. He felt in his pocket to find his mobile phone then remembered that he had been forced to get rid of it, as he could no longer afford the charges. He noticed a pay phone in the far corner of the room, and ignoring the pretty waitress, went over to put money in the slot. He looked around to make sure Gould had not returned and no one else could overhear him. "We've got to talk. I've had Gould hounding me. I'm sure he knows something," Jason spoke softly but intently into the receiver. "I'm not going down for something I've not done. You've got to come clean."

****

At Wormwood Scrubs that evening, Charles Anson was sitting on the bed in his cell awaiting the final lock-up of the night. He looked a pale reflection of the debonair executive he had once been, as he sat dressed in his prison fatigues reading a torn paperback he had managed to borrow from the prison library. He was one of the best-behaved inmates in the prison and had been given a comfortable librarian's job as a reward. His cell was on one of the wings that the guards rarely patrolled.

"Hello, Charles." Anson looked up as heard his name called. A fellow convict stood in front of him.

"Who the hell are you?" Anson asked, before recognition dawned. "My God, you're Miller, aren't you? I haven't seen you since that day in Macdonald's. What do you want?"

"I'm glad you remember me, but I have bad news for you. We have it on the best authority that you've been threatening to talk to Chief Inspector Gould. Mr Spendlove is displeased with you."

Anson began to look very scared and looked vainly around for help. "I'd never talk to the police. Someone's trying to get me into trouble. Tell Spendlove it's a put-up job."

"It was the police that told us."

"I knew it. Can't you see they're lying? They want us to fight among ourselves," Anson shouted, as he tried to escape.

Miller simply smiled, then pulled out a home-made dagger from his sleeve. Anson screamed as Miller stabbed him through the chest. Anson fell lifeless to the floor with his mouth still wide open. Miller looked down at the dead man. He was as proud of his handiwork as any professional craftsman. The wound was straight through the heart and it was obvious Anson had died immediately. Miller lifted Anson's body up onto the bed and carefully covered it with the blanket so it looked as if the dead man were merely sleeping. Miller put the dagger back into his pocket, then, opening the cell to check no one was watching him, walked casually back to his own cell arriving just before lock-up. As Miller washed his dagger in his toilet, Anson's lifeblood slowly seeped through the prison mattress onto the concrete floor below.

****

Before dawn the next morning, Miller was let out of his cell by a guard. Miller had a job in the prison kitchen and was one of those responsible for cooking the breakfasts each morning. Walking into the kitchen, he nodded respectfully to the supervising guard, and started to spread margarine onto slices of toast until he had finished the large pile in front of him. He explained to the guard that he needed some more bread from the delivery van that had just arrived at the prison. This was the transport that Spendlove had arranged for him. Walking through to the yard, he gave a sign to the driver and, checking no one was looking, climbed into the back of the van. The vehicle moved slowly away with Miller still inside.

****

The following morning, Gould waited in the hall of Kathleen Harvey's house. The walls were now painted a feminine pink, which Gould felt was Kathleen's bid to change the house to her own taste. A new au pair had ushered him in. She seemed much plainer than Tania, and Gould imagined Harvey would not have chosen her. Gould looked around to see if there were any pictures of Neil Harvey, but there were none. It was as if Kathleen wanted to eliminate any trace of her late husband.

"Chief Inspector Gould," Kathleen's voice came from behind him. Her voice startled him, as it seemed much weaker than before. "This is a surprise. Do you have some news for me?" she asked.

"No, Mrs Harvey, but I'm continuing to investigate your husband's death." Gould wondered if he saw relief or fear in Kathleen's face. "I'm seeing all the witnesses one more time. I'm sure you'll want us to bring whoever killed your husband to justice." Gould kept his eyes fixed on Kathleen's face, but she displayed no reaction.

"Yes, of course, come in, Chief Inspector, have a seat. Can I get you a drink?" Kathleen resumed her practiced role as a hostess as she ushered him into the sitting room.

"No, thank you," Gould replied when he was seated in a fragile-looking armchair. "Have you had any more thoughts on who might have killed your husband, Mrs Harvey?"

"No, not really. I still think it could have been some intruder who persuaded Neil to let him in. Or it could be some woman he was seeing. I wouldn't be surprised if it was that Lane woman. Perhaps she knew he'd had enough of her and she was jealous."

"What evidence do you have against Margaret Lane, Mrs Harvey?"

"None at all, I suppose," Kathleen gave a grudging reply.

"And how do you know your husband had had enough of her? You said you didn't know he was having an affair at all," Gould asked, leaning forward.

Kathleen looked frightened at his manner. "You asked for my suggestions, Chief Inspector, I don't see why I should be browbeaten in my own house."

"It's important to obtain all the facts in this inquiry, Mrs Harvey. I feel I'm close to making an arrest, but we need some more evidence. Has a man named Jack Spendlove been in touch with you at all?"

Kathleen looked blank. "No, I've never heard of such a person."

"And how about any girlfriends your husband may have had? He mentioned the name Samantha several times."

"I always tried to turn a blind eye to my husband's affairs. Men with money are so susceptible. I learnt to accept other women after a while. But in answer to your question, none of them have contacted me since the murder. I wouldn't expect them to." Tears came to Kathleen's eyes. "Really, Chief Inspector, I am sure all this has nothing to do with Neil's murder. You seem to take some delight in humiliating me. I know you have a job to do, but I must ask you to leave."

"How about the other case we're investigating. Have you any more ideas on who could have killed Annabel Ward? We're quite convinced it wasn't a normal hit and run."

Kathleen started to cry. "For God's sake, go, Chief Inspector."

Gould stood up promptly. "I'll be sure to let you know when we are close to making an arrest, Mrs Harvey." He stood up and left the sobbing woman behind him.

****

While Gould was returning from Haslemere, Philippa was standing outside a semi-detached house in Ruislip, idly reflecting on the contrast between her present surroundings and the City. She rang the doorbell of the house and waited patiently for a reply. After a minute or so, she saw a shape behind the stained glass in the door and Margaret Lane opened the door. Philippa instinctively gasped with horror when she saw her. Margaret was a pale reflection of the efficient businesswoman she had once been. She seemed haggard, as if she had aged several years in the three months since the murder.

"Hello, Margaret," Philippa said as brightly as she could when she had recovered from her shock. "How nice to see you again."

"Philippa," Margaret replied, surprised. "Come in." Margaret led Philippa into the sitting room. A very old lady was sitting in one of the armchairs, but she remained asleep. "Don't mind about Mummy, she's very deaf. I have to look after her now, but she won't bother us," Margaret said. "Take a seat."

Philippa waited in an armchair, while Margaret returned with a tray with two teacups. She poured a cup for Philippa and passed her some small cakes.

"Well, Philippa," Margaret said, with forced brightness. "What have you been up to since last year?"

"I've been working on other cases since we put the Harvey investigation on hold. But David has asked me to re-interview the witnesses to see if I can find anything new."

"David?"

"Chief Inspector Gould," Philippa clarified, blushing slightly.

"Oh, well, what can I tell you?"

"Do you still have any connection with Harvey and Ward, Margaret?"

"No," Margaret replied. "When Cassandra Harvey took over, she sacked me. I moved back home to look after my mother but I haven't found another job yet. Neither Mrs Harvey nor Cassandra will give me much of a reference. I suppose sleeping with Neil wasn't such a good career move after all." Her eyes filled with tears. Philippa found it painful to see the superior Miss Lane she knew before reduced to this state.

"Do you have any more ideas about who could have killed Neil Harvey?" Philippa asked, when Margaret had dried her eyes.

"Not really. I think your Chief Inspector Gould suspected me, but I didn't do it. I know I had a good motive from the way Neil treated me, but I couldn't kill anyone. Please try to find the murderer. Whoever it was has destroyed my whole life. All the neighbours here treat me as if I'm some sort of criminal."

"Can you remember anything more about the day of the murder?" Philippa asked.

Margaret seemed about to speak when the phone in the kitchen rang. She stood up apparently grateful for the interruption.

"Yes," Margaret said into the phone. "Hello, how are you … How did you know she was here? … Yes, I'll pass you over." She passed the receiver. "It's Chief Inspector Gould."

"Hello," Philippa said, picking up the phone. "It's me." She could feel Margaret looking puzzled, as her tone became warmer. "Oh, no … Very well I'll pick you up on the way there." Philippa put the phone down and turned to Margaret. "I'll have to leave you now. We've just heard some important news."

Philippa picked Gould up as she drove through London. While they were stuck in the rush hour traffic, Gould told her what he knew.

"They were opening the cells at seven o'clock this morning, when one of the guards noticed Anson didn't move," he said. "When the guard investigated a bit more he saw blood and realised Anson had been stabbed."

"Was he dead when he was found?"

"Yes, they think he'd been dead for several hours."

"Do you think Spendlove's behind this?" Philippa asked.

"He must be," Gould replied. "He's finally made his mistake and we can nail him for this, but we have to be careful. Spendlove's like a cornered rat now and that's when animals are the most dangerous." Gould said no more as Philippa drove through West London towards Wormwood Scrubs.

****

When Gould and Philippa entered the dark surrounds of the prison, they were escorted through long corridors to the Governor's Office. The Governor turned out to be close to retirement and almost as grey and gloomy as his prison. He shook hands with his two visitors, while two uniformed guards stood in the background.

"We called you because you were Anson's arresting officer," the governor said.

"Thank you for contacting me," Gould said. "Tell me what happened. Who was it who found him?"

A middle-aged guard came forward. "I called everyone out of their cells for breakfast, sir. After a while I noticed that

Anson didn't move. I shook him and noticed there was a lot of blood on the floor and he was obviously dead," the guard said.

"We had a roll call this morning and an inmate called Miller is missing – Nicholas Miller. He requested a transfer here a few months ago. It's unusual for anyone to choose the Scrubs. We're not yet sure how he escaped," the governor added.

"I know Miller. He was involved in the same gang as Anson. He tried to put the frighteners on DS Cottrell here. I'll bet he arranged the transfer here so he could keep an eye on Anson. Do the other prisoners know about the murder?" Gould asked.

"We haven't told them, but they must know something's up – they'll have seen the doctor and the ambulance arrive. They've been talking about nothing else all morning. You can guess what the rumour mill's like in here," the guard replied.

"Very well. I want to give whoever's behind this a shock. Tell the other prisoners that Anson was attacked but he's alive and recovering in hospital. They'll have seen the ambulance leave, so it could have taken Anson for surgery for all they know." The governor stared at him. "Is there any trouble with that?"

"No, sir. But what's the point? Won't whoever did it know Anson's dead?"

"If it was Miller who killed Anson, he did this on the orders of someone important. Miller's a professional hitman and he will be looking for payment. The man who's behind this will want proof Anson's dead before handing over any money. It is important that the rumour gets back to him that Anson's still alive. It might panic him into making another mistake. Is that clear?" Gould asked, turning to the governor.

"Yes, certainly, Chief Inspector. I'll pass that order on to all my staff. They'll make sure the inmates think Anson's just been taken to hospital. It'll give them something new to gossip about."

****

"Where to now, David?" Philippa asked as she drove out of the prison gates. "Back to the station?"

"No, I want to pass on the news to one of our suspects," he said. "Let's make a return visit to Spendlove Associates in Mayfair." Their journey continued in silence.

Within an hour, they were back in Jack Spendlove's luxurious office close to Park Lane. The same leggy receptionist greeted them. Her charm turned cold when she saw Gould's warrant card, but she ushered them into Spendlove's office quickly enough. Spendlove walked toward them with his arm outstretched – his politeness as false as it had been when they last saw him a year before.

"I have some bad news for you, Mr Spendlove," Gould said. "I believe you know Charles Anson is serving a sentence for drug dealing. I'm afraid he was attacked in his cell this morning. We are sure someone outside ordered the attack and we're anxious to find out who was responsible."

"Indeed, Chief Inspector?" replied Spendlove, with a polite smile. "Why have you told me this? As I told you last year, I know nothing of this Charles Anson."

"Then you won't be interested in the news that he is in hospital. He hasn't long to live. He realises he has nothing to lose, and he is prepared to make a statement setting out what he knows about the Harvey murder last year." Gould kept his eyes on Spendlove's face.

"That is good news for the police," replied Spendlove, in his customary suave fashion. "No doubt this will allow you to make an arrest." His words denied any interest in the affair, but to Philippa his eyes portrayed sheer panic.

"I hope so," Gould replied, keeping his eyes on Spendlove's face. "But there is little time to lose."

"Then I won't keep you, Chief Inspector," Spendlove replied. "You must be very busy."

"Don't worry, I'm just going." Gould turned to go and stopped as he came to the door. "Give my regards to Mr Rothenberg."

"I will, Chief Inspector," Spendlove replied. "Goodbye, Sergeant," he said to Philippa.

As they returned to the car, Gould turned to Philippa. "What do you think of Spendlove's reaction when we told him Anson was still alive?" Gould asked.

"He was rattled."

"That's what I think too. If we're right, he may be about to fall into a trap."

"What trap?"

"I'll show you. Park round the corner. I'll think you'll find this very interesting." Gould replied. When Philippa had parked, he got out and walked over to a telephone engineer's van. He opened the rear door and when Philippa followed him in, she was startled to see several of her colleagues inside listening to earphones. A pale youth she did not recognise was tapping into a computer in the corner.

"This is my little surprise, Philippa," Gould said, smiling at her startled reaction. "With any luck, this is the start of what they call in chess, the end-game." He indicated the youth. "This is Glyn Jones from South Wales. He makes a business of hacking into City businesses. We agreed to overlook a few technical offences in return for him helping us." He turned to an older man wearing earphones. "Turn it up will you, Bill?"

The man turned a few knobs and a phone line echoed in the van. Through the electronic crackle, Philippa could recognise Spendlove's voice. The first call she heard was to an unspecified subordinate. "I told you to kill Anson," Spendlove said. "Gould's just been round telling me he's still alive. I don't pay for shoddy work." She could hear Spendlove putting the phone down angrily, before the subordinate could speak.

Gould turned to Philippa. "We think he was talking to Miller – the man who put the frighteners on you and escaped just after Anson's murder. The call was too short to get a reading on the number he was phoning, but all the police forces in the country are looking for him now. He won't get far."

Spendlove dialled again. "Come here at once. I have some bad news … Yes, at once, there's been a development," he said. "Don't argue. You're in it deeper than any of us." They could hear Spendlove slamming the phone down.

"Who was he talking to there?" Philippa asked. "The voice sounded female, but it was muffled."

"That was Harvey's murderer," Gould said, looking at the list of phone number he held for all the main suspects in the case. "We'll just wait until she arrives, then we should be able to collar the whole gang at once."

****

Around two hours later, Gould and Philippa, accompanied by two uniformed constables, walked for the third time in the Harvey enquiry into Spendlove's plush office.

"I would like to speak to Mr Spendlove again," Gould said to the receptionist.

"I'm afraid that's impossible," the girl replied, with a sneer. "He has just left the office. About ten seconds ago, I think it was."

Gould took out a search warrant. "I should have said I demand to see him. I will let myself in." He marched past the receptionist and entered Spendlove's office without knocking. Two people seated in easy chairs in Spendlove's office jumped up.

"What do you mean by this?" Rothenberg shouted. "You're not allowed to barge into Mr Spendlove's office like this. Samantha shouldn't have let you in."

Gould and Philippa exchanged glances. "Samantha? That receptionist is called Samantha?" Gould asked.

"What of it? What do you want? I warn you, Chief Inspector, I am here to protect my client's interests," Rothenberg snarled.

"Robert Rothenberg, you are under arrest for tampering with the course of justice." The overweight solicitor looked at Gould with contempt.

"You think you've won, don't you, you and your girlfriend?" Rothenberg spat out the words. He smiled as he saw the look of concern on Philippa's face. "Yes, I know you spent the night together after Miller frightened you in your flat."

"You can't do anything now, Mr Rothenberg, you won't be spending much more time in Mayfair, more like Wormwood Scrubs, if you're lucky that is. Perhaps Spendlove will decide to have you killed, like Anson," Gould replied. "I can't see you working as a solicitor any longer. We should be able to pin conspiracy to murder on you, without much trouble."

"I'll bet you were scared, weren't you, little girl," Rothenberg continued, ignoring Gould and looking at Philippa. "Why do you think Miller let you see him on his last visit to your flat? We wanted him in the Scrubs just to keep an eye on Anson. And it was Spendlove who had Ward's wife run over. You should be grateful – I think Reg was anyway, gave him a clear run."

By this time, Rothenberg had been carried out of the room by two uniformed constables and his shouted ravings could be heard no more. Gould noticed Philippa shivering. "How did that man know so much about me? And why does he hate me so much?" she asked.

"Don't worry," Gould said putting his arm around her while no one could see them. "He's scum. Being hated by him shows you're doing your job."

Chief Inspector Gould returned to Spendlove's office and turned to the middle-aged woman crying to herself. "Kathleen Harvey, you are under arrest for the murder of Neil Harvey. You are not obliged to say anything but it may harm your defence if you fail to reveal evidence on which you subsequently rely on in court," Gould said.

Kathleen Harvey was crying too much to make any response and an officer took the sobbing woman outside to a police car. Gould and Philippa went outside to the receptionist. "Where the hell's Spendlove?" Gould demanded.

"I don't know what you mean," the girl simpered.

"I am investigating the murder of a Mr Neil Harvey," Gould said. "Now unless you want to be charged with conspiracy, I suggest you tell me where Spendlove is."

"I don't know what you mean," repeated the girl, in an insolent fashion.

"Before he died, Harvey was seeing a girl called Samantha," Gould went on, fixing his eyes on the receptionist. "I would be very interested in tracing this woman, who may be withholding information from my inquiry." The girl started to look scared. "I would be very interested to know how a respectable businessman like Mr Harvey came to be involved in drug-dealing. Was it a honey-pot operation, Samantha? Did Spendlove send you to seduce Harvey and get him involved? What did you offer him, Samantha? Did you promise him money or something he couldn't resist?" Samantha glared sullenly back at Gould. "You gave him sex, didn't you, Samantha?" Gould by this time had raised his voice and was leaning closer and closer to Samantha. Philippa put her hand on his shoulder to calm him down. "How close am I getting, Samantha?"

"You're right, that's what I do," Samantha sneered. "Mr Spendlove keeps me supplied with drugs and in return I'm his personal assistant. He reserves me for his favoured friends. Spendlove met Harvey at some social do – he said they were at school together. I was ordered to recruit him into the organisation. Spendlove thought Harvey's contacts in the travel trade would be useful. I am good at attracting middle-aged man. He told me I gave him the best sex he ever had. At least he died happy," Samantha laughed. "I could offer you the same, Chief Inspector. How would you like that?"

Philippa intervened, sensing that Gould was close to hitting Samantha. "That will do," she said. "Samantha Robins," she declared, noticing the girl's name on some papers on the desk, "I am placing you under arrest. You are not obliged to say anything, but it may harm your defence if your fail to mention something that you later rely on in court. Do you understand?" Philippa slipped handcuffs on the struggling girl's wrists.

"What are you arresting me for?" Samantha demanded as Philippa held her arms.

"Prostitution will do for a start," Gould replied. "And I expect we'll find some controlled substances when we search wherever you live."

"Do what you like," Samantha spat at the two police officers. "And I still don't know where the hell Spendlove is."

Philippa took Samantha, who was screaming obscene abuse, to the police car outside. Gould stayed behind for a moment, looking at the papers on Samantha's desk. He had three people under arrest, but Spendlove, the head of the drugs organisation, had escaped and Gould knew that Spendlove had the resources to make recapturing him as difficult as possible.

****

While Samantha was being transported in a police van, handcuffed to another female officer, Philippa drove Kathleen Harvey to Snow Hill police station. During the journey, Philippa asked her some questions for information, although she realised that with no written record, Kathleen's answers could never be used in court.

"Why did you kill your husband?" Philippa asked.

"The oldest reason in the book, I suppose," Kathleen replied, between her sniffs. "I went up to Neil's office unexpectedly – I thought I would give him a pleasant surprise.

I wanted to find out why he'd sacked Cassandra and persuade him to reinstate her. It sounds silly but I never realised Neil was having an affair with Margaret Lane. When he said he had been sleeping with her for years but was now ditching her for a younger woman, I saw red. I knew he had a gun in his drawer. While his back was turned I took it out and hid it in my bag. Then a few minutes later I shot him, dropped the gun and ran out in a panic."

"It was a perfect shot. We thought it must have been a professional hitman."

"It was pure luck, I assure you. Good luck or bad luck, I don't know which. I'd never used a gun before in my life."

"Was your husband involved in drugs?" Philippa asked.

"I wouldn't have believed that of him. That didn't come until later after he was dead. I started receiving phone calls from this man Spendlove. I'd never heard of him before. Spendlove said Neil owed him a good deal of money for a recent big shipment, and he expected me to pay. I didn't know what to do."

"You could have gone to the police," Philippa pointed out. "That would have been less suspicious."

"Not really. When I didn't respond, Anson told Jason all about it. Then Jason told Cassandra and then me. Just after the murder, it seems that Charles Anson saw me come out of the office, even though I didn't know he was there at the time. As I said, I just dropped the gun and ran. I learnt afterwards that Anson gave the gun, with my fingerprints on it, to Spendlove. He kept it to blackmail me. Anson planted a different gun and some cocaine just to confuse you, I imagine. I think he always kept drugs in his pocket and, because of the types he mixed with, he always carried a gun," Kathleen said.

Philippa sighed. "I used to be jealous of your fine house in Haslemere, Mrs Harvey. You'll be facing a life sentence, I'm afraid. The female prisoners go to Holloway – I don't think you'll enjoy it very much," Philippa said.

"No, one good thing is I have been diagnosed as having cancer, so it won't last for very long."

"I'm sorry," Philippa replied, giving a neutral reply, but feeling oddly moved. "How much did Cassandra know about it all?"

"About the drugs? Nothing at all. Neil loved her really," Kathleen said, dabbing her eyes with a handkerchief. "I'm sure everything he did was only to make money to give her a start in life. He just pretended to sack her to toughen her up, he told me on that last evening."

"What about Annabel Ward? How was she killed? We know you had a meal with Jason and Cassandra to discuss her visit. Did one of you arrange for her to be killed?"

"No, our family may have its faults but we would never do anything like that. But her murder is the only thing I'll never forgive myself for. Annabel came to my house with some cock and bull story that she knew about crime in Harvey and Ward's. I don't know if she was telling the truth or not. She wanted Reg to control the company – I think she felt they were still married. She was a staunch Catholic, you know. Stupidly, I panicked and phoned Jack Spendlove to tell him about her visit and what she said she knew. I'm sure Spendlove then had poor Annabel killed in a car accident." Kathleen cried openly. "I never wanted that to happen. I'd have stopped him if I could."

"I suppose that's what happens when you get involved with someone like Spendlove. He's a very dangerous man. You should have called us. It's what we're paid for," Philippa said, then looked out of the windscreen of the car. "We're at the police station now, Mrs Harvey. It sounds silly, but I'll do what I can for you."

"Thank you, Philippa, but I'm prepared to face the music. It's almost a relief to tell the truth at last."

When the car stopped, Philippa helped the prisoner through the reception area and into the interview room. Kathleen Harvey had stopped crying and with her head up, looked to Philippa like a French aristocrat on her way to the guillotine. Philippa told herself her dignity was a product of the expensive education her father had paid for all those years before.

Chapter 38

It was five o'clock – normal going home time for office workers – when Gould completed the arrest formalities on Kathleen Harvey, Rothenberg and Samantha. Kathleen had been charged with the murder of her husband, while Rothenberg was charged with conspiracy and Samantha with possession of a controlled drug. Warrants were issued for Spendlove and Miller, who were still missing. Gould then took most of his team out for a celebratory drink, but Philippa pleaded an imaginary headache. She finished work early and had time to complete what she wanted to do.

Gould made a detour on his way home that he had been looking forward to making. He knocked on the door of the terraced house in Enfield that he had visited a year before when this murder case had just started. He felt satisfaction at having warrants to charge Spendlove and Miller as he had promised.

Mrs Fitzsimons answered the door as she had the last time Gould visited. Her hair seemed even greyer than before. She gave no indication of recognising her visitor.

"I don't know if you remember me, Mrs Fitzsimons. I'm Detective Chief Inspector Gould. I've been investigating the murder of your daughter's fiancé."

"You'd better come in," Mrs Fitzsimons stood to one side to allowing Gould to enter, then ushered him into the front room where a television was on at full volume.

"Natalie," Mrs Fitzsimons shouted. "It's Chief Inspector Gould to see you."

A young woman with dark hair disentangled herself from the arms of a long-haired man who glared at the intrusion. Gould only dimly recognise her as Natalie. "Can we have a word in the hall, Chief Inspector," she said, leading Gould out to the pokey corridor.

"I thought you'd like to know I've got warrants out to charge two people for the murder of your fiancé," Gould told her, with professional satisfaction. "They're both professional criminals and it's good news they're going to prison for a long time. They'll soon be picked up. I know it doesn't bring Hugh back, but I hope it helps."

"It's kind of you to tell me, Chief Inspector," Natalie said, her face going red. "But I've got a new man now. This one doesn't know about Hugh and I'd like to keep it that way." She opened the front door, obviously anxious for Gould to leave. "Thank you for letting me know and all that, but please don't come again."

"I see. Goodbye, Natalie," Gould replied, walking out of the door. As he walked to his car, he felt oddly deflated. He realised it was natural for Natalie to want to start her life again, but he was still disappointed by her lack of gratitude. He directed his car towards his flat. He was looking forward to a relaxing, and hopefully romantic evening with Philippa.

When Gould's key turned in the lock of the front door of their Barbican flat, Philippa was waiting in the kitchen. "That was what you'd call a successful day, wasn't it, Philippa?" Gould called as he took off his coat in the hall. She stayed in the kitchen and made no response. "Where are you? ...What are these bags doing here?" he called when he saw several suitcases in the hall. Gould noticed the light in the kitchen and came in. "Hello, there.

How's your headache? What's wrong?" he said as he saw Philippa's face.

"I'm leaving you, David," she said, moving as far away from Gould as she could in the kitchen.

Gould gaped and stared as if stunned. "Why?" he asked after a long pause.

"How can you live with yourself after what you did to Charles Anson?" Philippa asked, unable to look at Gould's face.

"What do you mean?" Gould asked. "I arrested him because he was a drug pusher. He knew the risks he was taking. He went to prison. It's my job to put people like him behind bars."

"You killed him," Philippa said.

"What are you taking about? Spendlove ordered Miller to kill Anson. The two of them have managed to escape but we'll catch them soon."

"And why did Spendlove have Anson killed?" Philippa asked, though she knew the answer.

"Rothenberg heard in my office that Anson was going to turn evidence and told Spendlove. Rothenberg is under arrest too for conspiracy. He won't get long in jail but it means he won't be a solicitor for much longer."

"Whose idea was it, David?" Philippa asked, after a pause.

"What do you mean?"

"I am not a complete fool," Philippa responded with tears in her eyes. "We both know Anson wasn't going to turn evidence. That message Rothenberg overheard was phoney. You set Anson up to be as a patsy so you could catch Spendlove, as soon as he tried to kill Anson."

Gould opened his mouth as if to deny it, but then he changed his mind and revealed the truth. "You're right. It was my idea to catch all of them and it will be a complete success as long as we catch Spendlove and Miller. I'm sorry Anson was killed, but you know what sort of man he was. His criminal colleagues murdered him. He wore a fancy suit but he was still total scum."

"I know he was a criminal," Philippa replied. "He still shouldn't have died. Rothenberg told Spendlove who then ordered the murder and Miller actually killed him. But you know it only happened because you planted a lying story that Anson was going to turn evidence."

"I've done nothing to be ashamed of," Gould said, his voice rising indignantly. "I've arrested a murderer and a crooked solicitor. I've warrants out for two more, including one of the biggest crooks in the country. The streets are safer without Spendlove selling his drugs. I'm sorry that Anson died, but he was no more than a common crook."

Philippa stood up. "I'm afraid that's not good enough for me, David. I can't live with a man who could let a murder of anyone happen like that." She went into the hall and picked up her bags. "Goodbye, Chief Inspector," she said. "I'm taking a week's leave. I'll apply for a transfer when I come back." Gould knew her use of his police rank meant their personal relationship had broken down. He stood aghast at the door of the kitchen as Philippa closed the front door behind her.

★★★★

An hour after leaving the Barbican, as it was turning dark, Philippa turned the key in the door of her Greenwich flat. She was glad she had never got around to selling it, despite living with David Gould for a time. As she looked around, the flat looked reassuringly familiar to her after her long absence. Shivering a little because of the lack of central heating, she put down her case in the hall and went into the kitchen.

She opened the doors of the cupboard and took out a jar of instant coffee. She put the kettle on then went upstairs for a shower. In the bathroom, she pulled back the curtains and stood naked as the jets of water powered over her body. Just as the shower made her feel physically clean, she hoped that the break with Gould would lead to a more fulfilled future. Switching off the shower and picking up the towel, she expected to relax. Suddenly, she felt something was wrong. She thought she had heard breaking glass, but she could not be sure if it was a product of her imagination or not. Putting her gown on, she walked to the bathroom door and looked out.

Philippa listened for several seconds but could hear nothing. Reassuring herself she was imagining things, she decided to go downstairs to the kitchen. Standing on the landing, she put one foot on the first step, when suddenly she felt herself being grabbed from behind. A male hand grabbed her chin, forcing her head back, while she felt a knife held to her neck.

"One move, little girl, and I'll cut your throat," croaked a rough cockney voice. "Now, if you scream no one will hear you anyway, all you will do is scar your pretty little face. Are you going to be sensible? Nod if you agree." Philippa tried to imagine who the intruder might be, as she tried to remember her police self-defence training. Held by the unknown powerful man, she knew she had to concentrate on staying alive. Unable to open her mouth, Philippa merely gave a small nod of the head.

"Now, we'll be more comfortable down in the kitchen. I think I heard a kettle boiling down there. We'll go down the stairs together. You can't see your feet with your head held back, so you will do exactly what I say. You are coming to the first step now, down one step, two steps, keep going to the corner ahead of you then turn right. It's funny me giving you directions in your own house, isn't it?" The man kept his ghastly conversation going with Philippa desperately trying to breathe. "Three steps ahead … We're in your kitchen now. I think you're clever enough to know that I mean what I say. I will let you go – one move I don't like and you're dead."

The man let her go, and Philippa turned around, keeping a careful eye on his knife. She immediately recognised the intruder as she opened her mouth to breathe again. "My God, you're Miller," she exclaimed, after a pause. "You came here once before."

"That's right, Sergeant," Miller replied, with the sarcastic emphasis on her police rank. "You put me away then. Shall I tell you the difference this time?" Philippa nodded dumbly, hypnotised by his knife. "Did it ever strike you that bit of arson was a little amateurish – especially for someone with my long experience? Well, that's because I wanted to be caught," Miller laughed to himself. "Now why do you think that was?"

"I bet Spendlove put you up to it, to scare me off the case," Philippa said, keeping her eyes on Miller's knife.

"Sort of. Spendlove wanted me to get caught to go to prison. I was told to keep an eye on Anson while I was doing time in case he got scared and started to talk too much. And he was going to, wasn't he?"

"It was you who killed Anson, wasn't it?" Philippa gasped in a terrified voice. She thought wildly of what she could say to this professional criminal. "It would be best for you to give yourself up. We've arrested Rothenberg now and we have a warrant for you and Spendlove. You won't get far. Just hand yourself in, and say you killed Anson under pressure from Spendlove. If you co-operate, you could get away with a light sentence." She hoped she sounded convincing.

Miller gave a derisive laugh. "That's what you think, little girl, is it? But that's where you're wrong. I'm not giving myself up to the police. Mr Spendlove and I are both going overseas and you're coming with us as protection." He seemed pleased with himself when he saw Philippa's frightened face. "We know all about your affair with your Chief Inspector. He won't want to lose you. I followed you all the way here from his flat. Had some sort of lover's tiff, have you?"

"Sort of," Philippa said, thinking hard what line to take. "So it won't do you any good keeping me. Mr Gould doesn't want me anymore. I'm not valuable enough."

"We'll see about that. Now come with me while I phone Jack Spendlove – he should be near his mobile. I saw your phone in the hall when I came through. Now, move!" Miller indicated with his knife for Philippa to go toward the hall. When he got to the phone, he dialled a number, keeping his knife pointed at Philippa. After waiting a few seconds, he spoke forcefully into the mouthpiece: "Yes, I'm at the police bitch's flat now. I've told her we're taking her with us. She and Gould have had a lover's tiff. ... Yes, it is funny, isn't it? Yes, her address is in our files. OK, I'll see you here in an hour."

Miller put the phone down and turned to face Philippa. "Did you hear that, little girl? We've got an hour to wait until Mr Spendlove is coming by to pick us up." He chuckled to himself. "Now, what do you think a man and a woman could do to amuse themselves for an hour? Do you know what's going through my mind? Did I hear you in the shower when I came in? Would I be right in thinking you're naked under that gown you're wearing? Quite thin, isn't it? I'd like to see what Mr Gould finds so fascinating. You see, little girl, I've been away from female company for over a year, and a man's mind gets to thinking all sorts of things after that time."

Philippa moved away as Miller walked towards her with his knife outstretched. He roughly grabbed her robe and tried to take it off her. She screamed, held on to the robe and ran up the stairs, but Miller was too fast and too strong for her. He grabbed her half way up the stairs and started to pull back her gown. She lay protesting but helpless on the stairs as Miller grunted with excitement when he exposed her breasts. He put his hand out to grab them, when the doorbell rang.

"Who the hell's that?" Miller asked as he instinctively froze at the sound.

Philippa was as surprised as Miller but breathed a sigh of relief as she grabbed the robe back around her. "I don't know," she answered, trying to stand up, "but I'll have to answer it."

"Here's what we do, little girl," said Miller. "You open the door and tell whoever it is to go away. Do you understand? I can rely on you to make up some excuse. Now, I'll be standing just inside the door with this knife, so don't try anything clever."

Philippa nodded, and holding the robe tightly around her, walked down the stairs and went to the front door. Miller followed her and stood behind the door. He held his knife close to her ribs but out of sight of any caller. Philippa tried to imagine who her caller might be and, opening the door, she stood amazed as Reg Ward stood there. Philippa stared dumbly at him, too frightened to speak.

"I'm sorry to bother you at home, Philippa," Ward began. "But, I've heard on the news that you've arrested Kathleen. I thought now the case is no longer live, we could go out together sometime." He stopped, puzzled by her frightened look. "Of course, if it's inconvenient, I'll leave you alone."

"No, darling, how nice to see you, but it's such an awkward time," Philippa said, in a manner as unlike her own as she could manage. "It's just that I'm washing my hair tonight and you know how it is. But we must go to the cinema again next week. I enjoyed it before." She stared at Ward trying to convey panic without provoking Miller.

Ward stared, baffled by her words and unusual manner. "Of course, I should have rung first, I'll say goodbye," he said, his voice trailing off in his embarrassment. He turned away and walked down the path. Philippa, conscious of Miller's knife against her waist, was too frightened to call out, but willed Ward to sense that something was wrong. But he did not turn around and Miller closed the door before Ward had reached the pavement.

"Very good, little girl," Miller said, closing the door. "That stopped your boyfriend getting hurt. How many men have you got on the go, anyway?" He laughed, then looked Philippa up and down. "I think we still have some unfinished business, don't we? Perhaps we'd be more comfortable in bed than on the stairs."

Miller held his knife towards Philippa and advanced toward her as she wondered how to escape. Despite the self-defence training all police officers receive, she felt helpless – the kitchen knife held her hypnotised. She tried to remember

285

what her instructor had told her. 'Keep him talking for as long as you can. If that fails, remember that as a woman you cannot defeat a male attacker by strength – you have to use his strength against him.' She wondered whether to run but decided to face her attacker.

"I don't think Mr Spendlove will want me damaged," Philippa said to Miller, keeping a watchful eye on his knife. "I'm more valuable as I am. You're going to be caught anyway and, believe me, you don't want to find out what the police do to people who attack one of us."

"I don't intend to give them a chance to show me," Miller replied with a sneer. "Mr Spendlove and I are going a long way away." However, something in his voice indicated Philippa's threat may have made an impact.

"Turn evidence against Spendlove," Philippa said. "That's the only way out for you. Say you were only following orders. I'll put in a good word for you. We're not interested in you – he isn't either. You don't owe him any favours. You've already spent time in prison for him. You don\t want to spend any longer there, do you?"

Miller looked dubious. Philippa's arguments seemed to have made some impression on him. "OK, you can get dressed," he said. "But in front of me – I don't want any tricks."

Philippa nodded as he followed her upstairs to her bedroom.

Chapter 39

As Reg Ward walked back to his car from seeing Philippa, he stopped and thought. He told himself Philippa's manner had been distinctly odd. She had never called him 'Darling' before, indeed from what he knew of her, he could not imagine her using the word, with its dated Hollywood flavour, to anyone, let alone him. And what had she meant by going to the cinema again? He had never been to the cinema or any social date with her at all. And why had she looked so frightened when he spoke to her? He knew that, as a police officer, she was well able to look after herself, and she knew he had no reason to harm her. No, Ward told himself, something was definitely suspicious.

Ward retraced his steps and went back to look again at Philippa's flat. The curtains were not drawn, which was strange, as it was getting dark. She had been dressed in a gown and her hair was wet as if she had just come out of the shower; he would have expected her to close the upstairs curtains for privacy. But there was nothing really he could do, he told himself, as he walked away for the second time. He realised that Philippa was the sort of woman who valued her privacy and would not welcome strange men interfering in her life. But he told himself that, if only for a while, he had been her boss and he had a right to be worried about her.

By the time he had reached the corner of the street, Ward had decided he would call Chief Inspector Gould and ask him to check on her. He had no mobile with him and so he drove to the nearest call box. He asked to be put through to Chief Inspector Gould. It took a good deal of persuasion for the operator to connect Ward, but eventually, Gould came on the line.

"What is it, Mr Ward?" Gould's voice came on the phone, professional and slightly impatient. "I wasn't expecting to hear from you again. Our investigations into the Harvey murder are over."

"It's not about the murder, it's about Philippa. I went to see her at her flat and she seemed to be behaving strangely," Ward replied. "She looked scared. I've never seen her act like that before."

Gould sighed with annoyance. "Mr Ward, Detective Sergeant Cottrell is a professional police officer. I think you know that she only acted as your secretary as part of an important investigation. Now it's over, she doesn't need you pestering her at home."

"I'm concerned about her," Ward continued. "She seemed very worried about something. She wasn't acting like herself at all."

"She was probably upset about you bothering her." Gould paused. "Very well, I will investigate it. Thank you for phoning." Ward heard the sound of Gould's phone being put down abruptly and the line went dead.

Unsure what to do next but dissatisfied at Gould's response, Ward decided to have a coffee and went into a run-down transport café nearby. As he sat a table, sipping the unappetising brown liquid in front of him, he pondered again what to do. The more he thought about it, the less he was satisfied with Gould's dismissive response. Ward felt he had to return to Philippa's flat to satisfy his own curiosity about what was going on.

Leaving his half-full cup behind him, Ward drove back to Philippa's flat and decided to stay outside until she came out. He sat in the car keeping an eye on her front door, feeling slightly foolish and hoping no neighbour would report his suspicious behaviour to the police. After around ten minutes of waiting, Ward noticed a sleek BMW roll up outside the flat and a familiar figure step out. He immediately recognised his old enemy from school days, Jack Spendlove, as he walked up the garden path. Ward knew, from his conversations with Gould and Philippa, that Spendlove had developed into a major criminal. He could not have an innocent reason for visiting Philippa's home. Ward told himself he had no doubt Spendlove posed some sort of danger to Philippa.

Ward asked himself what he should do next. He did not know that the police had a warrant for Spendlove's arrest. He was fairly sure that Gould would be even more abrupt if Ward phoned again about Philippa. He asked himself what else he could do? Ward decided to tackle Spendlove head on. Ward strode up to Philippa's flat and rang the doorbell as hard as he could.

****

Soon after Ward left her front door, Philippa had managed to calm Miller down some more. By the time Ward returned to wait outside in his car, she had managed to dress herself while Miller kept his knife directed at her. The thought of Miller seeing her dressing revolted her, but she realised she had to keep the anger at her imprisonment under control. When she was dressed, Miller forced Philippa down the stairs again. He grabbed her arm while he opened the door when Spendlove rang the doorbell.

"Hello, Nick," Spendlove said. "I see you have your hands full," he added, chuckling to himself.

"Hallo, guv, yes, it's nice and cosy here. Our pretty sergeant lady is going to make a cup of tea for us, aren't you, love?" Miller said, with his knife pointed at Philippa.

"You'd both better hand yourself in," she said. "It's the only way out for you."

"I don't think so, Sergeant," Spendlove said. We are going on a private flight to Amsterdam. Everything's ready. We won't have time for that tea you were going to give us."

Suddenly Spendlove was interrupted by a ring on the doorbell. He pulled a small revolver from his suit pocket.

"Whoever that is, get rid of them," Spendlove barked at Philippa. She went into the hall and opened the door a scratch to see Ward there for the second time. Unable to speak, she merely stared at him in surprise.

"I came to see if you were all right. You were acting so oddly. I saw Jack Spendlove coming in. What's he doing here?" Ward asked.

"Come in, Reg," Spendlove called from the front room before Philippa could reply. "How nice to see you again," he continued, his voice filled with sarcasm, as Ward walked in. "Nothing for thirty years then I see you twice in a year. Sit down. I was just telling your girlfriend here that we're all flying abroad tonight. Sit next to Philippa, Reg. I don't think you've met Miller here. He can keep an eye on both of you as easily as one. Having an unfit civilian with us shouldn't be much of a challenge for him. We'll all get into my car outside and I want everything to look nice and normal. No sudden movements or screams for help; Miller might react badly. Grab hold of them, Nick. Here take this," Spendlove said, tossing the gun to Miller.

Miller stood between Philippa and Ward and grabbed their elbows. He directed them out of Philippa's front door and toward Spendlove's car. They looked like a normal group of three friends to anyone who could not see the carving knife that was hidden inside Miller's coat and the gun that was at Philippa's chest.

"Why didn't you call for help?" Philippa whispered to Ward.

"I spoke to Gould," Ward whispered back. "I don't think he believed me." Philippa shuddered then held Ward's arm as the two of them were pushed into the plush leather seats of Spendlove's top of the range BMW. Philippa looked around the street in the hope that Gould might have taken Ward's call seriously and sent someone to release them, but she could see no one at all in the street. She wondered whether to scream for help, but she knew that no one would hear them, and Miller was quite capable of killing one of his hostages if provoked.

Miller pushed them into the back seat of Spendlove's car. "What should we do now?" Ward whispered to Philippa as Miller walked around to the front passenger's seat.

"I've no idea, Reg, no idea at all," Philippa whispered back as the car moved into the traffic. Spendlove clicked the central door lock by the driver's seat so they could not escape, while Miller sat next to him and kept his revolver trained on the two captives in the back seat.

****

David Gould had been in the middle of a discussion with DC Fox when Ward had phoned and made it clear he did not appreciate being disturbed.

"That man's becoming a pest," Gould told Fox.

"Which man's that, gov?" Fox asked.

"Reg bloody Ward. He was a witness in a murder case I have just finished investigating. Does that mean I'm his personal policeman?"

"What did he want?"

"He says that Philippa acted oddly when he went round to see her. Probably told him to shove off."

Fox shrugged. "Is Philippa at home, gov? It wouldn't do any harm to check she's OK."

Gould thought. He did not want to phone her at the moment because of the abrupt way she had moved out of his flat. A phone call from him now could make her think he was putting pressure on her to move back with him. But Gould was still her senior officer with a duty to find out how she was, he told himself. Whatever their relationship, he was going to make sure she was safe. He dialled the phone in her flat, but it remained unanswered for several minutes.

"No reply," Gould said. "She's probably out. I'll phone again later. Now, how's the operation going. We really want to nab Spendlove and Miller as soon as we can. Have we got someone watching Miller's last address? It was in Mile End near where Marks's body was dumped."

"Yes, that's covered. There's no sign of him there."

"How about Spendlove?"

"He has a London flat above his office and a country house in Sussex that we know about. They're both being watched."

"There doesn't seem much else we can do. All airports are on the lookout for him."

Fox looked dubious. "Well, there is somewhere Miller's been seen before."

"Where's that?"

"Philippa's flat. He tried to burn her out once before."

"He'd be mad to go there," Gould said, then thought for a while. "Still, it's possible. Grab your coat, we're going to Greenwich."

After a half-hour's drive, Gould stood outside Philippa's flat. There was no response to the doorbell, but he told himself she could be out somewhere, innocently. Gould had no authority to force an entry to Philippa's flat. Her car was still in the parking area outside, so she could have walked to the shops. Then Gould had an idea. He picked up the radio in his car. "Find me the registration number of the car belonging to a Mr Reg Ward. He was interviewed in the Harvey murder case ... His address will be on file somewhere ... OK, I'll wait."

Gould thought some more. It was possible Miller might come back to this flat where he had tried to frighten off Philippa once before. Then again, if Miller had any sense it would be the last place he would visit. Just then, the radio crackled into life and Gould took down the details of Ward's car. After a short drive around, Gould and Fox spotted it parked nearby. It was empty but there was no sign of foul play. Gould talked again into the radio. "Any news on Spendlove's car yet? ... Add DS Cottrell and Reg Ward to the list – the descriptions are in the file ... There's something suspicious here... What's that? You think you've spotted Spendlove's car in Kent? OK, we'll be right there."

****

Philippa stared at the traffic through the tinted glass of Spendlove's BMW. She willed at least one of the people in the cars they passed by to call for help. But she told herself how unlikely that was, as they had no way of knowing that she and Ward were innocent people held hostage by two murderers. The driver had locked the doors and windows and Philippa knew that banging on the window could mean being shot by Miller's gun.

Philippa cast her mind back to the interview with Fred Tassell, written up by DS Clement of the Mile End police. He had talked about a big black expensive car gliding past, and she felt suddenly coldly certain that this was the car Tassell had seen. She imagined Miller dropping the murdered auditor's body into the canal and shivered.

After a while, worry over her predicament began to be matched by curiosity as to where they were going. She could tell they had been driving for over an hour and were starting to come to the further southeastern suburbs of London and seemed to be heading for Kent. Now the car was travelling faster, their chances of escape were becoming more remote. Although Philippa appreciated Ward's efforts to come to her rescue, the presence of an untrained civilian did not help matters. "Be polite. Keep on talking to them" had been the message from training courses for police in a kidnap situation, but she knew it did not always work.

After a further half-hour, the sky was starting to darken. The car turned off the motorway and travelled along minor roads until it turned down a track. They passed an old-fashioned windsock and Philippa realised that they were coming to a small aerodrome, filled with light executive aircraft. Miller drove the car up to the steps of one of the small planes and switched off the engine.

"Here we are, little girl," Miller said as he turned around and smirked at Philippa. "Next stop, Amsterdam."

"What about Customs?" Ward asked. "They'll want to inspect everything before you take off."

"No sweat," Miller replied. "We've filed a domestic flight plan to Glasgow and there'll be no checks on that route. When we're up in the air, we'll just change our mind and head for the Continent. I may lose my pilot licence but as I don't have one anyway, I've got nothing to lose," he laughed. "Ain't that right, boss?"

"It certainly is," replied Spendlove. "Now start putting those cases in the plane and we'll fly off." He indicated Philippa and Ward. "We'll put the human cargo in later."

Miller nodded and started to put Spendlove's luggage in the hold of the aircraft. He took no notice of an unmarked car driving slowly towards them until it was a few feet away. Then its headlights were suddenly switched on.

"Freeze! This the police." Philippa recognised Gould's voice coming from the car. Miller immediately stood stunned, but Spendlove grabbed Philippa in his arms and held the gun he was carrying to her throat. Gould came out of the car and advanced to within six feet of Spendlove.

"Don't be stupid, Spendlove, there's nowhere you can go now," Gould shouted.

"Move away or your girlfriend's dead," Spendlove ordered. "Get in the plane, Nick," he ordered Miller, who continued to prepare the small aircraft for take-off.

"Put her down!" Ward's voice came as a surprise to Gould as well as Spendlove.

"Stay out of this, Mr Ward," Gould ordered.

"Yes, leave it to us experts," Spendlove echoed mockingly. He pointed the gun to Ward. "You're coming as well."

When Spendlove pointed the gun back to Gould, Ward suddenly dashed forward and pushed Spendlove off his feet. Philippa then managed to crawl free of Spendlove's arms as he and Ward both fell to the ground. After a moment, a shot rang out and Ward cried out in agony. Gould sprang forward and, holding Spendlove down, managed to put handcuffs on him. Blood seeped through Ward's shirt as he lay motionless on the ground.

"Damn amateurs!" exclaimed Gould. "Phone for an ambulance now," he called to Fox, who was guarding Miller. "Put these two in the back of the car," Gould said, pointing to Spendlove and Miller. Then he turned to Philippa. "Are you all right?" he asked her.

"Of course, I'm not bloody all right," Philippa snapped. Despite all her police training, after her escape, she started to sob uncontrollably. "For God's sake, look after Reg. He tried to help me," she added before she fainted into Gould's arms.

Chapter 40

The following day, Gould looked at Jack Spendlove seated next to his new solicitor, Mr Cushing, a replacement for Robert Rothenberg, who was in a cell in another part of the City police headquarters. Spendlove was looking out of the window of the interview room, making a pretence of ignoring Gould.

"It doesn't look too good, does it, Mr Spendlove?" Gould said, spelling everything out for the benefit of the tape recording. "We have enough evidence to charge you with the kidnap of a police officer and Reg Ward, as well as the attempted murder of Mr Ward. Together with the murder of Hugh Marks, Annabel Ward and Charles Anson, you could face several life sentences."

"My client has no knowledge of the three murders you mention, if indeed they are murders," Cushing said. He was typical of the solicitors who can be called in to represent criminal clients with large funds – his public-school accent and pinstriped suit testifying to the large fees he could command for his services. "My client knows Reg Ward, of course, but I understand Mrs Ward was killed by a hit and run driver. Very tragic of course, but there is no evidence it was murder – certainly not involving my client."

"We have a full statement by Nicholas Miller confessing to the murders but saying he was only obeying your client's orders," Gould said. In fact, Miller had been as silent as Spendlove but Gould felt that any lie to have the two culprits implicating the other was justified.

"I doubt that, Chief Inspector," the solicitor said, brushing imaginary specks off his expensive suit. "In any event, unless there is any written evidence of an order, which there can't be, it is merely the word of an escaped criminal against my client. Hardly strong enough to convict." The solicitor folded his arms in a self-satisfied way as Spendlove nodded his agreement.

"What about the murder of Charles Anson?" Gould continued. "We have documentary evidence of Mr Anson visiting your client for discussions. He also paid for Anson's defence."

"My client is a rich man who is altruistic. There is no crime in paying to see that someone is properly represented in court."

"There is no doubt that Miller murdered Anson. He was seen going into the victim's cell then he escaped soon afterward."

"My client has no knowledge of what may have happened in Anson's cell," Cushing said with a sneer. "Some sort of argument between convicts, probably. I understand it happens all the time. But I have advised my client to plead guilty to the kidnap charges and to assault on Mr Ward as long as they are all the charges he faces."

"I don't do deals, Mr Cushing. Unless your client has anything else to say I suggest we terminate the interview now."

"I will be applying for bail as soon as my client appears in court. Unless you can produce more serious charges, I expect my client to be free within the next few days."

"We shall see. In the meantime, take the prisoner down to his cell," Gould instructed the uniformed constable seated by the door of the interview room. Spendlove was ushered out of the interview room after signing the cover of the tape.

Once Spendlove was gone, Gould sat on his own in the interview room to plan his next steps. He knew that it was going to be hard to pin any of the murders on Spendlove. Kathleen Harvey had already been charged with killing her husband. She had incriminated Spendlove in her statement, but Gould knew an expensive lawyer like Cushing would tell any jury that Kathleen was telling lies in the hope of a lighter sentence, and they might believe him. Even without a statement, there should be no problem with convicting Miller of the murder of Anson, but Gould knew Miller would never incriminate Spendlove.

Gould reflected that it would be hard to stick responsibility for Annabel Ward's death on anyone. There was thus only one murder with which Spendlove could be charged – that of Hugh Marks. The auditor must have noticed something suspicious about Anson's activities at the start of the case. But Gould was not sure he had enough evidence to convince a jury. He read through the file to see if there was some overlooked piece of evidence he could use to convict Spendlove. He had begun to read the first reports from DS Clement, when an idea struck him.

****

The same afternoon, Gould knocked on the high-rise council flat of Fred Tassell in Mile End. After a couple of minutes' wait, Tassell noisily pulled back several bolts and opened the door.

"How do you do, Mr Tassell," Gould said, showing his warrant card. "My name's Detective Chief Inspector Gould of the City of London police. I've come about the dead body that you found in the canal a few months ago," he continued, unconsciously raising his voice for Tassell's benefit.

"There's no need to shout, young man. I can hear you perfectly well," Tassell replied, in an impatient tone. "Of course, I remember finding the body. What do you want to know about it?"

Gould made a conscious effort to be as polite as he could. "We have two suspects for the murder, Mr Tassell. Unfortunately, the man we believe organised the murder denies it. Unless we can come up with some more evidence, we will have to let him go. We have him on other charges, but we really want a murder conviction to put him away for as long as possible. Is there anything you can think of about the body that you didn't tell us at the time?"

"Does the man you want to charge own a big black car?" Tassell asked.

"Yes, that's right, Mr Tassell. But you said you didn't spot the registration number when you saw the car. There are thousands of big black cars around London. We need more concrete evidence than that."

"Well, I think he must have been a smoker," Tassell replied after a moment's thought. "He threw a cigarette end and an empty packet out of the car window."

"Yes, the suspect smokes but again so do lots of other people."

"Well, I saw him throw a paper out of the window as well. I made a mental note to complain to the council about it. I'm on the neighbourhood anti-litter liaison committee, you see."

"Ah, well," Gould replied after Tassell had finished. "If there's nothing else that occurs to go, I'm sorry to have bothered you, Mr Tassell."

Tassell waited until Gould had started to leave then called him back. "If you see the man, you can give him his newspaper back."

Gould turned around sharply. "What did you say?"

"I pick up all the litter from that path and keep it. I'm going to show the council how much litter is dropped in a year," Tassell replied in a proud tone. "Come into the kitchen," he added, beckoning Gould to accompany him. "There, look at that," Tassell pointed to a black bin liner filled with rubbish. "My daughter keeps wanting me to throw it out, but I tell her we need evidence against these litter louts." Tassell pulled some litter out and peered into the bottom of the bag. "Yes, that's his paper. It's that pink one. We don't often see it round here."

"The Financial Times," Gould clarified, his eyes widening in excitement. "You didn't happen to pick up his cigarette end, did you?"

"No," Tassell replied, looking in to the bag. "Oh, yes, here it is – tucked into the empty pack inside the paper. Look expensive, don't they? But I don't see what you can tell from a cigarette end."

"That's where you're wrong, Mr Tassell," Gould said, unable to keep a smile from his face. "This might be just the evidence we need. Thank you very much indeed." Gould added as he picked up the bin liner. "I think I will take this, if you don't mind." He took a polythene bag from his pocket and placed the cigarette end and empty Gauloises pack inside. "If you could just sign across the seal to show where you picked it up, Mr Tassell, I think we're on our way to a result."

The next day, Jack Spendlove looked at Gould with an air of insouciant superiority. "Have you admitted defeat yet, Chief Inspector?" he asked. Both Gould and Cushing sitting beside Spendlove gazed at him in astonishment as these were the first words he had spoken in all their hours of interviews.

"I don't think so, Mr Spendlove," Gould replied. "I'm glad you're speaking again. Let me get you an ashtray." Gould passed him an upturned metal lid. "Make yourself at home."

Cushing looked panic-stricken as though he had walked into an avant-garde play in which the actors had suddenly changed their roles. Spendlove nodded his thanks and pulled out a cigarette packet from his pocket.

"Not many people smoke Gauloises nowadays, Jack," Gould said, in a conversational tone.

"No, I have to order them specially," Spendlove answered. "What's all this light conversation – the soft cop routine?"

"No, not exactly," Gould said, his eyes fixed on Spendlove's cigarette. "We know you killed Hugh Marks and dumped his body in the canal. I think you saw Neil Harvey the evening he died, before Kathleen turned up and killed him. What did you and Harvey talk about? Did he want more money, or had he decided he didn't want anything to do with your drug dealing?" Spendlove smoked furiously while Gould spoke.

"Then, when Anson gave you the gun Kathleen used to kill her husband, you blackmailed her into allowing the drug dealing to continue. You ordered Miller to kill Annabel Ward when Kathleen told you she knew something suspicious about the murder. I don't mind betting Annabel was bluffing when she told Kathleen that, but you couldn't risk Annabel going to the police and telling us whatever it was she knew. Finally, you ordered Anson killed when you thought he was going to turn evidence against you. You are guilty of three murders and one conspiracy to pervert the course of justice. How am I doing?"

Spendlove looked at Gould with contempt. "You say I'm a murderer. Very well, prove it," he said, stubbing his cigarette out on the makeshift ashtray.

Gould pulled a small polythene bag from his pocket and put the cigarette butt into it. "Would you sign to confirm that his cigarette was smoked by you, please?"

The solicitor gave a baffled nod to his client and Spendlove, with a shrug, signed the note on the bag.

"Thank you," Gould said, pulling the bag that Fred Tassell had signed from another pocket. "This was picked up from the canal near where you and Miller dropped Hugh Marks's body. Very similar, wouldn't you say? It's unlike you to get your hands dirty, but for some reason you did in this case. We'll analyse these for DNA to prove it, but for now, I am ready to charge you with a sample case of murder of Hugh Marks. You can go back to cells now, Mr Spendlove."

****

After charging Spendlove with the murder of Hugh Marks, Gould was feeling pleased with himself. One murder charge for Spendlove was less than Gould wanted, but he was prepared to accept it. He was sure Spendlove had also ordered the murders of Annabel Ward and Charles Anson but unless

Miller turned evidence against his former boss, it would be impossible to make any more charges stick. That evening Gould opened the door of his flat. He called out, "I'm back," before realising it was empty.

Walking through to the bedroom to change into casual clothes, he realised how much he wanted to go out and celebrate. He remembered his painful interview with the Commissioner. He thought wistfully of how Philippa made love to him then, probably as an act of commiseration. He thought of how much he would enjoy celebrating Spendlove's arrest with an expensive romantic meal with Philippa. They would come back and make love on the double bed he was sitting on now. He gazed at the phone by his bed and wondered whether he could call Philippa. Then he remembered how bitter she was when she had walked out a few days before, and decided it was too soon to make contact.

Gould shuddered again at the memory of Philippa's departure, then picked up the phone and dialled. "Hello, it's David here," he said. "Yes, I know it's a surprise… Great, Audrey, I'll see you at eight at the spot we always used to meet." He put the phone down. Perhaps this was for the best, after all, he reflected. He started to tidy up the flat in the hope that his wife might come back for a drink after their meal together.

Chapter 41

Four months later, Philippa was seated at her desk at the police station, working on a straightforward burglary when the phone rang. As she answered it she recognised the voice of her old employer.

"Hello, Reg here," came the voice.

"Yes, Mr Ward. Are you out of hospital yet?"

"Yes, I'm fine now. I wondered if you'd like to go for a meal tomorrow night."

"Reg," she said gently. "I am a police office on duty," she paused. "But the case is over and you're no longer a witness. I'd love to go out tomorrow night."

****

The following evening, Philippa found herself enjoying a meal in an expensive restaurant. Reg Ward was seated opposite. It was some time since a man had taken Philippa out and she decided to relax and enjoy herself. Both of them seemed to feel ill at ease. To break the ice, she asked him what was happening in the Harvey and Ward offices.

"Well, now Kathleen's been convicted of Harvey's murder, she's no longer allowed to inherit his shares. That means Cassandra and Jason are out of the picture," Ward said. "The Official Solicitor has found Neil posthumously guilty of drug smuggling so most of his estate has been confiscated. That means my shares control the company. I run the show now."

"You deserve it, Reg" Philippa said. "Old Harvey used to put you through hell. How's everyone else? What's Margaret Lane doing now?"

"I invited her back and she manages the office again in her usual efficient way," Ward replied. "Cassandra still works in the office. She was shattered when she found that her father was possibly a drug smuggler and everyone knew her mother murdered him because of his affairs. She's not as arrogant as she used to be and she's back as our chief seller."

"That must have been a comedown for her,"

"It was, but I didn't want to lose her. She's good at selling and she'll probably be a partner one day. Jason is still working for one of our competitors, but we recently beat him to a large contract, which was satisfying."

"You probably know Spendlove is serving a life sentence for the murder of Hugh Marks. It hasn't stopped him running his old gang from prison, but at least it's cramped his style. Miller's back in prison where he belongs, too."

"I always hated Jack Spendlove, even when we were at school together," Ward said. "It was strange crossing his path again all these years later. If I never see him again, I'll be happy. Are you still seeing David Gould?" he asked after a pause, attempting to sound casual.

"No, that's fallen through, but we still work together. I think he's back with his wife," Philippa replied, looking down. "Are you still chasing your secretaries?" she asked with a smile.

"No, I've just chosen the oldest and ugliest one I could find. It's safer that way. I've given up on good-looking ones. Unless you want your old job back?"

Philippa sipped the expensive wine Ward had bought her and decided that, after all, he was quite a charming man. She reflected that this man had probably saved her life. She smiled encouragingly at him. "No, I'll stay with my present job, thank you. I love the police too much to give it up. But I appreciate what you did for me at that airstrip." She looked happily around at the plush surroundings. "We must do this again sometime." She reached out her hand to touch Reg Ward's arm. All in all, she told herself that this date might be the start of something special.

EIN HERZ FÜR AUTOREN A HEART FOR AUTHORS À L'ÉCOUTE DES AUTEURS MIA ΚΑΡΔΙΑ ΓΙΑ Σ ΑΡΤΑ FÖR FÖRFATTARE UN CORAZÓN POR LOS AUTORES YAZARLARIMIZA GÖNÜL VERELIM RE PER AUTORI ET HJERTE FOR FORFATTERE EEN HART VOOR SCHRIJVERS TEMOS OS A ZÓINKÉRT SERCE DLA AUTORÓW EIN HERZ FÜR AUTOREN A HEART FOR AUTHORS À L'É ΑΚΑΡΔΙΑ ΒΣΕЙ ДУШОЙ К АВТОРАМ ETT HJÄRTA FÖR FÖRFATTARE À LA ESCUCHA DE LOS AI ΙΑ ΓΙΑ ΣΥΓΓΡΑΦΕΙΣ UN CUORE PER AUTORI ET HJERTE FOR FORFATTERE E ZÓINKÉRT SERCE DLA AUTORÓW EIN HERZ ÇÃO BCEЙ ДУШОЙ К АВТОРАМ ETT HJÄRTA

The author

Born in Washington D.C. in 1951, Ian Richardson
was educated at Highgate School and the Uni-
versity of Southampton. He spent most of his
career in the UK civil service, including HM Treasury
and the Cabinet Office, dealing with financial
matters. Since retiring, he has had more time
to enjoy his favourite activities of choral singing
and folk dancing and has also turned his hand to
writing with this being his debut novel. He has
three grown-up children and lives happily with his
wife in South Wales.

The publisher

He who stops getting better stops being good.

This is the motto of novum publishing, and our focus is on finding new manuscripts, publishing them and offering long-term support to the authors.
Our publishing house was founded in 1997, and since then it has become THE expert for new authors and has won numerous awards.

Our editorial team will peruse each manuscript within a few weeks free of charge and without obligation.

You will find more information about
novum publishing and our books on the internet:

www.novum-publishing.co.uk

Printed in Great Britain
by Amazon